Praise for Jesse Q. Sutanto's
Well, That Was Unexpected

"*Well, That Was Unexpected* is a delightful, hilarious, captivating love letter to Indonesia, and coming of age in a large meddlesome family, and the thrill of finding your person where you least expect it!"
—**Ali Hazelwood**, *New York Times* **bestselling author of**
The Love Hypothesis

"A hilarious, heartfelt rom-com with a refreshing take on matchmaking, complete with embarrassing, yet well meaning, parents and a social media twist."
—**Krystal Marquis**, *New York Times* **bestselling author of**
The Davenports

"Charming and immersive, this book feels like taking a trip to Indonesia. Jesse Q. Sutanto writes such vibrant characters, with gorgeous descriptions of setting, culture, and food. Don't read this on an empty stomach!"
—**Nicole Lesperance, author of** *The Depths*

"You will enjoy every minute of it."
—*E! Online*

"Sutanto is the queen of quirky heroines in borderline chaotic situations."
—*BuzzFeed*

Didn't See That Coming

Also by Jesse Q. Sutanto

FOR YOUNG ADULTS
Well, That Was Unexpected
The Obsession
The New Girl

FOR ADULTS
Dial A for Aunties
Four Aunties and a Wedding
Vera Wong's Unsolicited Advice for Murderers
I'm Not Done with You Yet

Didn't See That Coming

JESSE Q. SUTANTO

DELACORTE PRESS

Text copyright © 2023 by PT Buku Emas Sejahtera
Jacket art copyright © 2023 by Richard Mercado

All rights reserved. Published in the United States by Delacorte Press, an imprint of Random House Children's Books, a division of Penguin Random House LLC, New York.

Delacorte Press is a registered trademark and the colophon is a trademark of Penguin Random House LLC.

GetUnderlined.com

Educators and librarians, for a variety of teaching tools, visit us at RHTeachersLibrarians.com

Library of Congress Cataloging-in-Publication Data is available upon request.
ISBN 978-0-593-43401-7 (hardcover) — ISBN 978-0-593-43404-8 (pbk.) —
ISBN 978-0-593-43403-1 (ebook) — ISBN 978-0-593-70995-5 (int'l. ed.)

The text of this book is set in 11.25-point Maxime Pro.
Interior design by Michelle Crowe

Printed in the United States of America
10 9 8 7 6 5 4 3 2 1
First Edition

To my girls, Emmie and Rosie. If you ever choose to shorten your school skirts, I promise not to freak out.

CHAPTER 1

In the dim glow of the moonlight, nobody spots the cyborg assassin peeling herself off the back of a stone gargoyle's head. She moves with the liquid grace of a stalking cat, her eyes, one human brown and the other an electric blue, scanning the damp street before her. In one smooth motion, she raises the scope of her sniper rifle to the blue eye and peers through it. There. Her heat sensor picks up a small figure scurrying behind a building. The assassin smiles. From the way the figure moves, it's obvious that it's a dwarf. Dwarves are armed with machine guns, so it's in her best interests to eliminate this one before he spots her. Her finger caresses the trigger. Just one more step and the dwarf will be out of cover. She takes a breath to steady herself. The dwarf's hat comes into view, followed by his head. She pulls the trigger just as a huge shield appears in front of the dwarf.

What? It takes a second for the assassin to realize what's just happened. The shield is being held by a huge, hulking figure. A grinning giant of a man. The second it's taken the assassin to reassess the situation costs her. Before she can react, the dwarf swings his machine gun over the giant's shield and the world explodes. Machine guns are rarely accurate. But then, they don't need to be.

"VICTORY" flashes onto my screen as the assassin, along with the stone gargoyle, tumbles down onto the street. Grinning, I tap my fingers against my keyboard with practiced ease.

Dudebro10: Duuude!
Sourdawg: Yasss!

The robot assassin was the last of the enemy's team. Both teams started out with five members each, and the robot assassin managed to pick off three of my team members within the first ten minutes of the round. When our second member was sniped three minutes in, I told Sourdawg, who has chosen to play the machine-gun-toting dwarf, that we needed to stay well away from the assassin so we could kill off her teammates before getting to her ourselves. He agreed—he always agrees—and the two of us did what we do best, with me playing as the gigantic tank.

Sourdawg: Teamwork makes the dream work!

My grin widens. Sourdawg is such a dork, I swear. He's always ready with these little clichés that should be cringey but, coming from him, are adorable. Plus, he's not wrong. Ever since we started teaming up, Sourdawg and I have held one of the highest ranks in the Southeast Asian section of *Warfront Heroes.*

> **Dudebro10:** Ooh, watch the replay. Look at my shield.
> Looook!

On the screen, the replay starts, showing my ridiculously muscled character crouching behind his lead shield as he crawls behind Sourdawg's character. I was so careful to make sure that I was covered by the shield the entire time so that the assassin's heat scans wouldn't pick up my body heat.

> **Sourdawg:** You move very smoothly for such a big guy.
> **Dudebro10:** Hey, big guys can be graceful too.
> **Dudebro10:** Plus, I've been doing ballet since I was—

Oh shit. Delete, delete. Gah. I take a deep breath to recenter myself. What was I thinking? The well-earned victory must have gone to my head.

> **Sourdawg:** So anyway, you remember that sourdough
> starter I ordered weeks ago?
> **Dudebro10:** The one made from vintage grapes peeled by
> anointed virgins under a full moon next to Lake Como?
> **Sourdawg:** Okay, smartass. Plus, it's not a full moon. It has
> to be under a waxing moon.
> **Dudebro10:** I know you're kidding, but I don't actually
> know if you're kidding.

Sourdawg: SIGH. Anyway. It arrived yesterday, and guess what?

Dudebro10: Does it taste like the tears of anointed virgins?

Sourdawg: What do the tears of anointed virgins taste like?

Dudebro10: Iono. Like unicorn breath.

Sourdawg: Okay, that's not actually helpful. And it sounds gross. Anyway, no. I don't know what it tastes like, because it was DOA.

Dudebro10: DOA?

Sourdawg: Dead on arrival.

Dudebro10: I know what DOA stands for. But what do you mean?

Sourdawg: Exactly that. It was dead by the time it arrived. Maybe it got too hot during shipment or something, but all I got was rancid goop. 😨

Dudebro10: Oh nooo! RIP, unicorn breath starter.

Sourdawg: I was so bummed.

Dudebro10: I bet! You've been looking forward to that starter for months. Let me guess: You want to send them a strongly worded email.

Sourdawg: VERY strongly worded. I can't do it alone.

Dudebro10: Of course not. The level of passive aggression we're aiming for requires teamwork. Okay. Let's see. "To Whom It May Concern . . ."

Sourdawg: "I would just like to flag—"

Dudebro10: "—as a matter of utmost importance—"

Sourdawg: "—the fact that my order was DOA and is very definitely not made of unicorn breath."

Dudebro10: "I thought I'd bring this to your attention."

Sourdawg: "Looking forward to your timely reply on this
very serious matter."
Dudebro10: "Regards, A Disappointed Customer."

I lean back in my seat and review the email we've composed together.

Dudebro10: One of our best works, I must say.
Sourdawg: I like how you managed to slip in "as a matter
of utmost importance." A true masterstroke.
Dudebro10: /bows. Thank you. I appreciate that. I
thought "Looking forward to your timely reply" was a
particularly nice touch.
Sourdawg: I thought it would put some pressure on them.
Dudebro10: It definitely will.
Sourdawg: Truly, the perfect email.
Dudebro10: You're not sending it.
Sourdawg: Of course not.

I can't help but snort at this. Then I realize that my cheeks hurt, because I've been grinning nonstop since our round ended.

Dudebro10: You should send them something, though.
Like, a real complaint. I mean, you don't have to be a
dick about it, but they should know that their product
arrived dead.
Sourdawg: IDK, bro. Can't I just order another batch and
hope they do it right this time?

Aaand now my smile's gone. Not because Sourdawg is such an adorkable pushover but because of the word "bro." Every time he calls me "bro" or "man" or "dude," it feels like a needle pricking into my skin and letting air out. Erm, blood? Okay, gross. All I'm saying is, it makes me feel deflated. And it makes me want to scream "I'm not a dude!" at him, which is stupid, because whose fault is it that Sourdawg thinks I'm a guy? Who was it that chose the most cis male–sounding name in the history of names?

/raises hand

In my defense, I didn't do it for shits and giggles. And I definitely didn't do it thinking I would form any meaningful friendships on, of all places, *Warfront Heroes*. Don't get me wrong: as far as gameplay goes, it's right up there with the best of them. The weapons are so creatively varied there's no way anyone will get bored, and the character designs are the most diverse in the history of games. Plus, there are no overtly sexualized female characters with watermelon-sized boobs bouncing wildly as they run, which is saying something in the gaming world—a world dominated by very, very frustrated guys. (And I don't mean frustrated as in "Gah, my coffee machine broke!" I mean the other kind of frustrated. The sexual kind, in case that wasn't obvious.)

Despite all these progressive steps that the makers of *Warfront Heroes* have taken to be more inclusive, they still haven't managed to win the last battle: harassment. Sure, a few of the more overt trolls have been banned. But in order to get banned, a player would have to make truly awful, abusive comments that count as threats. Anything less than that and all they get is a gentle reminder from a mod.

When I first started playing, I naively chose the name Doom&Bloom. Okay, maybe it was sort of a stupid name, but whatever, most people's handles aren't serious. There are people called Puffbug and LightningLord, so I was sure I'd blend right in.

Except the thing with Doom&Bloom was that the word "bloom" apparently marked me as a girl, and I was quickly inundated with messages from the other players. The messages ranged from "Girls can't shoot. This is a REAL game, so fuck off and stick to your dolls" to the more succinct "Boob pic?" to actual rape threats. And that's only in the game's waiting room. Once a round began and the adrenaline started flying high, the abuse became so much worse. Most players interact with one another verbally. I have a headset, and the first few battles I played, I made the mistake of speaking to communicate with my team. As soon as they realized I was a girl, people I was grouped with reacted in one of the following ways:

1. "Great, we're gonna fucking lose 'cuz the algorithm grouped us with a chick. Fuck it, I'm just gonna sit in the starting area and wait until we lose this round so I can join a new group."

2. "You're a girl? And you're not playing a healer? Fuck you! Switch to a healer!"

3. "Ignore them. I really don't mind girls playing this

game. I think it's hot when girls are into guns. How old are you?"

And sure, I can block people, which I do, liberally, but for once in my life, I wanted to be treated as just a team member. As a human. I just wanted to play the freaking game without having to click the Block or Mute buttons.

I stopped speaking into my microphone, communicating with my team via chat messages alone. But that didn't stop my screen name from giving me away. Each time I was harassed, I reported the player to the moderators, who promised that they would look into the matter. But each week, when I checked the status of the players who had harassed me, I saw that they were still active. Nothing had happened to them. They'd likely been reprimanded and then left alone. And I noticed that the algorithm was starting to group me with the lower-ranked players. I was winning the majority of my games, so I knew I shouldn't be ranked with the bronze-tier players, and yet here I was, moving down the tiers with each complaint I made. Maybe the company thought it was protecting me by tweaking my profile so I was less likely to encounter the people I reported, but at the end of the day, the result was still the same: I was being punished for reporting the harassment.

For a while, I considered quitting the game. There was so much resentment festering inside me, and I was also exhausted. Every time I logged on, my stomach clenched painfully, my shoulders rose to my ears, and my neck muscles went completely rigid. I wasn't enjoying it anymore.

Then one night it hit me: I could be whoever the hell I wanted to be. Goodbye Doom&Bloom, hello Dudebro10.

When I logged on for the first time as Dudebro10, my shoulders were rigid, my hand clutching my mouse as usual. I kept expecting someone to shout "IMPOSTER" at me. And then mods would swoop in like Valkyries and, I don't know, hit me with the ban hammer. But nothing like that happened. People just went "Hey" or "'sup?" before launching into a discussion on strategy. Nobody asked me to play a healer. I chose my character, a warrior tank, and nobody told me that girls can't play tanks.

Nobody said, "Why're we following a chick around?" Nobody asked why I was going west instead of east. Everybody just followed my cue. It was only when the round ended that I realized my cheeks were wet. I'd been crying as I played, and it was as though the tears were part of a thawing. My shoulders were relaxed, my neck muscles no longer hurt, and my jaw wasn't clenched as per usual. I was . . . enjoying myself.

Overnight, I went from fielding dozens of shitty messages every day to invisible. Just another dude.

That was a year ago. Over time, I joined a guild, and being part of a team brought *Warfront Heroes* to a whole new level of enjoyment. After playing a few rounds, the team and I would hang around and chat. I told them that I couldn't do voice chat because my parents would kill me if they knew how late I was staying up, and they accepted it, no questions asked. They probably thought I was a twelve-year-old kid instead of seventeen.

The later it got, the more players logged off, and soon, it was just me and one other teammate left online: Sourdawg. Our chat flowed so seamlessly that I didn't realize it was just the two of us left. And when I did, I didn't mind. Sourdawg was great to talk to. We chatted for ages about the game—our stats and how to improve them, the various weapons we preferred, and so on. When I logged on the next day and saw the green light next to his name, a glow of happiness warmed my chest. It brightened when my computer *boop*ed with a message from him. That night, we played and chatted for four hours straight. I could barely stay awake in school the next day, but it was totally worth it. And we've been chatting every day ever since.

I never planned to make a real friend on *Warfront Heroes*. I just wanted to play in peace. I never meant to deceive—I mean, of course I knew I was deceiving, but I thought it would just be me logging on, playing a few rounds peacefully, without being harassed, and then logging off for the night. No harm done. I never expected to befriend someone like Sourdawg, and even after we started chatting with each other, I never expected to be so close to him. We're, like, properly friends now, which is freaking weird, and we share stuff about each other outside of *Warfront Heroes*. Well, I share under the guise of Dudebro10, which sucks, because it feels really slimy doing that. Here's what I know about Sourdawg:

1. He's 17 and he lives in Singapore.
2. He has some kind of obsession with sourdough, hence his screen name.

3. His dream is to get into the CIA—the Culinary Institute of America, that is, not the other CIA.

4. He's maybe the only decent guy on *WH*. One time, we were grouped with a player whose screen name was, and I kid you not, SexyLexxi. I winced when I saw it. Sure enough, the other guys started heckling her as soon as the chat opened, but Sourdawg said, "STFU, guys," and they did. Why couldn't the algorithm have teamed me up with him when I was Doom&Bloom, damn it?

5. He's got seven different kinds of sourdough starters. Have I mentioned his obsession with sourdough?

6. He's a swimmer. He recently competed in the national swim meet and came in second. He was bummed about not getting gold, but he is honestly more bummed about the dead sourdough starter. Oh my gosh, I can't believe there are already six things on this list. I could go on for ages, but I'm going to stop here because it's starting to feel kind of weird.

Given that I know so much about Sourdawg, it might seem weird that I don't know his actual name, but I've never dared to ask, because what if he asked what my real name is? Then I'd have to dig myself deeper into my lie and tell him that my name is Bob or Tom or whatever, which feels even slimier. The closer we get, the guiltier I feel. It's a good thing that Sourdawg lives in Singapore and I live all the way in Jakarta. We've got a whole sea separating us, so at least I can be confident that we'll likely never bump into each other in real life.

My computer dings.

Sourdawg: Another round?
Dudebro10: Gah, I'd love to, but I should probably get to
    bed. And you should too, isn't it super late over there?
Sourdawg: Okaaay, Uncle.

I bite my lip, smiling again as I imagine Sourdawg saying "Okay, Uncle" in that typical Singaporean way. Then that stab of guilt again. *He should be calling you Auntie, not Uncle.* I shake it off and type back.

Dudebro10: Sorry, it's just my first day at school tomorrow.
Sourdawg: Got it. Go get your beauty sleep. Later!
Dudebro10: G'night!

The moment I log off, all the joy that usually comes with chatting with Sourdawg dissipates. First day of my stuffy, super-traditional, elite private school tomorrow. Ugh. I still can't believe that Mami and Papi did this to me. But I shan't despair, for I am the Fabulous and Marvelous Kiki Siregar. The other students at Xingfa School aren't even going to know what hit them.

CHAPTER 2

As much as I hate to admit it, when it comes to my new school, its uniform gives me a lot more to work with than Mingyang's did. Mingyang High, my old school, is also a Chinese school, but it's all about integrating as much of Indonesian culture as possible, so its uniform is an atrocity made of batik-inspired cloth—with a pattern that I think is supposed to be seashells but has ended up looking like amoebas—cut into a bizarrely shaped blouse and skorts. It was voted Worst Uniform in Jakarta five years in a row. One would think that winning this nebulous award would've encouraged the folks at Mingyang High to revisit the uniform, but nope.

Xingfa's uniform, on the other hand, is the cute Japanese-style sailor uniform: white skirt and top with a large blue collar and a red sash. It makes me look like a manga character, and I fully approve of this. I admire my reflection after I've put it on with my regulation white socks. The skirt was the only thing I was meh about. According to Xingfa's rule book, it should be four fingers' width below the knee, which . . . uh, no. The day the package containing my new uniform arrived, I quickly sent the skirt out to be shortened so that it fell an inch above my knees. That's one thing Mingyang did right: our amoeba-covered skorts were at least allowed to be thigh-length. I'd be lying if I said I wasn't a tiny bit worried, though. Mingyang is known for being one of the most liberal, progressive schools in Indonesia, a country filled with conservative, traditional schools. Xingfa, on the other hand, is known for its "discipline," code word for super-strict traditional school. Which again raises the question of why Mami and Papi have chosen to transfer me to Xingfa.

I woke up half an hour early this morning so I could pull my hair into a messy braid and twine it around my head into a braided headband, and dare I say it: I look super cute. I pick up my phone, which is wearing a custom phone case I designed myself. It says *gamer goddess* in a beautiful cursive font, surrounded by an explosion of flowers. Just because I can't be publicly a girl in-game doesn't mean I'm not proud of being a girl gamer in real life.

I strike a pose and take a selfie before sending it to my WhatsApp group chat. A second later, my phone buzzes with replies.

Sharlot: WHAT! Your uniform is SO cute! I hate you!
Cassie: I love it! And your hair! Aah! You're going to slay them!

Over summer break, my cousin Sharlot visited us from Los Angeles. At first, it was a complete trainwreck. She and I didn't hit it off, and to make matters worse, she got roped into fake-dating George Clooney.

Well, George Clooney Tanuwijaya. Only male heir of the Tanu Group, one of the nation's biggest corporations. Their fake dating was exposed in the most humiliating way possible, and it was awful. Sharlot was devastated, but then she climbed out of her cave of sadness and we became a lot closer than before. Plus, the fake dating actually evolved into real dating, and now Sharlot and George Clooney are one of those couples who seem to have everything together and will no doubt get married once they finish grad school. I introduced her to Cassie, my BFF, and they got along so well that the three of us formed a group chat called the Bad Betches, and since then, we chat on it almost every day.

Kiki: I miss you guys so much. 🥺

Cassie: I know! Lunchtime is going to be so weird without you.

Sharlot: Hey, at least you guys are still living in the same country! I'm all alone in Cali!

Kiki: Your boyfriend literally flew halfway around the world to be with you. You're hardly all alone

Cassie: Srsly! #relationshipgoals

Sharlot: Yes, but I miss you guys! Female friendships > boyfriend

Kiki: Gasp! George would be heartbroken to see that

Sharlot: Why would he see it? 😇

Kiki: Screenshotted and saved for future blackmail 😎

Cassie: Kiki, pls look out for cute girls at your new school for me

Kiki: Always!

Cassie: Love you!

Sharlot: 💀

I'm beaming when I tuck my phone into my skirt pocket (my skirt has pockets! Yay!) and glance up at my reflection once more. I nod to myself. "Looking good, Kiki." Maybe I sound slightly deranged, talking to myself like this, but I'm all for positive self-affirmation. Mami says that even when I was a baby, it was obvious I thought I was the shit. At my baby class, I was always the first to crawl toward the ball or whatever the teacher was holding up.

I swipe on some tinted lip balm, pull out a few strands of hair from my braid to keep it from looking too severe, and release my breath. Okay, time to slay.

Mami and Papi are downstairs in the dining room, already halfway through their breakfast. Well, if one can call a glassful of alarmingly green veggie juice breakfast. No, wait, today's concoction isn't witch's-brew green; it's actually more mud-colored.

Noticing my look of disgust, Papi lifts his glass and wiggles his eyebrows. "Bayam, kale, bok choy, and kunyit." Spinach, kale, bok choy, and turmeric.

I give him the ugliest sneer I can twist my face into, and he laughs.

"Hey, this stuff's going to make us live to a hundred! Just you wait and see."

"I'd rather die young than drink that," I shoot back without any venom. I think it's kind of adorable that Papi is so into his disgusting vegetable juice.

"Aduh, choi! Touch wood!" Mami cries, knocking hard on her wooden chair. "Kiki, how many times must I tell you not to say such inauspicious things?"

Papi and I share a look. Normally, I would've been a bit more considerate and not said such things in front of Mami, but honestly? Just a tad resentful toward her this morning, because moving me to Xingfa was her idea. I should've known she would do this after the way she reacted when she found out that George Clooney (the knockoff, not the original) goes to Xingfa. But how could I have known that even my ambitious mom would be ridiculous enough to take me out of Mingyang High and enroll me in Xingfa for the last year of school? I mean, really now. When she told me a month ago, she was, like, "Mami and Papi made a mistake enrolling you in that hippie school. Now you can barely speak Chinese, you have no manners, and you're too—too prideful!"

"It's called confidence, Mami," I snorted.

"You see!" she crowed. "You're talking back to your elders. You need a good, traditional school instead of Mingyang, which is too—too liberal. Xingfa is a very traditional school. It'll get you in line."

I looked at Papi then, expecting him to step in and tell Mami to back down, but instead, he gazed at me, unsmiling, completely serious. I realized then that he was on Mami's side.

"Mami's right," he said after a second. "You're too—too . . . what's the word? *Pede*?"

Pede is short for *percaya diri,* which literally translates to "belief in oneself." It means confident but in an arrogant way.

"This is such BS," I groaned.

"No, we want you to learn to be humble," Papi said.

"If I were a boy, you'd be praising me for being confident."

Mami glowered at me. "Maybe. But you're not a boy."

Papi sighed then. "It's not that I don't want you to be confident, Kiki. Unfortunately, our society is still very conservative, and I worry that you'll struggle in the real world. Learning to fit in with social norms is important."

Story of my life. Whether in-game or in my own house, things would be a lot easier if I'd been born a dude. Fastforward a few weeks, and here we are on this fine morning, with me making tiny passive-aggressive remarks and/or welltimed snorts to show Mami that I haven't quite forgiven her yet. Technically, I guess I should also be mad at Papi, but the bulk of the blame rests with Mami. She was the ringleader in this whole mess.

I pour myself a bowl of cereal the color of a radioactive rainbow and start eating in front of them. Mami winces as I eat. I know she's dying to tell me that I might as well be eating poison, that I'm going to give myself cancer, and so on, but she thinks better of it. Instead, she forces a smile and goes to the fridge. She brings out a takeaway cup of Starbucks caramel latte, which she sets down in front of me.

"I got it for you this morning."

Damn it. Why does she have to go and be nice to me now? I consider turning my nose up at it to make a point, but the point doesn't seem worth making anymore, and gosh, I can see that she's ordered extra caramel drizzle on the top. "You're playing dirty," I grumble.

"Fine, I'll throw it a—"

My hand shoots out and grabs the cup.

"What do you say to your mother?" Papi says, like I'm all of three years old.

"Thank you," I mumble.

She gives me a beatific Mother Mary smile. "You're welcome, nu er." *Nu er* is Chinese for "daughter," and my parents love using it when they feel the need to remind me that I came from their loins. "Now get going. You don't want to be late on your first day of school."

"Yeah, yeah." I stand up, slinging my bag over one shoulder, and hear Mami's sharp intake of breath. I close my eyes. I don't know what she's going to complain about this time, but she'll find something, of that I'm sure.

"Your skirt—"

Oh, crap. She's noticed that I had it shortened. I arrange my features into those of an innocent pup before turning around to face her.

Papi is craning his neck to see what the fuss is about. "What's up?"

"Did you have your skirt shortened?" Mami asks in a dangerous, low voice.

"No . . . ?" I look down like I'm just as surprised as she is. "It came like this."

Mami's eyes narrow. The tension in the room crackles. I can practically hear her mind whirring madly, rushing through her options. I wonder if she's going to make me wear shorts underneath. Just as I'm about to lose it, one corner of Mami's mouth quirks up. If I didn't know any better, I would think she's trying to fight back a smile.

"Never mind," she says suddenly. "Off you go, don't be late."

What the hell just happened? Papi and I stare at her for a couple of seconds, both of us equally bewildered, before I shrug. "See you kids later."

"See what I mean?" Mami grumbles. "No manners."

"We've failed as parents," Papi agrees, before giving me a wink.

I'm not sure what to expect from Xingfa, but I know what they can expect from me: awesomeness. Not to toot my own horn or anything, but I've got the confidence of a mediocre white man down pat.

In the car, Pak Run, our family driver, quirks a smile at me through the rearview mirror. "You ready for your first day?"

"You know I was born ready."

He snorts as he backs out of the driveway. Pak Run's been with our family since I was a baby, and he might as well be a blood relative by now. "Buckle up."

"Yes, sir." It's not the law here to buckle up when sitting in the backseat, but Pak Run's made it clear he won't go anywhere unless I'm belted, which, you know, props to the man for having integrity.

My phone buzzes again. This time, the message goes through Discord instead of WhatsApp, and my heart does this little skip, because the only person I chat with on Discord is Sourdawg.

Sourdawg: First day of school! Knock 'em dead, kiddo!

I laugh silently.

Dudebro10: Are you secretly a sixty-five-year-old man?
Sourdawg: 👓 But forreals though, g'luck
Dudebro10: Thanks. Have you sent the email to the sourdough company?
Sourdawg: Ttyl!

As usual, my cheeks are hurting from grinning so hard. Typical Sourdawg, running away at the first sign of conflict. I tuck my phone back into my pocket and gaze out the window at the awful Jakarta morning traffic. Xingfa is in North Jakarta, and we live in the south, so at least we're going against the flow of commuter traffic. Still, it'll take us almost forty-five minutes to get there. I check my bag to make sure I've brought my textbooks and iPad and my aquamarine pencil case, then take out my compact to check my reflection. No spinach in my teeth. Not that I ate any spinach this morning, but I'm convinced that spinach was designed by Mother Nature to magically appear on teeth right before a big date or an important interview.

By the time the car arrives at the school, I'm surprised to find that my stomach is clenched into a tight knot. When I get out of the car, I almost stumble, because my legs are watery. I can't believe I'm so nervous that I literally can't walk.

"You're going to be okay. Just relax," Pak Run calls out.

I manage a weak smile, then turn around to face the

looming school building. Okay, so it's actually a really pretty building and doesn't do much looming, but I swear I can feel the school looking down at me and judging me. Right, I'm officially losing it. I tighten my hold on my messenger bag, take a deep breath, and mutter, "I'm the GOAT. I'm the GOAT." Except now I'm thinking of the animal instead of the acronym.

"Ci Kiki!" someone cries out from inside the building.

I look up and spot Eleanor Roosevelt, aka the little sister I've always longed for, waving crazily at me from inside the reception hall. Immediately, my muscles loosen and my legs spring back into action, taking me up the steps two at a time. "Eleanor Roosevelt!" When I first got to know her through her big brother, George Clooney, I made the mistake of calling her Ellie. She gave me this look that seared all the way through my blackened soul and said, "My name is Eleanor Roosevelt Tanuwijaya. You can call me Eleanor Roosevelt." I pointed out to her that even the original Eleanor Roosevelt probably didn't go by Eleanor Roosevelt, and she said, "Yes, but I do." And that was that.

She throws her skinny little tween arms around my waist the moment I get inside the building. "I can't believe we're actually in the same school!"

I hug her back, breathing deeply. Eleanor Roosevelt is probably the only good thing about switching schools. I can't explain the bond that we have. We each have friends our own age, but there's just something about Eleanor Roosevelt that reminds me of myself. I know it's a cliché, but it's so rare to come across someone just as loud and unapologetically obnoxious as myself. People are always telling Eleanor Roosevelt to quiet down, or stop talking, or stop meddling, and I totally get her frustration at having to make herself smaller and quieter for other people.

Even now, Eleanor Roosevelt is yammering a mile a minute. "Oh my god, you look ah-may-zing in the school uniform! Of course I expected nothing less from you, Ci Kiki." She stops and gasps, her eyes widening like an anime character. "Did you shorten your school skirt?" she whispers in a mock-scandalized tone.

"Maybe a little." I wink at her, and she squeals with laughter.

"I love it!" Then she hesitates. "But maybe others might not?" Just as my anxiety spikes once more, she quickly waves her hands. "Nah, of course they will. You're going to set a new trend, I know it. Save us from these eighteenth-century bags, am I right?" She gestures at her own pleated skirt, which goes halfway down her calves, making her look awkwardly tall.

"They are incredibly unflattering," I agree. I totally expected that all the older girls would have shortened their skirts, but Eleanor Roosevelt's reaction makes it obvious that no one else has, which is worrisome. Still, as she said, maybe I'll set a new trend.

I'm nothing if not an optimist.

"Anyway, there's someone I've been dying to introduce to you," Eleanor Roosevelt says. She doesn't wait for my reply before turning around and calling out, "Sarah Jessica Parker! C'mere!"

A bespectacled girl walks out from behind one of the ginormous pillars at the front of the school and approaches us with a shy smile.

I bite back my grin. "Sarah Jessica Parker, huh?"

"It's actually Sarah Jessica Parker Susanti. Sarah Jessica Parker is an actress best known for playing Carrie Bradshaw on *Sex and the City*," she says with all the earnestness in the world.

I want to hug this kid. "Yeah, I know who SJP is."

"My mom is a huge fan."

"I figured," I say solemnly.

"Anyway," Eleanor Roosevelt says, "we've been so excited about you starting here at Xingfa, because we have the most amazing opportunity for you. C'mere." She links her arm through mine and leads me firmly through the large reception hall and into a side corridor that's a bit less crowded.

Uh-oh. George has always said that his little sister is going to either appear on the cover of *Forbes* one day or end up in prison for running a worldwide scam. I mean, I love the kid like no other, but I can totally see it. "Yeah?" I say warily.

Eleanor Roosevelt gives Sarah Jessica a signal, and Sarah Jessica taps on her phone with a flourish. Sad violin music wails from the phone. I glance around us as students stream past. A few of them are definitely giving us curious side-eyes, but most of them are busy reading books or scrolling through their phones as they walk. Still, I do wish that Eleanor Roosevelt and Sarah Jessica Parker hadn't chosen this very moment to do this strange presentation.

Eleanor Roosevelt clears her throat and starts talking in a dramatic voice. "Life can be so lonely sometimes, especially when you're in school."

I want to point out to her that when you're in school,

you're *least* likely to be lonely, because you're surrounded by friends all the time, but I'm dying for this to be over, so I just nod and give her an encouraging smile.

"You're snowed under tons of schoolwork—projects, tests, and exams, oh my! How utterly depressing. Is this the fate of our youth? Are we destined to spend our best years languishing away, studying and studying and studying?" she moans. Then she brightens and holds up an index finger, just as the sad violin strings are replaced with a jaunty, uplifting tune. Wow, she's practiced this. "But it's okay, because Lil' Aunties Know Best is here to solve all your dating problems!"

I laugh and clap before I realize I have no idea how Lil' Aunties is going to solve anyone's problems. But Eleanor Roosevelt is delivering her speech with such passion that I'm, like, heck yeah, solve world hunger, Lil' Aunties!

"We may be young, but the Lil' Aunties will find the perfect match for you. You want someone tall, pale, and handsome? Done. You want someone who's into algebra? We got you covered. You want someone who will be respectful toward your elders and has at least one athletic extracurricular activity? We've got just the right person for you! WhatsApp us today and meet your soulmate tomorrow!" Both Eleanor Roosevelt and Sarah Jessica do jazz hands, and the music ends.

I clap, though not too loudly, because I'm super aware of all the stares from other students as they make their way to class.

"What do you think?" Eleanor Roosevelt says, her eyes shining with barely restrained excitement.

I have to fight to keep the grin on my face. "I mean, yeah,

that was great. Very, ah, very convincing. But I think we should go to—"

"Yasss!" Eleanor Roosevelt turns to Sarah Jessica, and the two of them bump fists. "I knew you'd love the idea. I just knew that you'd get it."

I have to smile at that. "If anyone were to run a successful matchmaking service, it would be you. But, um, are most parents going to be okay with their thirteen-year-olds dating?" Most parents in Indonesia don't even want their sixteen-year-olds dating.

"Oh!" Eleanor Roosevelt cries. "It's not for us, gosh no." Sarah Jessica Parker shakes her head vehemently. "It's for you seniors!"

"Uh-huh . . . Again, if anyone can run a successful matchmaking service, it would be you. But how many seniors do you know?" I can't see anyone going for a matchmaking service run by two thirteen-year-olds, but I don't say that out loud, because she'll probably find it patronizing.

Instead of deflating at the very legit point I've just made, Eleanor Roosevelt's grin widens. "Yeah, that's where YOU come in, Ci Kiki."

Uh-oh. "I'm . . . not following."

"Well, you're a senior. And you're new. This would be the perfect way for you to get to know more people at Xingfa!"

"I—I don't know . . . I'm going to be pretty busy with college apps—"

"Exactly!" Eleanor Roosevelt cries. How is it possible that her eyes are literally wider than before? I swear her face is

70 percent eyes right now. "This will be so good on your college apps!"

"Um, yeah, I don't think that using a matchmaking service—"

"You wouldn't just be using the service," Sarah Jessica says. "As our first-ever participant, you'll be granted a position within our company."

"I don't know—"

Eleanor Roosevelt holds up a thumb. "Organizational skills." An index finger. "Communication skills." Her middle finger. "Social networking." Her fourth finger. "Marketing skills." Her pinky. "And later, once we've conquered Xingfa, we can expand to other schools, and that shows entrepreneurial spirit. It's going to blow your college app profile out of the water."

"Uh . . ." Despite myself, I'm pretty freaking impressed. How are these kids only thirteen? When I was thirteen, all I did was play shooting games. Oh wait, I'm still doing that.

"But the icing on the cake," Eleanor Roosevelt adds, "is our app."

"Wha?" I can't believe I'm the elder here and I'm the one who's lost in this conversation.

She gestures with a flourish at Sarah Jessica. "You might not have guessed from how fabulous she looks, but our Sarah Jessica Parker is a programming genius. She's going to make an app for it."

Sarah Jessica curtseys. "I do like making apps. I've made a couple of them before, just to try my hand at it. It's really easy."

I nod slowly. "Really easy to make a phone app, huh?" I echo, still struggling to follow what's happening.

"Piece of cake. It'll be like Tinder," Sarah Jessica says with all the confidence in the world.

"Okay, I'm not even going to get into the fact that you two are way too young to know about Tinder." I frown sternly down at them, and they roll their eyes. "But there's also the fact that, uh, premarital sex is really—I mean—" I struggle for the right words. "It's, you know, you—you kids are too young!"

"Oh my gosh, Ci Kiki," Eleanor Roosevelt groans. "Of course it won't be about the sex. Ew. I mean, it's like Tinder but a lot more innocent. Like an innocent, parent-approved Tinder."

I narrow my eyes at her. "George will kill me if you get into any trouble, you know that?"

Eleanor Roosevelt smiles sweetly up at me. "Then you better make sure I don't get into any trouble."

I know when I'm defeated. "All right, I'll help you guys out with it, but I do *not* want to be involved in the actual dating."

"Are you sure?" Sarah Jessica says. "Going on dates will really help your social life."

I toss my hair over my shoulder and wink at them. "I don't need help finding dates."

Eleanor Roosevelt raises her brows at Sarah Jessica. "See?" she says. "I told you Ci Kiki is the best."

Sarah Jessica looks like she's about to continue arguing, but just then, the bell rings.

"That's the first bell," Sarah Jessica says. "Means we've got eight minutes before classes formally start."

"Okay, well, I've gotta run," I say.

"We'll revisit this later," Eleanor Roosevelt calls out to me as I hurry down the hallway toward the Secondary School building.

"Sure!" Phew—saved by the bell.

CHAPTER 3

I know from hours of watching Netflix shows that in the States, the students move around to different classrooms throughout the day. But in most Asian schools, the students stay put and the teachers are the ones who move around to different classrooms according to the timetables. So every year, students pray that they're placed in the right class, because if you happen to be placed in a class with someone shitty—a mean kid, or cliquey athletes who dominate the class—then you're shit out of luck.

At Mingyang, our classes were given animal names, and I was in Year Eleven Dragon, which was hands down the coolest animal out of the lot. I relished being referred to as "the Dragon kid" rather than, say, "the Orangutan girl." At Xingfa, the classes are given virtues as names. Ugh. They go by Year Eleven Charity, Eleven Diligence, Eleven Faith, and so on. Who'd want to go from Dragon to (ugh, my new class) Purity? This feels like a bad omen. Why is "purity" even a virtue? What kind of purity are they referring to? Racial purity?

'Cause that just sounds like straight-up racism. Or do they mean sexual purity, which is a whole other kind of gross.

Okay, so maybe my mind is spiraling and glomming on to anything it can focus its anxiety on. Now that Eleanor Roosevelt has scurried away to her class (Year Seven Justice), I'm left to find my class on my own. In a way, I'm glad that I'm not being escorted by some elderly admin lady, but Xingfa is really huge and I'm sort of lost.

"I'm the GOAT," I whisper to myself as I make my way through the crowds of students filing into their various classrooms. My eyes ping-pong between the classroom labels and the other students, all of whom glance at me as I pass by, their eyes crawling from my head down to my legs. Crap, none of the other girls have shortened their skirts. What the hell?

Never mind. Focus on finding your classroom.

Outside the classrooms are these huge bulletin boards. A few of them are filled with exemplary projects—there's one about the chemical composition of popular shampoos and why they may or may not cause cancer, another about the physics of eggshells and why they're so much stronger than we think they are. Other boards are filled with medals and paintings and other memorabilia. All of them proudly announce which class the students who made them are from: Year Eleven Wisdom, Year Eleven Hope, Year Eleven Kindness—they're not even in alphabetical order? Gah! But finally, I see it: Year Eleven Purity. My home for the next year.

I take my time standing outside the class to study the bulletin boards. Well, okay, I take my time standing outside because I'm sort of scared shitless to go in. But also, I'm gathering intel on my future classmates. The first bulletin board is filled with two projects, one of them an English Lit project (a study on Shakespeare's patronage), the other one a calculus project. Both of them were done by someone named Jonas Jayden Arifin. The name rings a bell, and I take my phone out and do a Google search. Which is kind of creepy, I know, but knowledge is power, and I need all the power I can get today.

When the search loads, my breath catches. There are a ton of news articles about Jonas Jayden Arifin, because his family owns TalkCo, the nation's biggest telecommunications corporation. Holy shit. Okay, wow. So Jonas Arifin, teenage billionaire, is the class nerd. Did not expect that, but I can respect it. But then I go to the second board, which is filled with medals for tennis, and I see that they were all awarded to Jonas as well. Okaaay. I adjust my mental picture of Jonas from a gangly, pimply nerd to a less pimply nerd with tennis shoulders. The third bulletin board is filled with photographs taken from various events, groups of sailor-uniformed students with their arms around one another, laughing. There's one of them at some sort of arts and crafts and baking fair, another of them wearing protective goggles in what looks like a woodworking class.

As I stand there checking out the board, a couple of girls walk past me. They glance at me with passing curiosity, and when our eyes meet, they smile. Before going inside the classroom, they take out their phones and plop them into a basket hanging off the wall. On top of the basket is a sign that says PHONES HERE!

Wow, okay. I guess we're not allowed to take our phones

into the class. That's pretty hardcore. With a lot of reluctance, I fish my phone from my pocket and place it carefully inside the basket. I feel naked without it. I won't be able to pretend to look busy without my phone. But maybe I won't need to pretend to look busy; maybe I'll be swarmed with so many new friends that I won't even remember that I don't have my phone on me. With that, I take a deep inhale, grip the strap of my messenger bag, and walk into my new classroom.

The first day of every year is harrowing no matter what, but being the new kid makes everything so much worse. I've had enough experience by now to know that the first step into a new classroom is a make-or-break moment that sets the tone for the rest of the year. It's imperative that I make the best possible first impression right now, or everything's going to go down the toilet.

Even though every muscle in my body is tense and wants to push my head down and hunch my shoulders forward, I force myself to stand straight. Chest out, shoulders back, chin up. A small, confident smile plastered on my face like war paint. *Everybody else in here is just as intimidated as you are,* I remind myself.

"Heads up—new girl!" someone hoots.

Okay, so not everyone else is as intimidated as I am.

Immediately, heads turn toward me like meerkats, and I find myself the subject of about a dozen interested stares. I freeze. I swear my heart forgets to beat. But somehow, I manage to nod in the general direction of the boy who hooted at me. "Hey." My voice comes out small and squeaky.

"You're sitting behind me," he says.

"Uh. That's okay, thanks." I lower my head slightly and make my way to the back of the classroom. Why am I saying no to him? He's actually not bad looking, but my instinctive reaction is to say no to him. Instead, I find an empty desk in the back row and put my bag down on it.

"Hey," a girl next to me says.

I turn to her, relieved that someone's talking to me. People here seem really friendly. "Hi."

Instead of the introduction I'm expecting, the girl says in a matter-of-fact way, "You can't just sit there."

"Oh?" I gape at her stupidly.

She sighs. "That's Grace's seat."

"Oh. Sorry, I thought—" My mind goes blank. I thought that since this is the first day of a new term, no one's claimed a desk yet.

"You can't just sit anywhere you want. We have assigned seating."

"Oh!" Okay. That makes more sense.

She nods at the front of the classroom. "The seating plan's there."

"Thanks."

She gives me a close-lipped smile and goes back to reading a book. The walk to the front of the classroom feels never-ending. I scan the roster quickly. All the seats are in pairs. I find my name next to someone named Liam Ng, and in front of me is the famous Jonas Arifin. I don't know how I feel about being seated behind the all-around star, but maybe his shine will distract the other kids from me. But when I turn around and head for my desk, I realize that Jonas is the guy who hooted at me when I entered the room.

He's sitting with his arms crossed in front of his chest, a smirk on his face. "Told you."

Heat flushes my face. When he told me to sit behind him, I assumed that—what? He was hitting on me? Turns out he was just letting me know, as a matter of fact, where I'm supposed to sit. Now I feel really stupid, like duh, of course he wasn't hitting on me or anything. Gah.

As though he read my mind, Jonas says, "Did you think I was hitting on you?"

My entire face bursts into flames. How did he guess what I was thinking? A small part of me wants to curl up and disappear, but hey, I'm Kiki Siregar, damn it. Today is intimidating as hell, but I'm as confident as they come. So I grin at him and say, "Yeah, obviously. Were you not?" Okay, that came out a lot more flirtatious than I intended. I went for Challenging in a Friendly Way and somehow landed on Very Suggestive. My insides squirm with embarrassment.

Jonas's eyes widen, his mouth parting slightly, and I'm torn between laughter and further embarrassment. Then his eyebrows knit together and he smiles and goes, "Okay, I see how it is."

I sense people watching us, and when I turn, sure enough, a handful of the other kids are staring, some of them looking less than friendly. A guy like Jonas must have his share of admirers, and I'm not here to step on anyone's toes, so I give him a reserved smile before turning pointedly to my bag. I make it clear that I am Very Focused on unloading books from my bag and therefore too busy to continue our chat. I turn to face the girl across from me, hoping to strike up a conversation with her. More than anything, my first goal here is to make female friends. Boyfriends come and go, but female friends are the ones who will stick around.

"Really? You're just gonna leave me hanging like that?" he teases. Or at least I think he's teasing? But I catch just a tiny hint of an edge in his voice, like he's not used to having girls turn away from him. Or maybe that's just my imagination running wild, because I'm the one who's on edge despite the numerous times I've reminded myself of how confident I am.

I glance back at him as I take out my pencil case and arrange it neatly on the top left-hand corner of my desk. "Sorry, I didn't mean to leave you hanging. You're Jonas, right?"

"That's me," he says with obvious pride, like I'm supposed to have heard of him. I suppose, technically, that I have heard of him—or, rather, read about him—from the bulletin boards outside. "And you're Kristabella."

"Kiki," I say quickly. "It's what everyone calls me."

He gives me a calculating look. "You look more like a Kris to me."

"How does a Kris differ in appearance to a Kiki?"

His expression turns thoughtful. "Well, Kiki's kind of a silly name, like something you'd call a tiny, yappy dog, you know?"

"Wow, okay, not holding back any punches, I see."

He laughs and holds up his arms, giving me a good view of

his tennis forearms and straight white teeth. "No, I'm trying to say that you're not at all like a tiny, yappy dog. You're more like a Kris, sophisticated and . . ."—he pauses meaningfully before meeting my eyes straight on—"pretty."

Despite myself, I feel goose bumps crawling up my arms and my cheeks turning red again. I'm used to flirting with guys, but flirting with a cute guy on my very first day at a new school is a whole other level of stressful/exciting that I wasn't quite prepared for. I do what I always do when I'm uncomfortable: my sense of humor slams into place like a shield, and I dramatically flip my hair over my shoulder and say in my best dramatic voice, "Why, thank you for noticing."

He laughs, thank goodness, and I laugh as well before looking pointedly down at my bag and unpacking the rest of my stuff. I wonder when my seatmate is going to turn up. Liam Ng. It's an interesting surname, not at all Indonesian. I'm weirdly nervous about meeting him. I wouldn't say I'm shy or introverted, but being the new kid in school is way out of my comfort zone, and I'm so wrapped up in making a good first impression that every muscle in my body is tense.

"Yo, Liam!" Jonas calls out. "You're next to the new girl."

I look up, the back of my neck burning, to see a super-tall guy striding in. He gives Jonas a close-lipped smile, then he turns and sees me, and phew, I must have the best karma ever. Because Liam Ng is devastatingly handsome. Cheekbones for days, thick eyebrows, a jawline that, if Greek gods were still in operation, would've gotten him struck down out of envy. Our eyes meet. I swallow. My mouth creates more drool. I swallow again. Altogether, not a great start for me. I wish I could tell my saliva glands to stop salivating. Wow, this boy is literally drool-worthy. And he's my soul—er, seatmate! I tell myself not to stare as he walks toward me.

"Hey." He flashes me a friendly smile. An earnest one, not the kind of condescending smirk that I half expected from someone this hot. Dimples appear in his cheeks. He has dimples? How dare he.

"Uh." No words come out. My brain has given up and is currently rocking back and forth in a tiny dark corner.

"I'm Liam." He flushes a little. "Sorry, you probably knew that from the seating chart. Anyway, nice meeting you, Krista-bella."

"Kiki!" I bark. Oh my god. I clamp my mouth shut and glare down at my lap. I have forgotten how to human.

"Cool," he says easily, as though I haven't just yipped at him like a nervous chihuahua.

Thankfully, the teacher walks into class then.

"Class stand," Jonas barks in such a loud voice that I jump in my seat.

Chairs scrape back against the floor. I look around, confused. Everyone's standing up. I quickly follow suit.

"Greet the teacher," Jonas says.

What the hell?

As one, the whole class bows and intones, "Good morning, Teacher."

The teacher waves at us without bothering to return the greeting. "You can sit."

Everyone sits back down. Okay, that was interesting.

As the teacher takes stuff out of his bag, I use the chance to check out my classmates. Subtly, of course.

The differences from the kids at Mingyang are small, but they're there. At Mingyang, we were allowed to wear whatever shoes, socks, and hairbands we wanted. But here at Xingfa, there's a very strict dress code in addition to the sailor uniform: white socks (no visible brand names or logos), black shoes (again, no visible brand names or logos), and hairbands only in navy blue or black. All female students with hair past their shoulders have to tie it back. No "outlandish hairstyles" allowed. All male students have to maintain their hair above their ears. No dyeing of hair, no nail polish, and absolutely no makeup allowed. Mingyang has the same rule about makeup, but I know just about every girl wears something. Most of us wore tinted lip balms, at the very least. I usually darken my eyebrows too, because I have the unfortunate kind that only go half the width of my eyes before thinning out. Without eyebrow pencils, my brows would look like sad little thumbprints.

But here I don't see any tinted lips or mascara-plumped lashes. Every face is naked. Unless these girls have fully mastered the art of natural makeup? But the teacher starts talking, so I'm forced to stop staring at my classmates like Joe Goldberg from *You*.

"Right," the teacher says. "I hope you all had a wonderful holiday. Some of you may know me already. For those who don't, my name is Mr. Francis Tan. I'm your Form teacher, and I'll also be teaching you English Literature." He pauses to give us all a small, businessy smile. I guess "Form teacher" here is what we know at Mingyang as our Homeroom teacher. I regard Mr. Tan more carefully.

As though reading my mind, Jonas turns to me and whispers, "Don't worry, Mr. Tan's chill. I had him for English Lit last year."

"Jonas, we've been over this." Mr. Tan sighs. "No talking in class unless I give you permission."

Jonas gives him a sheepish grin. "Aye, Shifu."

A handful of students laugh at Jonas's calling Mr. Tan the Mandarin word for "master," and Mr. Tan shakes his head with an affectionate smile. Then he seems to notice me for the first time. "Oh yes. And we have a new student joining us this year." He pauses, scrolling through his tablet. "Kristabella Siregar?"

"Yes," I say quickly. "Just Kiki will do."

"We don't do nicknames here, Kristabella."

"Wow, okay," I mutter, and immediately regret it. I hadn't meant for it to come out so full of attitude. "I mean, sure, that's fine."

One corner of Mr. Tan's mouth quirks up, though I'm not sure that I would call what he's doing smiling. "I'm glad you think that's fine, because those are the rules. Well, I hope you settle in here just fine. Anything you need, you can come to me." He swipes down on his tablet and turns on a screen projector. "Right! We're diving right in." He glances over his shoulder at me. "I'm assuming you've read our guidebook?"

Negative. Very much so. Who reads those things anyway? Xingfa's welcome booklet included a stupidly heavy guidebook, which I tossed aside and forgot about completely until this very moment. But I hesitate for only a split second before nodding with enthusiasm. "Yep, totally. Riveting."

Next to me, Liam stifles a snort. I can't tell if it's a friendly one or a derisive one.

"Good," Mr. Tan says. "So you know that Xingfa isn't just an academically oriented school; we take pride in our students learning to think outside the box. Forty percent of Year Elevens' final grade will come from projects instead of exams. Last term, we were assigned Science as our project topic, which most of you aced."

A few students hoot. One of them shouts out, "Yeah, Jonas!" Jonas, in turn, gives a smug smirk. I think of the bulletin boards outside the classrooms and how Jonas dominates the one outside ours.

"This term, I've advocated really hard for Purity to be assigned an interesting topic. No Geography or, god forbid, History."

There are a few snickers.

"I hope you didn't get us assigned to Science again, Mr. Tan," Jonas calls out.

A corner of Mr. Tan's mouth quirks up, and he taps on his computer screen. The projector screen lights and brings up a vibrant collage of—oh my god—games. There are lots that I recognize: *Borderlands, Assassin's Creed, Stardew Valley, Fortnite,* even lesser-known ones like *Bugsnax* and *Slime Rancher.*

"Video games!" Mr. Tan says with an exaggerated flourish, and everyone breaks into applause.

"That's awesome!" someone shouts out.

"Great job, Mr. Tan!"

I clap along with them, grinning hard. A project about games, heck yeah! That's my jam. Maybe Xingfa isn't going to be as dreary as I feared.

"I've assigned you to groups based on your seating chart."

I meet Liam's eyes and flush, breaking eye contact immediately. Am I glad to be in the same group as someone who's obviously too beautiful to be human? I mean, I'm not NOT glad. But damn, it's going to make focusing that much harder.

The projector goes to a different slide and shows our assigned groups. I'm in Group B: Kristabella Siregar, Liam Ng, Jonas Jayden Arifin, Peishan Wongso. The four of us look at each other, and Jonas grins.

"We're going to kill this," he says.

Well, we're definitely going to kill something.

CHAPTER 4

Mr. Tan spends the next few minutes going through our project guidelines. At the end of each term, the school holds a project exhibition. Only the top projects are picked from each class and shown proudly inside the hall for parents and other students to admire. Each Purity group has to come up with a new game, including a concept, a cover, and a business plan. Despite myself, I'm really impressed by this. At Mingyang, the only projects we were ever assigned were your traditional science or history ones, but as Mr. Tan explains, the global gaming industry is, in fact, bigger than the movie industry, and it's still not done expanding, so it makes sense for us to tackle this as a topic.

Well, I'm not complaining. By the time Mr. Tan is done with his talk and we break off into our respective groups, I'm raring to go. Seriously, I couldn't come up with a better topic if I tried. I'm practically rubbing my palms with glee as Jonas and Peishan turn their chairs around so we're facing one another.

"So," Jonas says, grinning, "how awesome is this?"

Liam nods. "I think it's the first time I'm actually excited about my term project."

Only Peishan looks unimpressed. "I don't really play games."

I'm about to say something when Jonas says, "That's fine. I'm a serious gamer. I've got this down pat. You guys just have to follow my lead."

I stare at him. "Okaaay."

Maybe that came out slightly more caustic than I expected, because a small frown crosses Jonas's face for a second. Then he clears his throat and takes out an iPad from his bag. Right, I'd forgotten that Xingfa is so fancy that every student is lent a school-sanctioned iPad. The iPads have been programmed so that we're unable to download any apps aside from the school-regulated ones. Jonas places his iPad on the table with an air of importance, opens up a drawing program, and begins sketching. I look at Peishan and Liam out of the corner of my eyes, waiting for either one to say something, but they both seem perfectly happy letting Jonas run the show, so I bite my lower lip and make myself stay silent as Jonas draws a quick sketch.

"So I'm thinking an FPS, right? That's first-person shooter," he adds in a tone so patronizing that my teeth clack together loudly.

"I knew that," I snap.

Jonas raises an eyebrow in obvious disbelief, then shrugs and continues sketching. Liam meets my eye again, and this time, his thick brows knit together. Gah, well, I'm sorry some of us aren't just going to stay silent while Jonas patronizes us.

After a painfully quiet minute, Jonas flips the iPad around and proudly shows us his sketch of the cover concept. "Ta-da!"

Oh god. It's the most stereotypical sketch that has ever existed: a skinny woman standing with her back super arched, so that her super-round butt is more pronounced, looking over her shoulder at us so we're treated to a view of her duck lips and the curve of a huge boob peeking out beyond one arm. I mean . . . need I say more? I can't help the small scoff that escapes my mouth.

Jonas's gaze snaps toward me. "You don't look impressed, new kid." There's a challenging note in his voice, like he's both amused and annoyed.

"Well . . ." I struggle to come up with the most diplomatic words. "Ah, your drawing skills are like, amazing, obviously. But the sketch itself . . . I think it's kind of overdone? Plus, haven't you heard about the whole *Overwatch* controversy with Tracer's art design? Blizzard had to remove a photo of her doing this exact pose, because fans complained that it was overly sexualized and reduced her to nothing more than a sex symbol. And, let's face it, it's just a really lazy pose. It's the most overused, obvious pose you can get for female characters."

The moment the words leave my mouth, I wish I could swallow them back. I didn't mean to give a whole speech about it, but wow, I guess I had Feelings about the over-the-shoulder pose. But it's not just that. It's also the way that Jonas has taken the helm so quickly, dismissing the rest of us as mere peons, that's rubbed me the wrong way.

For a moment, they all just stare at me. Then Jonas snorts and says, "Wow, okay, tell us how you really feel."

It's the smirk that does it. That and the snort. And what he said. It's just so much. "Yeah, I will, actually," I say. "And given that it's supposed to be a group effort, you could, you know, consider working as a team rather than bossing us around?"

Jonas's mouth drops open in mock surprise. "I would never think of bossing anyone around. I'm just taking the helm because I'm a gamer, so I have the most experience in this field."

"I'm a gamer too," I say, and it's a testament to my patience that I don't add, "asshole."

Jonas rolls his eyes. "*Candy Crush* doesn't count as a real game."

I swear I'm this close to leaping across the table and throttling his little neck, but just then, I notice that Liam is glaring at me. When I meet his eye, he gives a small shake of his head. What is he, Jonas's stooge? But then I see that Peishan is also glaring at me, and my anger crumbles into guilt. I'd assumed that since she's a girl, she would also object to the art. I didn't mean to start a fight with a group mate on what seems like a really important term project, and on my very first day at school, no less. Crap. I take a deep breath and lean back in my seat.

"Liam here used to game, but not anymore," Jonas says, "and Peishan's too busy studying, so I think it's for the best if I'm team leader. Everyone agreed?"

No! my mind screams. But neither Peishan nor Liam says anything, and it hits me that maybe I'm the one being unreasonable. Maybe I'm the one being disruptive and they're all annoyed at me, not Jonas. It's an ugly feeling, twisting deep down in my guts. The bell rings then, and Mr. Tan tells everyone to return to their seats and prep for the next class.

We get a five-minute break between each class, so as soon as Mr. Tan leaves the classroom, I don't spare anyone a single glance before leaping out from behind my desk and practically sprinting out. I can feel eyes skittering across my back like spiders. Outside the class, I brisk-walk to the bathroom, lock myself into the farthest cubicle, and sag against the wall with a bone-deep sigh. I rest my forehead against the cool tiled wall. My inner Mami screeches at me about how unhygienic doing that is, but I don't have the strength to lift my head from the wall.

How in the world did I manage to tank my first-ever class so badly? I don't get it. Where did I go wrong? I close my eyes and immediately, the excruciating scene replays in my mind. My voice echoes through my head.

It's the most overused, obvious pose you can get for female characters. God, could I sound more pretentious? Why did I say that? Why couldn't I have just said it in a more mature, palatable way, like "I think you could definitely come up with a better pose." Or, better yet, why couldn't I just keep my mouth shut and follow Jonas's lead? As Mr. Tan pointed out, Jonas killed it last term with his project, so he obviously knows what he's doing. Why do I always have to act like I know better?

But even as I think that, a not-so-small part of me growls: Because I do. In this instance, I know I was in the right. I'm a gamer too, I keep up with gaming news, I know that the gaming industry needs to be more inclusive and start listening to everyone, not just hetero, cis male gamers.

And Jonas . . .

Ugh, he caught me so off guard. How the hell did things go south so quickly? I mean, right before the class, we were flirting with each other! He told me I was pretty, and I thought he was cute, and it was all exciting and fun, and then—what the hell happened? I should've backed off. No! I shouldn't have backed off. At Mingyang, I wasn't even considered one of the more outspoken pupils, because we were always encouraged to speak our minds.

Okay, so this cinches the deal. I can't carry on at Xingfa. I'm gonna go home and tell Mami that I crashed and burned in the most horrific way possible and that she has to re-enroll me in Mingyang right away. I take a deep breath, then recall that the last thing I want to be doing is to take a deep inhale in a public restroom. Gah. Of course, as soon as I think about telling Mami to take me out of Xingfa because I made a fool of myself on not just my first day but my first class, I can already imagine her reaction.

Aduh, Kiki, I didn't raise you to be a quitter. Or a loser. You were born to be a queen bee, my darling girl.

Then I'd be like: *But Mami, these kids are so different. They're not the kind of people I'm used to. They just want me to keep my head down and follow the rules.*

Then Mami would be like: *Well, there are two ways this could go. One, you could prove them wrong and show them that speaking up for your beliefs is important. Or two, they teach you some manners. Either way, it's a win-win.*

And I'd be like: *For you, maybe. Grumble, grumble.*

Damn it, even Imagination Kiki can't win against Imagination Mami.

A bell rings, probably to signify the start of second period. I take another deep breath, remember belatedly *again* where I am, and lift my chin. I come out of the cubicle, smiling politely at a couple of girls who are washing their hands. They glance at me with some interest but don't say anything before leaving.

That's okay. I'm going to go out there and freaking slay. I check my reflection and nod to myself. That first class was just an anomaly. Now that I have a feel for the culture here and who to avoid (i.e., Jonas), the rest of the day will be fine. I'll just keep my head down, stay away from Jonas, and maybe try to feel out which of the girls in my class are more approachable.

My newfound confidence is short lived. As soon as I get into class, I know I've made a huge error, because the classroom is deathly silent. The teacher is already there, and she stops talking mid-sentence when I step inside, which of course means that every student immediately turns to look at me. A few pairs of eyes roll. I can practically read their minds. Ugh, the new girl can't even get it together to be on time.

The teacher, a rake-thin woman in her late thirties wearing a pencil skirt, gives me a cold glance. "Glad you could join us," she says in a clipped voice. She glances at the clock. "Two minutes late. Go to your seat." She turns to address the rest of the class. "Some of you had me in precalculus last year, but for those of you who don't know, the rule is, if you're more than three minutes late, you can't attend my class. You'll have to stand outside the whole period. I won't have anyone disrespecting my time."

Silence. I swear my seat is leagues away from me. Eyes follow me as I scamper toward it like a hunted hamster. Then I jump when the teacher suddenly barks, *"Understand?"*

As one, the class choruses, "Yes, Ms. Tian."

I finally reach my seat and scramble into it. My heart may as well be a tennis ball caught in my throat. I clench my hands on my lap and find them so clammy that my fingers keep slipping. None of the teachers at Mingyang ever shouts. Is this what Mami was referring to when she waxed on and on about Asian discipline? I've seen the funny TikToks and all the memes about it. Some of my cousins have been kept in check with the dreaded feather duster or sandal, but Mami and Papi were more into ordering me to the "Thinking corner" or, at worst, grounding me, so I've always thought the memes were exaggerated. Having a teacher shout at an entire class like this is a whole different experience.

Ms. Tian gives a short nod and turns back to the front of the classroom. She gestures to the screen, on which are the words CALCULUS WITH MS. MARIE TIAN. "As I was saying, calculus is very different from precalculus. Compared to precalc, this class is a lot harder. You're going to need to pay full attention. Expect ten hours' worth of homework every week."

No one groans at this, which kind of blows my mind. At Mingyang, we would all throw our heads back and give the most dramatic groan whenever any teacher announced homework, though of course we'd do it. We just liked our teachers to know that they were ruining our lives. But none of my Xingfa classmates even sighs or shows any signs of annoyance. In fact, most of them are writing down everything Ms. Tian is saying. Maybe I should do the same?

"There will be a test every two weeks. If you fail more than two in a row, you will be taken out of this class and put in . . ." Ms. Tian waves her hand flippantly at the corridor. "Wisdom, or Charity," she says with open derision.

Maybe I'm missing something. Why is she being so horrible about those two classes?

Sensing my confusion, Jonas whispers, "Those two are the bottom-tier classes. That's where all the dumb kids go."

I must have looked horrified, because he smirks and adds sarcastically, "But I'm sure you belong with us smart kids."

Seriously? The classes are tiered? I can't believe they do that, and also, which tier is my class in and how do I find out? *Also, kind of ironic that the class named Wisdom is for "the dumb kids,"* my mind titters at me nervously.

"Jonas Arifin!" Ms. Tian snaps, glaring at us. "Are we going to have a problem with you talking in class?"

Jonas quickly shakes his head. "No, Teacher. Sorry, Teacher," he says without any trace of mockery.

Wow. I've never seen a student so quickly cowed before. Not to say that we were ever disrespectful at Mingyang, but our teachers were the kind that would be, like, "Stop it, you animals," in a long-suffering way instead of actually snapping at us.

"And you?" Ms. Tian turns her terrifying attention to me.

"Uh." I have no idea what to say. "No?"

"No, what?" Her voice is now dangerously low.

"No, Teacher," Liam whispers under his breath.

Seriously? "No, Teacher," I say.

She narrows her eyes at me for another second before nodding and turning back to the rest of the class. Oookay. I feel like I'm in some sort of high school boot camp. I sneak a glance at Liam, wondering if I should thank him, but he's staring with rapt attention at the board. I should probably follow his lead.

For the rest of the class, I keep my head firmly down and my attention fully on taking in everything Ms. Tian says. Her class sounds like a real ass kicker, and by the time the period ends, we have an unbelievable amount of homework. Brutal, considering it's the first day of the semester.

Fortunately, after our second class, it's time for recess. Or maybe I should say unfortunately, because after the disaster that was my first two classes, I'm left with very little confidence. Me, the Fabulous and Marvelous Kiki Siregar, feeling unsure? Yep. And all it took was two classes at Xingfa.

Still, I rally. I'm sure this school isn't as bad as my morning made it seem. I mean, there are people like Eleanor Roosevelt and George Clooney enrolled here, so how bad can it be? Eleanor Roosevelt is, as previously mentioned, a future conqueror of the world. Meanwhile, her brother is so incredibly nice. The way he treats and looks up to Sharlot would melt even the coldest heart. Of course, unfortunately, George is spending this semester in California on a study abroad program. He's told everyone that it's to further his studies in business management, but we all know it's because he wants to be close to Sharlot.

I glance around the classroom as everybody stands, some of the students stretching. People start streaming out in pairs or bigger groups and everybody's chatting and I feel so impossibly alone. Liam turns to me and looks like he's about to say something, but Jonas leans back in his chair and says, "Well, you made quite the statement." He's still wearing that smirk, and I can't decide if this is him trying to be friendly or just him being a jerk.

I have no idea how to respond to that, so I just shrug.

Liam gets up from his seat and says, "Take it easy," as he leaves, and I have no idea if he was saying it to Jonas or to me.

Jonas gives me a once-over. "You have a really pretty smile. You should do it more often."

"Excuse me?" I blurt out. Seriously? Did he really just tell me to smile?

"Okaaay. Don't freak out, I was just trying to be nice." He widens his eyes and looks over his shoulders like he's expecting an audience. And, to my horror, there are a couple of guys who I've just now realized are waiting for Jonas. They both smirk and shake their heads. "Jesus," Jonas mutters, shaking his head.

"C'mon, let's get out of here," he says to his friends, cocking his head toward the door, and the two guys follow him out of the classroom.

What just happened? I don't get it. I thought it's pretty much universally accepted that telling a girl to smile more is an asshole move. I'm still standing there, stunned, when Pei-shan, on her way toward the back door, leans close to me and mutters, "The fish rots from the head."

"Sorry?"

She pauses, sighing like she's annoyed that she has to explain something so obvious to me. "It's a saying. If the head's rotten, the rest of the body will follow suit. And Jonas is our head. He's the class monitor, star tennis player, richest kid here, yada yada."

"Uh. Right." This is a lot of information, and I'm struggling to remember everything. I look at Peishan with hope. "Um, but you're not . . . like, part of the Jonas fan club?"

She shrugs and adjusts her glasses. "I guess you could say I'm not part of the fish's body." She frowns. "Okay, the fish thing is a bad analogy, but let me stay with it. So, Jonas is the head and most of the other kids here are the body, and the body follows the head. I'm . . ." She waves her hands, trying to think of the right word.

"The sea turtle?" I suggest.

"Nah, that's too cool for what I am. I'm more like the sea-weed. Just hanging out in the background."

I laugh, feeling much better than I have all morning. "That doesn't sound so bad. I could be seaweed too."

Instantly, Peishan's eyebrows knit together. "No. You're done for. You're not even seaweed. You pissed Jonas off. I mean, that whole thing during the project discussion . . ." She sighs. "Yes, you're right, that pose is overdone and clichéd, but you don't just say that stuff to Jonas. You're krill."

"Krill?"

"Those little shrimp that fish eat."

"I know what krill is. I just—"

She doesn't wait for me to finish talking. She says, "Cool. Okay, see ya." And with that, she walks off, leaving me alone in the classroom.

Outside, there are the distant, familiar sounds of students filing out of their classrooms, chatting and laughing easily. In here, there's just me and my own heartbeat, thumping a manic, stressed-out rhythm in my ears. I make myself take a deep breath to slow down my rushing thoughts. Peishan must've been exaggerating. Yeah. Stuff like this doesn't happen to me. I'm not krill. I'm not even seaweed! Back at Mingyang, I was, if not the fish's head, then damn near to the head. I was at the very least the fish's neck. Do fish have necks? Okay, the gills. I was definitely at least the gills.

This fish analogy sucks.

Okay, focus. So the morning hasn't gone as well as I'd hoped. But not everything is lost. I can still come back from my bumpy start. I just need a strategy. A battle plan. Let's see, I've tried going head-to-head with Jonas, which was apparently a really bad idea. Okay, from now on, I am ignoring Jonas. Nothing he says is going to get to me. Good plan.

With that, I stride out of the classroom and follow the last of the students streaming toward the cafeteria. Xingfa's cafeteria is huge, about three times the size of Mingyang's. The noise is overwhelming. Due to the school's immense student population, recess time is staggered into three groups, but still, there are over a thousand pupils in the cafeteria, and all of them seem to be talking and shouting and laughing. There are over twenty different food stalls, each one boasting healthy, organic foods. I walk past the stalls, my mouth watering at the various foods on offer. There's a nasi and mee goreng stall (fried rice and fried noodles), a nasi uduk stall (coconut rice), a Hokkien mee stall, and even a grilled cheese stall. It's the first difference from Mingyang that I actually appreciate. At Mingyang, there's just one serving station, and it rotates between hot dogs, pizza, and frozen nuggets.

I join the line at the soto ayam stall (Indonesian chicken soup). I'm scanning the menu when I hear the familiar sound of Jonas's voice. Crap. I was so distracted by the food stalls that I completely forgot to look out for Jonas. But seriously, what are the odds that we'd be near each other in this vast food hall? Why, Universe? Why are you doing this to me? I manage to stop myself from turning toward the sound of his voice and, instead, look down at my phone and pray to the universe that he won't notice I'm there. A subtle glance tells me that he's in the grilled cheese line to my right. I turn to my left, hiding my face, but my ears are pricked, following his voice the same way that a rabbit listens for the sound of its predators.

"—for tonight?" one of his friends asks.

"Of course, bro," Jonas says. "We're going to dominate the Silmerrov Gulch! I bought a new skin—that limited-edition Goldwater Dragon one."

It feels as though my skin has gotten too tight for my body. Because Silmerrov Gulch is one of the battle arenas in *Warfront Heroes*. Ugh, Jonas plays *WH* too.

"I even paid to change my handle so it goes with the new skin. I'm now—"

I don't quite catch what his handle is.

"Cool," Jonas's friend says. "Yeah, I'll add your new character to my Friends list. Anyway, you wouldn't believe what happened today. Miss Teen Indonesia is the new girl in our class. Crazy hot."

Jonas says, "Dude, what? Seriously? Which one is she?" There's a pause as—I assume—he and his buddies spy on some girl. There's a low whistle, then he says, "Yeah, I'd hit that." Gross. The other guys laugh in agreement. "Man, how is this fair? Your class gets Miss Teen Indonesia and mine gets the crazy feminazi from hell. Bro, you should've seen this girl when we were talking about our term project, she was, like, 'Ew, like, this is so gross, you guys.'"

Something inside me breaks, and before I can stop myself, I turn around and march toward Jonas. He's only a few steps away from me, and all of a sudden, I find myself standing face-to-face with him. His face is frozen in a half-laugh, his eyes wide with surprise, and I don't think I've hated a guy quite as much as I do him in this moment. Next to him, two guys with popped collars and manicured faces—trimmed eyebrows, ultra-moisturized skin—are snickering and elbowing each other.

"Shit," one of them whispers, barely containing his laughter.

I ignore them all and stab a finger in front of Jonas's stupid face. "For the record, you're a misogynistic asshat and a little squealer who only dares to talk shit behind people's backs. Next time you want to call me names, say it to my face."

"Oooh," one of his friends says, obviously delighted by this.

I shoot his friends a withering glare, and they both snap

their mouths shut, looking cowed. I spin around and stalk off. Or try to, anyway. My legs are so trembly that walking is a real effort. I focus all my energy on moving my feet. Right foot, left foot, right foot. Keep going.

Behind me, I hear Jonas say, "See? What did I tell you? Crazy."

More laughter. The students around me are either quietly staring or whispering behind their hands. Oh god, what have I done? Why did I do that? Krill can't eat fish!

But you're not krill, a small voice at the back of my mind pipes up.

No, you were a big fish in a small pond and now you're suddenly in the ocean. You might as well be krill, and krill stay the hell away from the big fish. Don't go right up to its mouth and announce their presence.

My breath releases in a shudder. This isn't good. But I couldn't just stand by as he called me a "crazy feminazi" to his friends. Except I've probably just proven him right. God, I really thought that my first day at school would've gone way better than this.

I end up spending the rest of recess in the bathroom, doing deep-breathing exercises in the cleanest cubicle I can find. I peel myself away from the bathroom only when the next bell rings. When I get to my seat, Liam leans over and says, "Hey, so I think you should—"

But the teacher strides in then, and it's just as well, because I've had enough about what I should or shouldn't be doing. I turn away from Liam pointedly and keep my gaze on my books.

The rest of the day isn't much better, but at least I manage not to make any more of a spectacle of myself. I keep my head down and focus on writing everything my teachers say in my notebook. Two more classes, and finally, the day comes to an end. I stuff everything into my bag and keep my eyes down as I trudge out along with everyone else. Am I imagining it or are people glancing at me and then looking away as soon as our eyes meet? Whatever. I look down at my hands and realize I'm white-knuckling the shoulder strap. I force them to release their grip. I'm okay. I survived my first day. I'll be fine.

CHAPTER 5

I can't get my hands on my phone fast enough. As soon as I retrieve it, I swipe up and check my notifications. There are almost 100 messages in the Bad Betches WhatsApp group between Cassie and Sharlot. A mess of emotions swirls through me. I'm torn between feeling happy that my two besties are getting along so well, but also ARGH! that I've missed out on so much conversation. I locate my car in the lineup of idling cars, get in, say a quick hi to Pak Run, and scroll all the way to the top of the messages.

Cassie: Kiki, look how buff Axle got over summer

Image sent of previously scrawny Axle looking like a mini Hulk

Sharlot: Holy . . .
Cassie: Right?
Sharlot: He's kind of rly hot? Lol, sorry George

Cassie: Eh, only if you're into that whole broad-shouldered, chiseled-jawline look, I guess. I heard that he went to LA and worked out on Muscle Beach the whole summer. I bet he was chugging protein shakes and taking steroids

Sharlot: Welp, they clearly worked on him!

Cassie: Yeah, but they'll also make his penis smaller

Sharlot: What? Srsly? No, you're messing with me

Cassie: I'm serious! I read about it in this article. Steroids affect your hormones. If guys take them, their voices get really high and their dicks get tiny!

Sharlot: ROFL

My eyebrows are all the way up in my hairline by now. My thumbs hover over the screen, ready to type a reply, but instead, I scroll lower and see that the conversation has already moved on to Cassie telling Sharlot about Mrs. Prasari, our notoriously eccentric biology teacher, who wears two pairs of glasses: one over her eyes, the other perched on her forehead. Even after two years of biology, we still don't know if she's aware of the second pair of glasses on her head. Apparently, she brought a dead pig to lab, and nobody was sure whether it was school-sanctioned or Mrs. Prasari bought it at the wet market earlier that morning. Knowing Mrs. Prasari, it could really go either way, and the thought of her compared to Ms. Tian makes my breath catch. I never thought I'd miss Mrs. Prasari with such ferocity, but oh, how I do.

Again, replies fly through my mind—already I can think of at least four jokes I can make out of the situation—but as I scroll, I see that the conversation has moved away from that and on to something completely different. By the time I reach the end of the messages, Cassie and Sharlot have covered at least five different topics of conversation, and I've missed every single one of them. All because of Xingfa's rule about keeping phones in a stupid basket outside the classroom.

There's a surprising lump in my throat, and I gaze out the window, taking long, deep breaths that come out ever so slightly juddery. My thoughts keep coming back to *It's not fair. Not fair, not fair. Not. Fair.*

I'm fully aware that this train of thought makes me sound about four years old, but truly, this is such a great injustice. I had friends at Mingyang. Good ones, girls I can see myself growing old with. But what if I'm wrong? What if Cassie and I were only ever so close because we just happened to be in the same class for years and years? And now that I'm no longer there, maybe she'll decide that we never had that much in common before. Why did Mami and Papi think it would be okay for them to yank me out of the only school I've known for the past ten years and plonk me into a cold, unwelcoming environment where I'd have to start from scratch. Why? All because George Clooney goes there and so it must be the premier school in Jakarta. It's not fair. Why should I be punished for my parents' ambitions?

By now, I'm so upset that I can't even muster up the energy to respond to the messages. What's the point? The last message was sent over an hour ago. Cassie is probably doing her extracurriculars right now—she plays the cello in the school orchestra. And Sharlot's probably in bed. I plop my phone onto my lap and rest the side of my head against the car window.

As soon as I get home, Mami is all over me.

"Kikiii!" she cries, swooping down on me and dragging me through the living room and into the kitchen. "I got ube cheesecake, your favorite, and an oat latte—I know how much you love those. Come in here and tell me everything about your day!"

I look at her, and the awfulness of today crashes down on my shoulders. With it comes the anger, glowing like hot coals. "My day was shit. I hate my new school. I still don't know why I had to switch out of Mingyang—oh wait, it's because you want me to be a social climber like you."

The smile freezes on Mami's face, and I feel a stab of guilt, but it's quickly flattened by my anger. Because where's the lie in what I just said?

Mami takes a deep breath. I can tell she's trying to control her temper. She hates it when I talk back, will usually remind me I've become too westernized. Still, she rallies on, forcing a smile. "Well, I'm sure it was just first-day jitters. It's not at all like you to be cowed by other kids. I know you: you'll learn to fit in just fine."

"Not sure if I want to fit in with this bunch."

The corners of her mouth twist down. "Kiki—" she sighs.

But I can't deal with her, not right now. So much resentment is festering in me. My entire head is pounding, my heartbeat a constant rhythm of *All her fault, all her fault.* I mean, I just got called "crazy," for god's sake. Who does that? "I'm going up to shower," I say, interrupting Mami. Then the guilt overcomes me and I add, "But thanks for the cheesecake and the latte." Before Mami can argue, I hurry up the stairs and breathe a sigh of relief only when I'm inside my bedroom. No doubt Mami is going to complain about this whole exchange to Papi, and then they'll both tell me off for being rude to my elders blah blah blah.

Just then, my phone beeps. It's the Discord notification tone, which makes me jerk straight up and snatch my phone out of my pocket.

> **Sourdawg:** How was your first day at the new school? Survived it?

I suddenly understand the saying "My spirits lifted," because everything inside me feels a little less heavy at this. Smiling, I type out a response.

> **Dudebro10:** I'm literally flopped all over my floor, that's how soul-sucking my new school was
> **Sourdawg:** Haha, what was so bad abt it?
> **Dudebro10:** Where do I even begin? OK, first of all, there's this ass in my class who's, like, this ridiculous misogynist.

I pause. I almost said that Jonas was sexist toward me, but that would be giving myself away.

> **Dudebro10:** There's a new girl in our class and he called her "crazy"
> **Sourdawg:** Srsly?

Dudebro10: Right? I mean, it's not just me? That's pretty freaking offensive?

Sourdawg: It's not just you. I would've called him out on it. What did the girl do?

Dudebro10: She told him where to stick it, basically. And she was, like, "Next time you wanna talk shit about me, do it to my face."

Sourdawg: OK I'm kind of falling for her

I abruptly take my fingers off the keyboard and stare at the screen, my face tingling. Ugh, I hate this feeling. So slimy. I'm literally talking about myself in the third person to my online bestie. That's super creepy, right? But what else can I do? And after the events of the day, I really wanted to talk to Sourdawg about it, even more so than to my WhatsApp group. Maybe because I wanted to make sure that he wouldn't react like one of those guys. I already know how Cassie and Shar would react. They'd explode into indignant cries of "How dare he mistreat you, Queen?"

Dudebro10: Haha, dork

Sourdawg: I'm just saying. She sounds cool. Anyway, what's the rest of the school like?

Dudebro10: Omg, unbelievably strict. For example, we have to call the teachers "Teacher," not even, like, "Miss Chan" or whatever

Sourdawg: Okay, well, that's what we have to do at our school too

Dudebro10: And none of the girls shortened their skirts, WTF?

Sourdawg: Uh. Okay, kind of creepy that you want the girls to shorten their skirts

Shoot. I'd forgotten that I'm supposed to be a guy. Okay, coming from a guy, that comment about girls not shortening their skirts would sound really creepy. Although I can totally see Jonas saying something like that. Not great.

Dudebro10: I didn't mean for it to come off that way. I just meant, like . . . it's weird not to see any sort of pushback on the uniforms. Back at my old school, we were always pushing the boundaries on our uniforms

Sourdawg: I get it. My school has really strict rules when it comes to the uniforms too. When we first started in Year Seven, a handful of us rebelled, but we're in Year Eleven, we're used to it by now

Dudebro10: Oh, and get this: We have to bow to the teachers and to the prefects whenever we pass them in the hallways. And when classes begin, the prefect says, "Class stand." And we stand, and then the prefect says, "Greet the teacher." And we have to bow and say, "Good morning, Teacher." And when classes end, we have to go through the whole thing again: "Class stand." "Thank the teacher."

Sourdawg: You've just described my school to a T. Except the prefects here say, "*Please* greet the teacher."

Dudebro10: Seriously? And you're all okay with this?

Sourdawg: Yeah. Why wouldn't we be?

Dudebro10: Because it's like . . .

I pause midsentence and midbreath, trying to find a way to convey how weird I'm finding all this.

Dudebro10: It's the kind of thing I would expect from a YA dystopian movie, you know?

Sourdawg: LOL, okay bro. We don't get sorted into different factions or districts, if that makes you feel better

Dudebro10: You sure about that?

I smile as I type that. Only Sourdawg can make something like an overly strident system sound okay.

Dudebro10: Are all schools in Singapore that strict, or is it just yours?

Sourdawg: ??

I frown. Did I just say something weird?

Dudebro10: What's up?

Sourdawg: Why Singapore? I wouldn't know

Dudebro10: Uh, don't you live in Sg? Your location says Sg

Sourdawg: Oooh. My location just says Sg because I was there visiting my mom over summer break when I downloaded the game. But the rest of the time I live in Indo.

Wait, what?? To say I'm in shock would be the under-statement of the year. I can barely feel my hands as they move across the keyboard and start typing. I don't even really know what I'm about to type until I hit Enter.

Dudebro10: Cool. Which sch did you say you go to again?
Sourdawg: Xingfa, why?

What. In. The. Hell?! I sit there, frozen, gaping at the screen for what seems like ever, my fingertips hovering over the key-board, not moving a single inch. My breath is held completely still. Scrambled thoughts whizz through my mind like broken bits of asteroids, crashing and exploding into smithereens.

Sourdawg: U there? Are we gonna play or what? I rly want to hit Silmerrov Gulch tonight.

Somehow, the mention of Silmerrov Gulch wakes me up enough to move my fingers across the keyboard once more.

Dudebro10: Sorry, I gtg. I have a ton of homework. From school.

Oh god. Of-freaking-course any homework I have would be from school. Where the hell else would it be from? Before I can say anything dumb and accidentally out myself, I hit close on the app. I lean back in my chair and release a ridiculously long breath. Holy shit. What just happened? I try to slow down my thoughts. Okay, so Sourdawg is at Xingfa—

Just the thought of it triggers my mind into a hundred thousand squealing thoughts screaming *Omigod whaaaat!*

Yep, this is it. This is how I perish. Through my heart climbing up my rib cage and esophagus and lodging in my skull and then exploding. Because of course. Of COURSE Sourdawg is at Xingfa, where I am considered the loseriest loser that ever lost. And he's definitely going to find out that I'm Dudebro10 and that I've been lying to him this whole time. Then another horrible thought crawls its way into the center of my brain: *I know at least one other person at Xingfa who plays* Warfront Heroes. *Jonas.* GROSSS ARGGGH ARGH ARGH! What if Sourdawg is Jonas?!

Oh god, this is a huge freaking mess, and I have no idea how I'm going to fix it.

This is hopeless. I need help. I can't process this on my own. I pounce on my phone and send a text to Cassie: SOS!!!!

Cassie's reply is almost immediate: Meet at Cake Ho?

Despite the explosions going off in my head, I have to smile at that. There isn't much that can't be made better by a cake from Cake Ho and a good scream with my bestie.

According to Papi, Jakarta's food scene used to be pretty boring—nothing but traditional Indonesian and Chinese restaurants everywhere. I mean, not to say that Indonesian and Chinese food isn't good, but there was very little variety. Here and there, you'd find the odd Italian or French restaurant, but they weren't well-known, and they were really overpriced.

When I was a kid, Mami and Papi only ever took me to Chinese restaurants. But in the last few years, Indonesians who went to college overseas came back and opened up new restaurants, and suddenly, the food scene in Jakarta exploded. We went through a fusion phase, where everything was fusion—Italian Japanese, Indonesian Vietnamese, Indonesian Italian, Chinese Indian, Korean American, and so on. Then we went through a café phase, where you couldn't throw a stone without hitting a picturesque shop boasting local, artisanal coffee. Now we're in the cake phase, and I fully approve of the cake phase. I mean, I fully approved of all the previous phases too, but the cake phase is particularly delightful.

Because there isn't much to do in Jakarta other than eat, restaurant owners pour all their money into making sure their restaurants and cafés are beautiful places you want to spend hours at. Take Cake Ho, for example: it looks like Willy Wonka's dream come true, if Willy Wonka were French and had actual good taste. Okay, so maybe not at all like Willy Wonka. The walls are painted a luxurious green, and there are soft pink peonies everywhere and hardcover books with pastel spines lined neatly in the bookshelves. Then there are the cakes. Towering behemoths slathered in rich buttercream, displayed proudly in their glass cases, the cakes look almost too pretty and too decadent to eat. Each has at least eight thick layers, and usually, Cassie and I would go straight from Mingyang after school and share a slice between the two of us and still have enough to take home.

The bell above the door chimes as I enter, and the owner,

Tessa, glances up from behind the counter. She smiles when she sees me, then cranes her neck with a quizzical expression when nobody comes in after me.

"Where's Cassie? You two usually arrive together."

My throat closes up ever so slightly. I know it's stupid to get emotional over such an innocuous question, but it's been a long day. "Oh, Cassie will be here in a minute."

She must have caught something in my voice, because her expression turns soft, understanding lighting her eyes. "Take a seat. The usual drink?"

My usual drink is what Cassie affectionately calls the Embarrassment of Indonesia. It's an iced latte but with just half the espresso shot. No self-respecting Indonesian café serves decaf, and if I drink coffee past noon, I'll stay awake the rest of the night, so as a compromise, I order half shots.

"Yeah, and Cassie's usual, please. And can we have a slice of . . ." I hesitate, scanning the glass display case. There are the usual favorites: carrot cake, red velvet, German chocolate, nastar crumble (nastar is an Indonesian butter cookie filled with thick pineapple jam), and pandan coconut. Today, there's also a giant cake that's a deep purple.

"Japanese ubi," Tessa says, following my gaze. "With palm sugar frosting."

"Ooh, yes, that one." Of course, as soon as I say it, I realize my stomach is in such a tight knot that I don't really have much of an appetite, not even for one of Tessa's magical cakes. Still, no harm in trying to fix my problems with cake.

"Okay, coming right up."

Cassie arrives just as our drinks and stupidly huge slice of cake arrive, and I practically leap up from my seat to hug her.

"Uh-oh. Okay, so it's a *real* emergency. Oh god. Are you—please tell me you're not, like, seriously ill." She actually looks like she's about to cry.

"No! God, nothing like that." Great, now I feel terrible for making Cassie worry. "It's just—Sourdawg."

"Oh?" Cassie looks confused for a second before understanding dawns. "Oh no! Did your starter die?"

"My starter?" Now it's my turn to look confused.

"Your sourdough starter. Remember? We all made one during the pandemic, and yours was the only one that's lasted this long. Aww, I would hate for Francine to die!"

"Oh, right. No, Francine's okay . . . I think." To be fair, Francine's probably close to death. I wouldn't know; I threw her in the freezer a couple of months ago and have pretty much forgotten about her. "This isn't about sourdough, it's about Sourdawg."

"Sour . . . dog." Cassie eyes me warily. "Is that some weird sex position you just read about on Reddit?"

"Oh my god, you perv. No, Sourdawg is my online friend, remember? The one in *Warfront Heroes*?"

"Ooohhh. Right, yeah. The rando you've been chatting with for—what, a year now? The one who thinks you're a guy? You do realize he's probably a fifty-year-old dude living in his mom's basement in, like, Arkansas or something?"

It's been an ongoing joke between Sharlot and Cassie that my online bestie is some old creeper pretending to be a teenage boy. I guess, on the bright side, I'm about to prove them wrong.

"Actually, he's a bona fide teen boy."

Cassie's eyes widen. "Ooh! You finally have a photo of him? Yasss! Oh my god, is he hot?"

"No!"

"Oh." Her shoulders slump. "Yeah, I should've known that a gamer guy wouldn't be hot. No offense to you. Gamer girls are, like, scalding hot. But the guys, eh."

I have to laugh at that, because it's kind of painfully true. "I don't know what he looks like."

"Then how do you know he's not a fifty-year-old man?"

"Because—" I take a deep breath. Here it comes, the unlikeliest news of the year. "He's in Year Eleven, like us. And . . . he's a student at Xingfa."

Cassie's jaw thumps to the floor. "Whoa, wait—"

News out, I lean back, spent. Even saying it out loud feels ridiculous, like, seriously, what are the chances?

Cassie's mouth closes a little, then opens again, then closes. Then opens. "But—" she sputters.

"Yeah, exactly." I'm glad I'm not the only one freaked out by this.

"Shit," she whispers, then out of nowhere, she giggles. The giggle turns into a laugh, and before long, it morphs into a full-body cackle. And I can't help but join in, because really, what else is there to do aside from laugh-cry? "Are you freaking serious?"

I nod, and the two of us devolve into yet more boneshaking laughter.

"Oh my god. Oh my god!" she shriek-laughs. "Wait, but— oh my god. Who is he?"

"I don't know!" I moan. "He could be anyone. Xingfa is a huge school! There are, like, three hundred students per year group."

Cassie dissolves into laughter again. "What are you going to do? He thinks you're a guy!"

"I know that. I don't need you to remind me of that. Every single time I talk to him, I'm reminded of the fact that my online best friend thinks I'm a dude."

Cassie's laugh softens into a sad smile. "Aww. Your online bestie! That's so cute. It's so, like, circa 2000. Like that ancient Meg Ryan movie that our moms are always watching."

"Okay, it's kind of different from *You've Got Mail*."

"Really, in what way?" Cassie cocks her head to one side.

I narrow my eyes at her. "Well, first of all, Sourdawg and I actually do something together? We don't just sit around emailing each other."

"Oh, right." Cassie smacks her forehead dramatically. "Sorry, how could I forget, you guys play that shooter game together. Yeah, total couple goals."

I glare at her. "Anyway, that's not the point. The point is, what am I going to do? We're in the same school! In the same year group!" I repeat, just in case the direness of the situation hasn't sunk in.

Cassie nods. "Okay. Well, anyway. Here's what you do. You ready?"

I lean forward, ready to absorb whatever suggestion she comes up with.

Cassie takes a deep breath. "Nothing."

I blink. "Nothing?"

"Nothing. He doesn't know who you are. Does he know you go to Xingfa?"

It takes me a minute to consider this. "I don't think I mentioned it by name, no. I just told him that it's one of the biggest Chinese schools in Indonesia. He might've figured it out—"

"Dude, how many Chinese schools are there? Like, a freakton. There's Huayang, Nanyang, ACS, SIS, National High, Tzu Chi—actually, Tzu Chi is probably the biggest one. Or maybe ACS? So he's probably assumed it's one of those two."

I nod slowly, digesting her words. Despite Cassie's cavalier attitude, what she's saying actually makes a lot of sense. "Okay, so Sourdawg doesn't know I'm at Xingfa. But what if he asks Dudebro to meet up?"

"Who's Dude—oh god, is that your screen name? Seriously?" Cassie grins.

"I wanted to pretend to be a guy, so . . ."

"So you used the most stereotypically male nickname ever? But I get it. I would never have guessed that someone named Dudebro is a girl." Cassie gives me this *You did well* smirk. "Okay, so let's say he asks Dudebro to meet up. You could fess up? Nope, never mind. Too big of a risk. Okay. You've got a couple of options. One: Be a normal person and come up with some excuse, like 'I can't, because I'm panicking in introvert.' Or two: Send some guy to go and pretend to be Dudebro."

"Right, because it would be so easy to find someone to pretend to be Dudebro."

"It is, actually. We could ask my brother. He'd do it for a fee. He games too, so he'll know what he's talking about."

I shake my head. "I already feel awful enough about duping Sourdawg into thinking I'm a guy. I really don't want to have to take the con any further than that."

"Okay, so just come up with excuse after excuse. You got food poisoning, because this is Jakarta and we get food poisoning every other month. You have an exam coming up, because you go to a super-competitive Chinese school. Your parents are stereotypical tiger parents and don't let you go out of the house, ever. There are myriad reasons why you can't meet up with your online friend." Cassie looks satisfied by her reasoning, and I can't blame her, because they're actually really good excuses. Listening to her makes me feel like I can pull this off, that Sourdawg being here isn't even that big a deal.

But that night, as I lie in bed wide awake and staring up at the ceiling, my confidence melts away, and the fear laps at me once more. What if Sourdawg finds out the truth?

CHAPTER 6

The next morning, I get ready for school with renewed purpose. The purpose being: *Well, if Sourdawg is my schoolmate, I really need to not be such an outcast. Bad enough if he ever found out I'm Dudebro10; I can't have him thinking I'm a total loser in real life too.*

I take extra time to blow-dry my hair until it's so shiny that when I put a comb in it, it just slides through the silky strands of hair on its own. Then I swipe on a light coating of mascara and tinted lip balm and smile at my reflection. I look so cute. "Me? Pretty?" I say to my reflection. "Oh, I just woke up like this."

Then it's down to the breakfast of champions: cereal that's basically made out of cardboard and sugar but pretends to be healthy, and a cup of coffee so strong that my right eyelid starts twitching about halfway through. I swear, Indonesian coffee is so potent it might as well be crack cocaine. And now I'm ready to go and slay. Even Pak Run tells me I look particularly "neat" this morning, which is a serious compliment coming from him.

My renewed confidence lasts only until we drive through the towering Xingfa gates, then it fizzles away with a sad squelch. But I glare up at the building and silently remind myself that I've got this. I've handled far worse. I may not be able to think of what situations I have handled before that were far worse than being bullied at my new school, but I'm sure I've been in worse situations.

As I trudge up the stone steps, I spot two familiar figures in the distance: Eleanor Roosevelt and Sarah Jessica. A smile takes over my face. It's impossible to not be in a good mood when I see Eleanor Roosevelt. "Hey, guys," I call out. They spot me and start coming toward me, grinning. As they come closer, it hits me that their matchmaking service might just be the answer I need. As soon as the idea appears, it sinks its little claws inside me and refuses to let go. Why not? It's a brilliant idea. With the help of Lil' Aunties Know Best, I'll be able to take my time figuring out who Sourdawg is without attracting too much attention.

"Hey, Ci Kiki!" Eleanor Roosevelt gives me a hug, and my desiccated husk of a heart melts a little. For the millionth time, I wonder what amazing karma George Clooney must have to have a little sister like Eleanor Roosevelt.

"Hey, kid. Hey, Sarah Jessica."

Sarah Jessica raises her chin and says, "'Sup."

I'm a little bit disarmed by a bespectacled thirteen-year-old in a school uniform that goes below her knees saying "'Sup," and it takes me a moment to gather my thoughts. "Hey, so I was thinking . . . you know, about Lil' Aunties."

Eleanor Roosevelt's eyebrows knit together in clear disappointment. "Oh. You don't wanna do it after all?"

"No, actually," I say quickly, "I would love to be a part of the whole thing. Including the matchmaking."

It's as though the sun has just come out from behind the clouds. Eleanor Roosevelt's whole face lights up, and she turns to Sarah Jessica, who's already grinning, and the two of them grasp each other's hands and squeal. The sight of it twists my heart; I miss Cassie and Shar so, so much.

"Really?" Sarah Jessica says.

"Yeah. I mean, I think we need to go over some ground rules, but sure, I think it'd be fun."

"Ah!" Eleanor Roosevelt shouts, wrapping her arms around me. "It's going to be amazing!"

Sarah Jessica pushes her glasses up her nose and clears her throat. "Let's be more discreet about this, please, since dating is not technically allowed at Xingfa." She looks so serious and matronly that I have to bite my lip to keep from smiling. God, was I ever this confident when I was their age? "Don't worry, we'll send you our guidebook before you go on a date."

"You have a guidebook?"

They both roll their eyes at me. "Duh," Eleanor Roosevelt says, tucking a stray lock of hair behind her ears. She's wearing her hair in a braided headband and looks so adorable. The fashion industry needs this kid. "It has everything: a code of conduct, rules of engagement, an NDA—"

"An NDA?"

"That stands for nondisclosure agreement," Sarah Jessica says with all the earnestness in the world.

"I know what an NDA is, I just—why do we have to sign one?"

"Because like Sarah Jessica said, we're not technically allowed to date at Xingfa, and Sarah Jessica and I need to protect ourselves."

I nod slowly. "You know, when George told me to keep an eye out for you, I think he got it wrong."

Eleanor Roosevelt grins. "Oh, he one hundred percent meant keep an eye out ON me, not for me. See you, Ci Kiki! And welcome to Lil' Aunties!" And with that, Eleanor Roosevelt and Sarah Jessica leave, chattering excitedly.

My second day at Xingfa isn't as bad my first; in fact, it's worse. I arrive at my classroom with renewed resolve to be my awesome self and make new friends, but as soon as I step inside the room, Jonas calls out, "Hey, Gigi, c'mere. I need to talk to you."

Gigi? Fuck this guy. Then I recall that—oh god—there is an actual real possibility that Jonas might be Sourdawg, and my insides twist so tightly I almost hurl.

"No thanks," I say, ducking my head, refusing to even meet his eye. I head straight to my table, keeping my head down. I don't even bother saying hi to Liam.

"Hey, seriously, I'm not joking around," Jonas says, louder this time. "This is me talking to you as your class prefect."

The easygoing noise in the classroom suddenly subsides. Everyone is watching us. Liam straightens in his chair, and I get the feeling that he's trying to catch my eye, but I'm too busy glaring at Jonas. I grip my shoulder strap tightly and take a breath before saying, "Yeah? What can I help you with, Jonas?"

"Here at Xingfa, we take our school's reputation very seriously."

What is this guy doing, giving a speech? "Okay," I mumble.

"Have you read your student handbook?"

"Jonas, take it easy," Liam says.

I glance at Liam, then back at Jonas, who's apparently still waiting for an answer. "Yeah." Well, I've definitely read the cover anyway.

Jonas says the most theatrical "Huh" in the history of huhs, like HUH, REEEALLY? "That's funny, because on page thirty-seven, section fifty-one A, it clearly states that you are not allowed to wear your school uniform out in public."

"What?" My gaze snaps up to his face, and I immediately regret it, because there it is again, that ever-present smirk that makes the back of my neck prickle with the need to punch him in the face. I shake my head. "That doesn't make sense. Are we supposed to change out of our uniform before leaving the school?"

Jonas rolls his eyes. "No, when you're in transit—that is, traveling between your house and the school, that's fine. But you're not allowed to make stops at the mall, or the supermarket, or a café, while you're wearing the Xingfa uniform."

"What?" I spit out. My head spins with how ridiculous this rule is. Back at Mingyang, the girls and I were always going straight to the mall after school. Jonas must be making this up.

"Hey, I don't make the rules," he says, as though reading my mind. "I'm just saying, it's embarrassing that you got caught breaking the rule your first day of school."

"What?" I say again. I seem to have run out of other words to say. Around me, my classmates are still staring.

"Jonas—" Liam says with a sigh. "Come on, man."

"Stay out of it, okay?" Jonas says. "I'm trying to make sure the new girl knows the school rules. What if a teacher had seen her out in public in her school uniform? Do you want her to get suspended?"

Next to Jonas, Peishan is shaking her head at me, like, *Girl, you should've known better.*

With a long-suffering sigh, Jonas takes out his phone and opens up TikTok. He taps a couple of times before brandishing the phone at me. Music blares from it.

My mouth drops open. It's a TikTok of me and Cassie at Cake Ho, laughing over cake. The caption reads: "Anak jaman skrg, pulang sekolah langsung ngopi ngabisin uang. #Xingfa." *Kids nowadays, as soon as they get out of school, they go straight to a café to waste their money.*

"Wha—" It feels like my mind has imploded. There's so much to unpack here. "We were at a café having cake. It's not like we went to a karaoke lounge and started flinging cash at everyone. And who the hell took that video? That's so creepy."

"You were at a café called Cake *Ho*," Jonas says, emphasizing the "Ho" with obvious relish. "And the rules are clear: you can't wear your uniform outside the premises, aside from when you're traveling to and from your home."

"I think she got it," Liam growls, but Jonas isn't done with his speech.

"When you wear the Xingfa uniform, you represent our

school. You have to wear it with pride, not besmirch our hard-earned reputation."

"How the hell did I besmirch your stupid reputation by having fucking *cake*, you obnoxious twat?"

There's a collective gasp, and too late, I realize I haven't just overstepped my own personal rule of not letting Jonas get under my skin; I've smashed right through it. And just then, things go from bad to catastrophic, because someone at the door clears his throat, and we all turn to see Mr. Tan, glowering at me.

"Did you just call a fellow student a 'twat'?" he says in a tone of voice full of poison.

I know I should be groveling, I know what the culture demands, but my insides are boiling: someone took a video of me, for god's sake, and posted it on TikTok. Surely that's the most messed-up thing here? "Yes," I say, raising my chin and meeting Mr. Tan's eyes.

"Kiki," Liam mutters, "don't—"

"But don't worry," I continue, "it's only because he fully deserved it."

Mr. Tan's mouth drops open. A couple of students gasp. The tension in the room solidifies. Then Mr. Tan says, "Come here."

Dread coils up my leg muscles, and I swear I practically forget how to walk, but somehow, I manage to make my way to the front of the classroom. *Whatever*, I tell myself, *so he'll give me detention. Big deal.*

But when I get to the front, Mr. Tan says, "If you like being the center of attention so much, you can stand here for the rest of the period."

A few of my classmates groan. "Mr. Tan," Jonas says, "she's kind of blocking the board."

"Well, you have Miss Siregar to thank for that."

My cheeks are burning so hotly it's a wonder my entire head hasn't exploded into flames. Of course they wouldn't just give me detention at Xingfa, oh no, they believe in public humiliation here. I look down at my shoes, my toes curling with shame, and Mr. Tan says, "No, you can look straight ahead at your classmates so you know exactly how disruptive your behavior was."

Tears prickle my eyes, and I focus on sipping air in through my mouth to keep from crying as I raise my head and stare straight ahead. *Just focus on the back of the classroom*, I tell myself. *Ignore everyone else.* But I can't pretend not to see their judgmental faces as Mr. Tan begins the lesson. Thankfully, after about ten minutes of lecture, Mr. Tan tells us to break into our groups to continue discussing our group projects. I take a relieved step to join my group, but Mr. Tan tells me I have to remain standing where I am.

"But my group—"

"—will just have to survive without you for this period." Mr. Tan narrows his eyes at me. "You have to understand, here at Xingfa, we take students' conduct very seriously. 'Purity in character, diligence in practice'—that's our school's motto. You can spend the rest of the hour thinking about what that means and how your actions have affected your group."

I glance at my group, the only one with three students instead of four, and my stomach lurches. Because it hits me then that maybe they're actually glad to not have me in there fighting with Jonas about our game. Maybe without me there, they can get on with it and go along with Jonas's awful game idea. And maybe that's for the best. "Purity in character, diligence in practice." Ugh, what the hell kind of motto is that? Mingyang's motto is "Service and Truth," which is kind of meh, but also, no one ever quoted it. I doubt that half the school even knows what the motto is.

When the bell finally rings, I hurry to my seat, keeping my eyes down as I pass by the rows of students. Some of them whisper as I walk by, and I mentally go *lalala* so I don't have to hear whatever mean thing they're no doubt saying about me. I refuse to meet Liam's eye as I slide into my seat. For the duration of the next class, I keep my eyes firmly on my desk.

But somehow, despite the no-phones-in-class rule, someone has managed to record me shouting "You obnoxious twat!" at Jonas.

By recess, it's all over TikTok. A looped clip of me shouting "Obnoxious twat! Twat! Twat!" over and over, with Gwen Stefani singing in the background "This shit is BA-NANAS! B-A-N-A-N-A-S!" tagged with #CrazyKiki. I can hear it as I walk through the hallway. I'd been planning to go to the canteen for recess, but after the fourth time I hear "B-A-N-A-N-A-S!" I'm so overwhelmed that I duck into the nearest bathroom instead. Of course, because it's break time, the bathroom is filled with girls fixing their hair and chatting, and they all have their phones out, so even in here, I can't escape Gwen Stefani's voice. They all look at me. Someone giggles, and I rush out of the bathroom and hurry down the hallway, barely aware of where I'm going. I turn one corner, then another, until I find myself in a quiet part of the school.

I look around me. My breath is still coming in and out in rapid spurts. There are no classrooms in this part of the building. I vaguely remember that Xingfa had a new extension built a handful of years ago, and that's where their library and science labs are located. I guess this is where I'll have my physics and biology classes tomorrow. I wander down the deserted corridor until I find the entrance to the library, then I walk inside, reveling in the air-conditioned silence. A librarian looks up and gives me a quick, polite smile before turning her attention back to her computer screen.

Xingfa's library is impressive: modern and bright, with high ceilings and shelf after shelf of books. The entire space somehow smells both clean and yet heavy with book scents, and I immediately love it. I guess I'm now someone who spends her recess time in the library. I release a shuddery breath and wander down a narrow space between bookshelves, trying to shake off the memory of everyone laughing at me. To my horror, now that I'm in a space that finally feels safe, I feel my nose tingling and my eyes filling with tears once more. *Stop it,* I scold myself, but one tear rolls down my cheek, then another and another, and I can't believe I'm crying in the library on the second day of school.

Someone taps me gently on the shoulder, and when I turn around, I'm met with a piece of baby wipe. A baby wipe that's being held by Liam. Oh god, *whyyy?*

He looks just as mortified as I feel as we stand there, staring at each other, my face streaming with tears and snot. Then he clears his throat and says, "This has cucumber extract on it."

Okay, so of all the things I thought he might say, this might possibly have been the last.

"The wipe, I mean," Liam says. "Um. So. Yeah."

I take it from him and wipe my face with it. "I can't smell the cucumber extract." I have no idea why I just said that, other than that my brain is probably misfiring neurons all over the place.

"Well, I doubt they put actual cucumber extract on it. But the package comes with a very refreshing image of cucumber slices."

"Ah, that's all that matters." Despite myself, the corners of my mouth turn up in a small smile. "Thanks." I look down at the wad of damp baby wipe. "Didn't expect anyone to walk around with a packet of baby wipes on them."

Liam shrugs. "It became a habit during the pandemic."

I nod. Our eyes meet, and we immediately look down again. "About Jonas—"

"It's fine," I say quickly. I'm still smarting over everything that's happened today, and I still remember how Liam shook his head at me yesterday. I don't think I would be able to stomach another lecture about how I should respect my class-mates.

"Xingfa's kind of an adjustment, huh?" Liam says.

My breath releases in a shaky laugh. "Yeah." I scramble for a subject change. "How did the group discussion go?"

Liam wrinkles his nose, and I have to tear my eyes away from how adorable he looks when he does that. "It went fine.

I think Peishan and I don't much care as long as we get good grades." He winces apologetically. "Sorry, I know you really didn't like the design that Jonas came up with, but . . ."

My face heats up again. The unspoken part is obvious. "But you guys just want to get it done and over with. I get it." And I'm only now realizing that maybe this is what I have to do too, in order to survive Xingfa.

Liam grimaces. "I hate how that sounds. But yeah, I guess. And since Jonas is a gamer and all . . ."

Oh god. Don't remind me. The possibility that Jonas is Sourdawg punches me in the stomach like a sledgehammer once again. Argh. "You know, I game too," I mutter.

"Really? That's so cool. What do you play?"

"Mostly FPS." I don't want to tell him that I play *WH* too, just in case it somehow gets round to Jonas, so I rattle off other FPS games I've played. "*Borderlands, Gears of War* . . ."

"I love those!" Liam's eyes light up, and his mouth curls into a soft smile that makes my stomach turn. In a good way, I mean. "You know what I love about *Gears*? Its amazingly clichéd lines."

" 'Get ready for the pain train!' " I growl, and Liam guffaws.

Someone shushes us, and we both clap our hands over our mouths, trying to stifle our laughter. The bell rings then.

"Come on, five minutes before the next class starts," Liam says, and leads the way out of the library. We walk out in amicable silence, but as we near our classroom, my good mood dissipates and is quickly overwhelmed by a rush of anxiety. The anxiety gives way to anger, because why am I letting anyone make me feel like this?

By the time we go inside the classroom, I'm ready to face anything. When I spot Jonas, laughing with his friends in that obnoxious way he has, something inside me boils over and I march straight up to him. When they spot me, he and his friends fall silent.

"Kiki, what are you doing?" Liam whispers, but I ignore him. At this moment, all I care about is making sure that my online best friend isn't a douche in real life.

"Jonas," I say.

"Yeah?" Jonas is still smirking. Everyone else is so silent that I can hear the inward rush of my own breathing. They're all staring at me, bug-eyed, and I know this isn't helping my case, I know it's only going to make #CrazyKiki even more on-brand, but I can't help myself.

Are you Sourdawg? Just say it, damn it. But what if he is? What if he says, *Yes, I am, why?* Then I would lose Sourdawg. I would lose my online refuge. I could never play *Warfront Heroes* without being reminded of him. "Are you—" Just. Say. It! My eyes rove around wildly, seeing everyone's expectant faces, and that's when I see it.

Jonas's notebook. How did I miss it before? He's stuck a massive sticker on its cover—one of Titanimus, a character from *Warfront Heroes*, presumably his main. And across Titanimus's chest, he's written "@GoldenDragonLord." That's it. That must be his handle.

Relief surges through my entire being. I almost collapse in a puddle.

"I'm waiting for that apology," Jonas says.

I blink. "Huh?"

"I assume that's why you're talking to me?"

"Oh. Right. Uh . . ." Everyone is still staring. I should just apologize to him and get it done and over with. But my head's such a mess. I'm still angry at everything, and yet also rejoicing at the fact that Jonas is not Sourdawg, and I just—I can't do it. Nope. I give Jonas the sweetest smile I can muster up. Then I say, "I will as soon as you stop being such a twat."

The collective gasp is drowned out by an angry shout from the door. *"Kristabella Siregar!"*

Great. Of course the next period's teacher has chosen to walk in right this very moment. I guess I'll be spending this period standing at the front of the classroom again.

But unlike Mr. Tan, Miss Rumanou points to the door and says, "Go to the principal's office. Now."

I've never been sent to the principal's office before. Back at Mingyang, I was considered an asset to the school—outgoing, inclusive, liked by both students and teachers. Mingyang was a pretty small school, so our principal actually knew most of us by name. Whenever she saw me at school, she'd smile and say something like "Hey, Kiki, ooh, your eyebrow game is on-point!" At that time, I found it cringey, the way Principal Ramani was always trying to act chummy with us kids. Now look who's feeling stupid and hoping against hope that Xingfa's principal will be as chill as Principal Ramani?

Well, the principal here could be really cool, for all I know. Anything's possible, right? And maybe he might even side with me, especially after I use this chance to expose all the bullying that Jonas has been doing. I know it makes me sound supremely uncool, but it's time I tell one of the school officials what's been going on here. I've never been a narc before—I've never had cause to be—but enough is enough.

The admin lady glances up from her e-reader when I walk in, and her eyes widen slightly, like she's not used to students coming in here. She recovers quickly, though, putting down the e-reader and giving me a kind smile. "Hi. What can I do for you?"

"Uh . . ." Now that I'm actually here, I realize that I don't really know what to say in such a situation. "I was asked by my teacher to speak with Principal . . . uh . . ." Gah, of course I've completely forgotten the principal's name.

"Principal Lin?" She winces. "Okay. Wait here. I'll let him know."

Geez, she didn't need to wince like that. What did that wince mean? Oh god, she must feel bad for me, because she knows I'm in for a terrible punishment. What if I get suspended? What if I get expelled? Would that go on my permanent record? My rib cage constricts as the admin lady gets up and knocks on the principal's door. She pops her head in, says something, and a moment later, she turns back to me.

"Principal Lin will see you now."

I try to decipher the expression on her face, but I can't tell if that's a sympathetic smile she's wearing or a "sucks to be you" sort of smile. My knees wobble as I walk toward the office, and I grip the doorknob to steady myself.

I've seen Principal Lin's picture in the main hall of the

school. In the picture, he's smiling with confidence, both his hairline and jawline strong. In person, he seems somehow rather diminished, a little bit more crumpled, and both his hairline and jawline are softer. He glances up at me from behind his desk.

"Come, sit." He gestures at the chair opposite his desk, and oh god I wish to all the atoms in the universe that I hadn't been sent here. He must have seen the apprehension on my face, because he gives a close-lipped smile and says, "Don't worry, sit. We'll just have a chat."

Right. It'll be okay. Yeah. Mami mentioned to me in passing that Mr. Lin has been the principal here for almost thirty years, so he knows his shit. He'll see that I had a good reason for calling Jonas a twat.

Never mind my stomach—my entire body clenches as I walk into his office and sit down opposite him.

Principal Lin leans back in his seat, crossing his hands over his belly. Behind his glasses, his eyes are shrewd, and he speaks in a clipped, rapid way, like every word is something he needs to waste as little time as possible pronouncing. "So. You're new here, yes? Your name is . . . Siregar?"

I nod. My mouth is too dry to speak.

"And your teacher sent you here. Who's your teacher?"

"Uh." It takes a second to recall her name. "Miss Rumanou."

"Ah, yes." Principal Lin frowns. "Miss Rumanou is quite lenient. You must have done something really bad to be sent here. What did you do?"

Bile burns its way halfway up my esophagus, and I have to

take a deep breath before I'm able to answer. "Uh, I . . . sort of called one of my classmates a rude name."

The frown deepens. His eyebrows are practically touching each other. He places his hands—his fingers are very elegant, like a pianist's, I notice, and then immediately after noticing that, I'm like, *Why am I noticing his hands? That is so weird*—on the table and leans forward. "Okay, I understand that you're new, but here at Xingfa, you need to address your elders by using Sir or Madam or Teacher, do you hear me?"

"Oh! Right. Okay."

"Okay *what*?" Principal Lin says, enunciating the "what" so it comes out pointed and threatening.

Crap. "Okay, sir." My voice comes out in a mumble. I have never wished for anything more than an excuse to get out of here.

"Good." He leans back again, looking satisfied. I hate him already. "So why did you call your classmate a rude word? What was the word?"

"Uh. 'Twat.' Sir," I add at the last minute.

Principal Lin's upper lip curls in open disgust. "Maybe in your old school that kind of language is acceptable, but here at Xingfa, respect is everything. Purity of character and discipline, that's what we're known for. We cannot abide foul language, do you hear me?"

He says this with so much venom that one might think I'd kicked a puppy instead of calling someone a twat, and something inside me ignites. It's not right that I'm being punished for this while Jonas gets away with bullying me. "Yes, I hear you. Sir. But, um, in my defense, I was sort of being bullied? And I know that Xingfa takes bullying seriously too. Uh, sir."

Principal Lin narrows his eyes at me. "All right, tell me about this bullying incident." His tone is skeptical.

"Um . . ." Where do I start? This whole situation is so not what I expected, and it feels so bizarre to be telling this man about Jonas. Still, I'm here now, and the only way to go is forward, so I will myself to form the words somehow. "So this is only my second day here, and—"

"Where did you transfer in from?" he interrupts.

"Oh, uh, Mingyang."

The corners of his mouth go down, and he grunts. "Mm."

Okaaay, make it obvious that you disapprove of my old school, why don't you? Still, I soldier on, because my last school shouldn't matter, shouldn't even be part of this discussion. "Anyway, as I was saying, this is only my second day here, but the other students have been picking on me. Calling me names, like 'Crazy Kiki.' And there's this video of me going around, and someone even uploaded it onto TikTok and it's gone a bit viral—"

"TikTok," he groans, pinching the bridge of his nose. "You kids and your social media."

"Um." I'm not sure what to say to that. Am I supposed to apologize for the existence of social media?

"What's this video of you about?" He looks more irritated than concerned.

The thought of the video, with me on a never-ending loop, makes my insides coil. "It's kind of hard to explain . . . ,"

I mumble. Now I really regret having brought up the video at all.

"Show me, then."

For the first time, I'm glad that my phone is in the basket outside my classroom. "I don't have my phone."

"That's fine, I'll use mine." He takes out his phone, taps on the screen, and opens TikTok. Interesting that he claimed to hate social media but has the TikTok app. "What do I search for?"

The words fight me the whole way out. "#Xingfa #CrazyKiki." I keep my eyes on my hands, which are grasped above my lap, as he finds the video and plays it. My voice streams out.

"You obnoxious twat! You obnoxious twat!" And in the background, "B-A-N-A-N-A-S!"

The line between Mr. Lin's eyebrows deepens, and he pauses the video. "I don't understand. This is actually evidence of you being the aggressor. Are you reporting yourself for bullying?"

"What?" I stand up. Holy shit. I totally did not see that coming. "No, wait—"

"You really need to work on your manners when addressing your elders," he barks, and he's gone from looking irritated to looking incandescent with anger. "Look at yourself, your behavior—it's atrocious. And your skirt! Did you shorten it? It's supposed to be four fingers' width under your knee, not over it. You need to order a new size, you hear me? One that doesn't make you look so indecent."

My insides shrivel up, my neck and face burning with

shame. I feel so humiliated I almost burst into tears then and there. God, why did I shorten my school uniform? Why??

"I'm so sorry, sir. I didn't mean to—I just—no, I'm not reporting myself for bullying. Sir."

He grunts, leaning back slightly. "Well, all I see is you violating school rules—calling someone names. Shouting. It's all very disturbing."

"I—yes, but now they're all calling me crazy, and I don't think that's appropriate either, and it's all because of Jonas Arifin. He's the one who—"

"Ah, Jonas Arifin." The frown lines melt away from his forehead, and his eyes actually twinkle with affection. "I've known that boy since he was in K1."

"Uh . . ." Now that I know he's Jonas's number one fan, I have no idea how to proceed.

"So he's the one who started calling you crazy?"

I nod hesitantly.

Mr. Lin snorts. "Ah, that Jonas. He is a character, isn't he? Look, that's his way of showing you that he likes you."

"I don't think—"

"Trust me. I've been the principal here for thirty-two years. Thirty-two! That's almost twice as long as you've been alive, ya? And under my guidance, Xingfa has become the nation's top-tier school. Our reputation is known throughout the whole of Southeast Asia. We even rival Singapore's top schools."

I wish I could tell him that he sounds like a cheesy marketing brochure.

"Look, I know what I'm talking about, okay? Don't be so sensitive. Jonas is a very popular boy, and for him to be so attentive to you is a compliment. You kids nowadays are so sensitive, to the point that you can't even tell what's a joke and what's serious. Don't take it so seriously, ya?"

"But everyone is—"

He waves at me with a *tch* sound. "Don't worry about what everyone says. You need to have self-confidence. We are raising confident leaders of the future here, not weak-willed little snowflakes who melt at the slightest criticism. And 'crazy'? That's not even a criticism. To be honest, in your video, you do seem a bit—" He snorts and makes a seesaw motion with his hand. "You know?"

Did he just call me a bit crazy? I stare at him, open-mouthed.

"Now, what *is* serious is you using foul language. That's unacceptable. I'm going to let it go this one time, because you're new and your old school might be more lenient. . . ." His voice trails off, and I realize he's waiting for me to grovel and thank him for his leniency.

"Thank you, sir," I manage to bite out.

Principal Lin nods. "If this happens again, I won't be so lenient." He doesn't wait for me to reply before standing up. I guess our meeting is over.

I can't look him in the eye as I stand and head for the door.

The receptionist looks up from her e-reader and smiles at me, but I don't even have the energy to muster up a smile for her as I slump out.

CHAPTER 7

When I get home, Mami calls out, "Kiki? Is that you? I've got some madeleines from that new bakery—"

"I don't want any!" I snap, and rush up the stairs. I lock my bedroom door and lean against it, breathing hard. God, Mami better not come up here and try to talk to me. I listen through the door for a bit, but I don't hear her footsteps coming up the stairs. Good. With a sigh, I park myself at my computer and fire up *Warfront Heroes*. There's no other way to describe how I'm feeling aside from completely destructive. I'm angry. So freaking angry. My talk with Principal Lin keeps resurfacing in my mind, and each time I get a flash of his sneering face and patronizing tone, the rage inside me burns hotter, licking at my flesh and consuming all of me. And the feeling of helplessness on top of it only makes it even worse. I want to scream. I want to grab hold of the fabric of society and yank hard, watch everything come tumbling down.

And so I log on to *Warfront Heroes*. Sourdawg isn't online; he doesn't usually log on until after nine p.m. I join the queue for a round at Silmerrov Gulch and choose to play as Heartcrusher, an elf who dual-wields a sword and an axe. The next fifteen minutes are spent stabbing and slashing away with abandon at the enemy group, and by the end of the battle—which my team won—I'm feeling ever so slightly less murderous. But all that replaces the rage is bitterness. I don't feel satisfied. So what if I've taken out my anger on a stupid online game? So what if my *Warfront Heroes* ranking has just risen by a point? None of it matters. I'm still at the bottom of the hierarchy at my new school. My principal is still a misogynistic, patronizing ass. And my classmates are still under Jonas's spell.

Jonas. The thought of him makes my upper lip curl with revulsion. Ugh. I can't remember the last time I despised someone as much as Jonas. I think of his smug smile and his obnoxious voice, and that's when I recall the Titanimus sticker on his notebook, along with his *WH* handle. What was it again? It was something so very Jonas. Like BigDick or Huge-Asshole or . . . GoldenDragonLord. Yes! That's it.

I go into my Socials tab and type in GoldenDragonLord. And there it is. TheGoldenDragonLord, location: Indonesia. And the dot on the left side of his name is green. My heart rate increases dramatically. Jonas is currently online. An evil grin takes over my entire face as I move my cursor over to his name and click on the heart icon to its right. Liking TheGoldenDragonLord means that I enjoy playing with him, which would encourage the algorithm to increase the likelihood that TheGoldenDragonLord and Dudebro10 would run into the same battles.

With that settled, I join the queue for another round of Silmerrov Gulch. Heh-heh. I rub my hands together and twirl an imaginary evil mustache as I wait to be logged on to a battle. The moment I'm on, I quickly open up the list of players and scan it for Jonas. Damn it. No stupid dragon lords in this round. I log off the battle, go back to the home screen, and join the queue for a different round. It takes me a minute longer to get into a new battle this time, because the algorithm doesn't like quitters; the more you quit, the longer you have to wait to join the next game. But it's worth it.

This time, when I call up the players list, his name leaps out at me as though it were written in all caps and neon colors. THEGOLDENDRAGONLORD. My grip on my mouse tightens, and I bare my teeth at the screen. Maybe I'm grinning, maybe I'm growling, who knows? Jonas isn't even going to know what hit him. I choose my character: the Shadow Stalker. Heh-heh. My primary weapons are two short daggers, because I'm going to kill Jonas at close range. I want to see the look on his face when I—well, okay, I won't be able to see the look on *his* face, because this is just an online game, yada yada. But I like the idea of stepping very close to Jonas right before I kill his character.

Unfortunately for Jonas, the new skin that he's just spent a buttload of money on is very, very flashy. Titanimus is a huge warrior with shoulders as wide as he is tall, and his new armor is a painfully shiny gold plate. It's very impressive. It also means I easily spot Jonas within the crowd of players from a mile away. Heh-heh. As soon as the battle begins and everyone charges forward and clashes in the middle of the battleground, I guide my character to the periphery, away from the main action. Halfway through, I engage my character's superpower:

the shadow stance, which is a partial invisibility skill. I'm not quite invisible, as that would make me overpowered, but I fade into the background like a shadow, and only players who are looking out for me would spot me.

I move silkily, past fighting bodies, following the beacon of shining armor that is Jonas. He's waving his giant sword around and making all these showy moves. I creep up until I'm right behind him, then I disengage the shadow stance. There's a beautiful moment where Jonas's character stops moving, and I can practically see Jonas behind his computer going, "Oh, shit." Then I plunge my dagger into the back of his neck, at an exposed sliver of flesh between his helmet and his body armor. Just in case that doesn't do the trick, I press a couple of keys, bringing up my other dagger and slashing his throat with it. The words "No. of Kills: 1!" pop up onto my screen, and my grin is so huge that my cheeks legit hurt. I watch as Jonas's character tumbles onto the ground and slowly fades away. *Mwahaha!*

It takes thirty seconds for a character to respawn after they die, so I quickly engage the shadow stance once more, before Jonas's teammates can get to me. Luckily, they're all still distracted by the fierce battle around me. I walk past them and straight to the enemy quarters, where Jonas will respawn, and I wait patiently. Just as expected, there's a flash of light, and Jonas's character appears at the respawning station. I don't even let him take a single step before I rush forward and stab him multiple times. He crumples to the ground and disappears just as the words "No. of Kills: 2!" appear on my screen.

This time, the chat window explodes with a stream of expletives.

TheGoldenDragonLord: WTF??!! WHAT THE F***??!!!

Warfront Heroes automatically censors swear words, but I got the gist. Still smirking, I type out a short and sweet response.

Dudebro10: :)
TheGoldenDragonLord: F*** YOU, DUDEBRO, YOU
     F***ING LITTLE S*** I AM GOING TO REPORT YOU
Dudebro10: Why are you so sensitive? It's just a game.

I notice a flicker at the respawning station and bite my lip to hold back from laughing, because here is Jonas, about to reappear. It's almost too cruel. Almost. I giggle as I kill him for the third time.

TheGoldenDragonLord: F***!!!!!!!! YOU F***ING
     USELESS TEAM WHERE THE F*** ARE YOU ALL I'M
     GETTING GRIEFED BY SOME F***ING COWARDLY
     BACKSTABBER COME HELP ME YOU A*******!!!!!
Dudebro10: Wow, is that how you talk to your teammates?
     No wonder they won't help you. You know, you catch
     more flies with honey.
TheGoldenDragonLord: I REPORTED YOU FOR GRIEFING
     ME, YOU C***

Wow, he used the C-word. He must be really angry. I click on his name and select the Report button. When a window opens up, I copy/paste Jonas's chat message and hit Send. *Two of us can play the reporting game, Jonas.*

> **MMPlayer:** Hey, guys, stop f***ing around and join the actual battle. DragonLord, we rly need a tank here.
>
> **TheGoldenDragonLord:** HAVE YOU NOT BEEN LISTENING, I'M TRYING TO GET TO THE BATTLE BUT THIS LITTLE S*** IS CAMPING ON THE RESPAWN STATION
>
> **AryaStarkFan:** Uhh, so kill him. He's a little Shadow Stalker. One hit from your hammer will destroy him. God, you suck
>
> **Dudebro10:** Arya is not wrong. ;) It takes me a few stabs to get to you, but you could easily kill me in a hit. I guess you just suck at the game
>
> **TheGoldenDragonLord:** F*** ALL OF YOU
> **<TheGoldenDragonLord has left the battle>**

Oh. Oh ho ho. Jonas rage-quit. I stare at the computer in disbelief for a couple of seconds. I did that. I made him so angry that he quit mid-game, which would severely slash his ranking, because if there's one thing that's universally unaccepted on *Warfront Heroes*, it's people quitting mid-battle. It leaves your teammates seriously screwed, being one person short. With Jonas gone, I rejoin the main fight, and we defeat his team in record time. By the time the round ends, I'm breathless. I feel like I've come back to life.

I log off, feeling rejuvenated enough to take a shower and deal with the rest of the day's work, i.e., the ridiculous mountain of homework that Xingfa assigns us every day. When I complained about it to Sourdawg last night, he said it's something many schools do to make sure that their students don't have any time to go out and "cause trouble." I put on my headphones, play my "homework playlist," and get to work. I'm only halfway done when Papi calls out for me to come down for dinner.

Dinner is— How do I say this without coming off like a complete brat? It's awkward, because there's someone at the table who is extremely surly and grumpy. That someone is me, by the way. I'm surly and grumpy. But hey, I've got good reason to be this way. Mami, Papi, and I used to chat about our day over dinner, but tonight, when they ask me how my day went, I say, "Well, it was truly awful, if you must know. How much longer do I have to stay in this school from hell?"

Papi sighs. "Sayang, you must try to fit in. Xingfa is the best school in the nation. Its reputation is sterling."

"You know," Mami adds, "half of Xingfa's graduates go to Ivy Leagues or Oxbridge!"

"Right," I mutter, "uh-huh. So you're saying that I'm not settling in not because there's something wrong with the school. Oh no, it must mean that *I'm* the problem."

"That's not what we're saying at all," Papi says. His eyebrows are furrowed. "What's going on, Kiki? Why are you not settling in?"

I almost blurt out that I was, in fact, sent to the principal's office today. But then I recall how Principal Lin sneered at me, how he kept saying I needed to learn respect and honor, and for some weird reason, shame floods me. I don't understand it, but I feel red-hot guilt surging through me, like I've somehow let my parents down. Part of me is shouting: *No! This isn't at all your fault!* But the other part is going: *Well, actually, it is? What kind of idiot calls their classmate a twat? That's actually really shitty.*

No, I can't possibly tell Mami and Papi. For one thing, they'd both be horrified by me calling anyone a twat, and for another, if they were to find out that the person I'd called a twat was Jonas freaking Arifin, son of the Arifin empire, I think Mami would have an actual brain aneurysm.

I eat as fast as I can before telling them—grumpily—that I have to finish my homework.

Finally, *finally*, I'm done with my homework and can log back on to *WH*. The second I get on, my computer chimes with a direct message from Sourdawg.

Sourdawg: Hey, you're on later than usual

The sight of his screen name does things to my stomach. My heart lurches up, lodging itself in my throat and nearly choking me. I wonder if it's actually possible to be strangled by your own heart.

Who is Sourdawg? Inquiring minds need to know! My fingers hover over the keyboard, aching to type out: What's your name IRL?

But if I asked him that, he'd probably ask me the same question, and then I'd have to lie to him. Even more than I already have, that is. And also, what if he gets suspicious, like why the hell am I asking now, after over a year of online friendship? Maybe it might even get him to start wondering what could have triggered the question. Arrrgh! I shake off all the squeaking my mind is doing and make myself answer like I normally would.

> **Dudebro10:** Oh man, you wouldn't believe the amount of homework I just had to wade through. Brutal!
> **Sourdawg:** Haha, you mean you're finally getting the NORMAL amount of homework?

I can't help smiling at that. A few months ago, Sourdawg and I compared homework, and he was scandalized to find that his school was assigning double the amount of homework that Mingyang was. Of course, now that I know he goes to Xingfa, this makes a lot more sense.

> **Dudebro10:** Well, I don't know how you do it
> **Sourdawg:** You'll get used to it. How was school? Any better today?
> **Dudebro10:** God, if anything, it was even worse. I had to talk to the principal.

As soon as I hit Enter, my breath catches and I jolt up in my seat. Shit! I shouldn't have said that! Everyone at Xingfa probably knows by now that I was sent to the principal's office. Oh god, oh god, damage control:

> **Dudebro10:** It was my own choice, I wasn't sent there or anything.

Oh god, that's so painfully obvious. I pinch the bridge of my nose.

Sourdawg: Wow, okay. Why?

Dudebro10: Oh, just . . . well, I'm noticing quite a bit of bullying at my school. IDK, that kind of thing rly bothers me

Sourdawg: Yeah. That's rly good of you to report it. What did the principal say?

Dudebro10: That's the thing, tho. He was basically like, "Eh, the boy was just calling the girl names because he likes her. Don't make such a big deal out of it."

Sourdawg: Oof. That rly sucks, but I can't say I'm surprised

Dudebro10: Rly?? I was shocked

Sourdawg: That's 'cuz you've been spoiled by your hippie school. Haven't you read the news recently? There's that case in—I can't remember, it might have been Thailand—where this girl reported her classmate for harassment and got expelled

Dudebro10: WHAT?

Sourdawg: Yeah, dude. That's not even unique. She only got some press because she happens to be a YouTube star. Then there's that case in Malaysia where this boy said he was dunked in the trash by his classmate, and they were BOTH expelled for "besmirching the reputation of the school."

Dudebro10: Wait, WHAT? They expelled the poor boy for being bullied?

Sourdawg: Yesss. It's a thing! How do you not know this?

It's a problem all over Asia. And the thing is, when students report bullying, a lot of the time, the schools are only concerned about saving face. Otherwise the school might LOSE FACE #shockhorror

Dudebro10: Wow, okay. That rly sucks. I guess I sort of knew about it, but I had no idea it was this bad

Sourdawg: Yeah. I rly hate that about our cultures. You know how I've been going to therapy ever since my mom left?

Dudebro10: Yeah, you said it's been rly helpful, right?

Sourdawg: Yeah, I love my therapist. She's rly cool. But anyway, she's also a secret. Like, my dad basically told me I couldn't tell anyone else—not my cousins or friends or our relatives—about her

Dudebro10: Jesus

Sourdawg: Yep. Because if anyone knew that I was seeing a therapist, they'd be like, "Omg he's craaazy!" and then WHAT WOULD PEOPLE THINK OMGGG

Dudebro10: OMG WE WOULD LOSE SO MUCH FACE

Sourdawg: ALL OF IT, ALL THE FACE

Dudebro10: LMAO

Sourdawg: 😂

Dudebro10: Hey srsly tho, thanks for telling me. I feel honored and stuff

And really, really guilty, because Sourdawg has no idea that he's just told a schoolmate. God, I seriously need to find out who Sourdawg is IRL.

Just as I think that, my phone beeps. It's a message from a

group chat called Lil' Aunties. Ah, good timing. I open it with just a tad of trepidation.

> **Eleanor Roosevelt:** Ci Kiki! Guess what? You are all set to go on your first ever Lil' Aunties–sanctioned date

I hurriedly type "BBL" to Sourdawg before typing out a message to Lil' Aunties.

> **Kiki:** Cool, who's it with?
> **SJP:** Jeremiah Riady. He's an above-average specimen of the teenage male

My mouth quirks into a smile. These girls, I swear.

> **Kiki:** Above-average specimen of the teenage male, huh? Wow, you're really selling this hard
> **Eleanor Roosevelt:** That's actually our highest category. We have "Above average," "Average," "Below average," and "Unfit"

Was I ever this smart and cool when I was their age? Oh, who am I kidding? I'm still nowhere near as smart or cool.

> **Kiki:** Sounds good. I'm looking forward to it!

Operation Find Out Who Sourdawg Is is officially underway.

CHAPTER 8

The next morning, I keep my chin up as I walk inside my classroom, steadfastly averting my gaze from Jonas's corner. As I put my bag down on my chair and start unloading books and sliding them into the open mouth of my desk, I overhear Jonas talking to Tristan.

> **Jonas:** ". . . swear, that asshole was on me the whole night. It made the game unplayable."
>
> **Tristan:** "That sucks. Did you report him?"
>
> **Jonas:** "Of course I did. Do you think I'm a moron? But of course the mods did nothing. They don't care about these things."
>
> **Tristan:** "Well, I guess it's hard because, technically, the opposing side is supposed to kill you, so . . ."
>
> **Jonas:** "Yeah, but this was different. He wasn't doing it to win the game. He was hunting me down and camping on the respawn point."
>
> **Tristan:** "Why didn't you just kill him?"

There's silence, then Jonas says, "Ugh, you just don't get it. He was in freaking stealth mode the whole time! How the hell was I supposed to see him, never mind kill him?"

Heh-heh. Ah, this conversation is sparking such joy, as Marie Kondo would say. I imagine myself joining in and helpfully suggesting that Jonas use his warrior ability to strike around him in a whirlwind, which would render the shadow stance useless. Oh, to see the look on his face when he gets taught how to play better by a girl. But I need to focus on my goal, which is not to troll Jonas but to make myself a couple of friends. Right.

I look around. There's ten minutes before the first period starts, and half my classmates have already arrived. Most of them are chatting with their friends, but a couple of them are sitting quietly at their desks, reading. Introverts! Yesss. Okay, that came out a lot more creepy than I intended. Better still, one of the quietly reading ones is none other than Peishan. Surely a girl with the bad luck of sitting next to Jonas would be sympathetic toward me.

Here goes. I take a deep breath and tap Peishan on the shoulder.

"Hi, Peishan." Good. My voice comes out the perfect balance of chill and friendly.

She turns around and—get this—does what I swear is a tiny grimace. Gah! Not a good start. Still, I press on.

"Um, read anything good lately?" I say, nodding at her book. Oh god, that sounded so pathetic, like a pickup line some creep would try at a bar. Okay, maybe not at a bar. I wouldn't know, I've never been inside a bar, but I imagine they're full of creeps approaching women with stupid one-liners. Much like the one I've just approached Peishan with.

"No," she says. She shows me the cover of the book she's reading, and of course it's one of our textbooks.

"Oh, right. Yeah, studying hard, huh?" Inside, something shrivels up and dies. I believe it was my soul. Because could I sound more dadlike?

Peishan narrows her eyes at me. "What do you want, Kiki? I'd rather not chat with you for too long."

Wow, okay. That was very straightforward. "Uh, I just—I—" Eleanor Roosevelt's little matchmaking project jumps to my mind, and I hurtle toward it. "A couple of friends and I are starting this really cool app." That sentence is sort of, kind of misleading, I realize, because I'm not sure that Eleanor Roosevelt and Sarah Jessica count as "friends." I mean, are you even allowed to be friends with people four years your junior? It's definitely not going to help me rejuvenate my reputation, that's for sure. But nobody needs to know that the friends in question are only thirteen. "Basically, it's a matchmaking app for teens, and we were wondering if you'd be interested in joining?"

One side of Peishan's upper lip curls up, and she looks at me with the amount of disdain one might reserve for a particularly fat, wriggly earthworm. "Uh, no? Dating? We don't have time to date, Kiki." She says this really slowly, like I'm hard of hearing. "We've got exams and college apps to prep for. And not to mention dating's forbidden?"

"Right. Of course. Well, you know, if you wanted to be

involved in the business side of things, it could be good on your college apps?" Why am I even still trying? Part of me is shouting at myself to retain what few shreds of dignity I have left and leave already. But the other part of me is panting with desperation.

"No," she says simply, and returns her attention to her textbook.

Shot down, just like that.

Liam arrives then, plopping down on his seat and depositing his heavy backpack on the floor with a thump. He catches my eye and raises his chin. "'Sup?"

Ugh, did he catch the tragedy that was me trying to chat up Peishan? My face feels hot, so I turn away. I hope I'm not visibly blushing. I still haven't quite figured Liam out yet. I mean, at first, I thought he was one of Jonas's stooges, but yesterday he told Jonas to back off, so I don't know what his deal is. Whatever it is, I am not in the mood to try to figure out the horrible mess that is my group mates. I need a fresh start, someone who's completely new to me.

Okay. I look around. Thankfully, no one else has given us any attention. I want to thunk my head down on my desk until school is done for the day, but no! I'm not one to be so easily thwarted. I eye another student. A boy named . . . uh, I believe it's Jeff, or it might be Tobin. Wildly different names, I know, but he has a very Jeff/Tobin vibe. I saunter over, pretending like I'm perusing the bulletin boards at the back of the classroom. Luckily, Jeff/Tobin sits in the very back row. When I'm a couple of steps away from him, I summon up a smile and say, "Hey."

He looks up in surprise and smiles at me. "Oh, hey." Okay, this is a good start.

"Hey, what're you up to?"

He gives me a sheepish grin and leans back in his seat so I can see that he's got a textbook open, but hidden inside the textbook is a graphic novel.

"Cool!" I smile back to show that I'm definitely not the kind to rat out someone reading a graphic novel in class. Unlike Peishan, who is definitely that type. "Yeah, I'm really into graphic novels myself."

"Really? No way! Which ones have you read?"

"Well, my favorite is *Saga*. I know it's kind of old, but—"

"Oh my god," Jeff/Tobin says. "I loved that series. They weren't available here for the longest time, so I had to order them from Amazon US. I spent all my allowance paying for international shipping, but it was worth every cent."

I laugh. "Wow, that's hardcore. I asked my cousins in Singapore to bring me back copies. What are you read—"

"Oooh," someone hoots. Jonas. He's waggling his eyebrows at us while wearing this smirk that he probably picked up from a shitty rom-com with a shitty alpha male who thinks he's hot shit. "Is it just me, or is there something going on between you guys?" His smirk morphs into a grin, and he crosses his arms in front of his chest. "Nicky and Crazy Kiki. I like it. Has a nice ring to it."

"Jonas," Liam groans, but Jonas simply shrugs and gives this innocent smile before going back to his seat.

Okay, so my new friend's name is nowhere near Jeff or Tobin.

Even as I'm digesting this fact, Nicky's whole face turns red and he shakes his head jerkily. "No," he snaps. "There's nothing going on between me and Crazy Kiki." With that, he turns his whole upper body away from me. I've literally been given the cold shoulder.

And it stings. Holy crap, does it ever sting. It's not like I've developed feelings for Nicky or anything, but we were having an actual conversation. We were bonding. I thought he could be my first friend here, someone with whom I share a genuine interest, and we graphic novel nerds should stick together, right? There's an unspoken rule of loyalty between graphic novel fans and gaming nerds to have each other's backs in real life. But Nicky's gone and stuck a knife deep in my gut to preserve himself. He didn't even just say nothing's going on between us. He went the extra mile and called me the name that Jonas christened me with.

From the corner of my eye, I see Liam stand up and walk toward me. I bet he's going to tell me I'm being stupid or whatever.

Crazy Kiki.

God, I hate that name. Tears prick the back of my eyes. I can't bear to look at anyone. I keep my eyes on my feet and stalk out the door just as the first period teacher walks in.

"Class is about to start," Mr. Wong says.

I manage to choke out, "Toilet!" before hurrying away. No doubt I'll get reprimanded for this—tardiness, lack of manners, and other transgressions they'll come up with—but I don't care. I run to the blessedly empty bathroom and sob. I hardly know myself anymore. I didn't think that my confidence could be shattered this quickly, but then again, I've never been in a position where I'm the butt of an entire class's joke.

I can't wait to get home and give Jonas the thrashing he deserves on *Warfront Heroes.*

By the time the weekend arrives, my nerves are shot. I've never felt this way before, not even when I was in kindergarten. I've always been so confident, but my first week at Xingfa has left me feeling like I've been on the losing end of a fistfight. Normally, I would be half-excited, half-chill before a date—excited because I know I'm about to have a blast, chill because I know that even if we don't hit it off, it's all going to be okay. But now, before my first Lil' Aunties–arranged date, I'm actually nervous as hell. I have no idea what to expect. My phone beeps as I'm getting ready, and I practically pounce on it.

Sharlot: Hey, you have a date today, right?

Cassie: She does!!

Sharlot: Aaah! Excuse me, we need PICS! Show us your outfit!

That makes me smile despite my nerves, and I oblige, taking a mirror selfie and sending it their way.

Cassie: I LOVE

Sharlot: Yasss, I approve! The shorts say: I'm super casual, this is no biggie

Cassie: But the top says . . . wait, I don't know what the top says

Sharlot: It says: But take me somewhere nice

Cassie: Yes, that

Kiki: You guys are dorks, you know that, right?

I love these two so much for making me smile. Another message pops up at the top of my screen, from the Lil' Aunties group, and I tap on it.

Eleanor Roosevelt: Ci Kiki, did you receive the pdf we sent you yesterday?

Kiki: The 12-page pdf with over a hundred rules on dating? Yes, yes I did.

And boy, do I ever wish that I hadn't. The rules that these girls have come up with range from sensible ("No posting pics on social media without everybody's permission") to random ("No going to Starbucks or Coffee Bean") to ridiculous ("Family members may attend if it is the following: siblings okay on the second date, cousins okay on the third date, parents okay on the fourth date, grandparents and uncles/aunts only after the sixth date"). Okay, knowing the Chinese Indonesian culture, that last rule isn't actually that ridiculous; I've heard of many a first date where one party took their parents along.

SJP: Here's a link to a DocuSign. Pls sign it before you go on your date

Kiki: Ummmmm . . . dare I ask what it's for?

SJP: We mentioned the NDA before—don't worry, it's very

reasonable. You can talk about your date freely if you want, but you must leave Eleanor Roosevelt and me out of it. No one else can know of Lil' Aunties

Kiki: So you're like the Illuminati

Eleanor Roosevelt: But better, because we're actually doing good. The DocuSign also includes a waiver so you can't sue us if things go wrong :)

Kiki: UMMM, wait, just how wrong are you expecting things to go??

SJP: It's just a formality

Eleanor Roosevelt: Yep, just a formality. But sign it before your date pls

Welp, this is the first-ever NDA and waiver I have ever had to sign. Feels right that it would be, of all things, for Eleanor Roosevelt's questionable matchmaking service. I click on the link and sign where the program tells me to, then hit Send.

SJP: Got it

Eleanor Roosevelt: Thanks, Ci Kiki! Right, you've got sixteen minutes before Jeremiah picks you up for your date. Have fun!

Sixteen minutes is very precise timing, but I can picture Eleanor Roosevelt and Sarah Jessica holding an actual timer and watching it to mark the start time of my first date. I check my reflection in the mirror one last time before making my way downstairs.

I walk as quietly as I can past the living room, but Papi spots me and calls out, "Kiki, you off to see Cassie?"

I wipe the grimace off my face and plaster on a smile before turning to face him. "Just going out with a friend from school."

Mami appears from the kitchen behind him, grinning. "From Xingfa?" she practically squeaks. "A new friend!"

Anger leaps up my gut. She is the last person who has the right to be happy about anything that has to do with Xingfa. I scowl at her. "Not a friend. Just—" I struggle for the right words. I don't want to tell my parents that I have sunk so low that I had to enlist the help of two underaged matchmakers. But then I realize, why not? It's their fault I'm in a school so ill-suited to me that I'm now friendless. "I don't have any real friends at Xingfa."

Mami's and Papi's faces crease into frowns. "That's not possible," Mami says with a snort. "Even when you were in kindergarten, you were always popular."

It hurts because it's true. I've never had a taste of being a pariah, and the reminder of how loved I was in the past suddenly drains me. I shake my head. "Whatever."

Papi's smile fades. "Kiki." There's a warning tone in his voice, which angers me.

"Well, you clearly have friends, because you're going out now," Mami says brightly.

It's too much, all of it. Mami's peppy, hopeful voice. Papi's disappointment. I shrug and say, "Anyway, see you," and before they can say anything else, I practically rush out the front door.

The last thing I want to do is have to walk back inside the house and be faced with more questions, so even though

Jeremiah isn't here yet, I walk down the driveway and wait outside our gate. I check my phone. It's two minutes past the official start time of our date. I chew the inside of my cheek and scroll through TikTok for a bit. Five minutes pass, then ten. Technically, this isn't a rarity; Indonesians are notorious for being late. We call it "Indo time." But Eleanor Roosevelt and Sarah Jessica have been so insistent on punctuality, I really wasn't expecting this. I'm about to send a WhatsApp message to the Lil' Aunties group chat when I see a car trundling down the street.

It stops right in front of my house. My mouth goes dry, and I have to swallow to keep from coughing. This is it. My first-ever Lil' Aunties date. The back door opens and out comes Jeremiah. Niiice. I make a mental note to commend Eleanor Roosevelt and Sarah Jessica for making a good choice: broad shoulders, firm jaw, a mop of curls that's just begging for fingers to run through it. Jeremiah is totally a sight for sore eyes.

But apparently he doesn't feel the same way about me, because when he sees me, his expression falls. It's such a drastic change that it's impossible to miss. His mouth actually drops open, and his eyes go dark, his brows slamming together. Good god, do I really look that terrible? Maybe I have a giant piece of spinach stuck to my teeth? No, the way he's staring at me with such despair, I would have needed to have a whole bunch of spinach stuck to my face.

"Um, hi," I somehow manage to say.

"No," Jeremiah says.

"Sorry?"

"This is not happening. I am NOT going out with Crazy Kiki."

It feels like he's just kicked me in the stomach. The breath is knocked out of me, and I want to crumple to the ground.

Jeremiah is shaking his head. "Ugh, I should've known better than to trust those kids. No wonder they didn't want to tell me who my date was. Jesus, what a waste of time." Sneering, he climbs back inside his car. He doesn't even bother speaking to me. Everything he's said has been to some invisible audience. Before I know it, the car is reversing. My head is a screaming, scrambled mess. What is happening? He just got here! I didn't even get to—

"Wait!" I shout, running toward the car. It halts, and the back window rolls down. Jeremiah peers out at me, still frowning.

"Sorry, but I'm not interested," he says.

"I figured," I snap. "I just—" What the hell was I going to say to him? What is there to say? It feels like my brain is hiccupping. "Do you play *Warfront Heroes*?" I blurt out.

"What?" The frown on his face deepens. "What's that?"

"It's ah—an online game?"

"Like I said," Jeremiah says, enunciating every word like he's talking to a toddler, "I'm not interested." And with that, he presses a button and his window starts closing again. But before it closes all the way, he chuckles and says, "You really are Crazy Kiki."

I stand there shaking, watching his car disappear around the corner, and no matter how many times I tell myself that it's okay, it's his loss, I don't think I'll ever believe it.

CHAPTER 9

By the time Monday arrives, I feel so defeated that I can barely summon the energy to get myself out of bed. Eleanor Roosevelt and Sarah Jessica have texted me multiple times, asking me for updates, but I can't bear to tell them how the date went. I don't even have it in me to snark back at Mami and Papi when they tell me to have a good day. And at school, I keep my eyes down and refuse to look at anyone.

This morning, we have a group project session, and I realize that I just don't care anymore. I don't. I sit there, completely silent, as Jonas tells us that the painfully voluptuous female character on his poster has to carry two humongous guns to "show that this is a feminist game." He smirks at me and pauses, as though waiting for me to voice my disagreement. Liam is staring at me with a frown, but I simply let my gaze drop to my lap with a shrug. Jonas can do whatever the hell he wants. I'm not going to stick my neck out again over a project I don't give a crap about.

As soon as the recess bell rings, I hurry out of the classroom and make my way to the library. No disrespect to bookworms, but I've never been the sort of person who spends her break time at the library. But now, only wild horses can drag me out of this hallowed, quiet, safe space. Well, wild horses and the fourth-period bell. I breathe in deeply as the doors slide open. I'm quickly learning to love that unique smell that libraries have: a cloudy scent of dusty pages and ancient ink. I go past the more popular kid lit section and bury myself deep among the forgotten shelves. The books back here are a mishmash of forgotten genres: travelogues, old textbooks, and a smattering of memoirs. None of it interests me, to be honest—I doubt I'll ever be a serious enough reader—but their presence comforts me.

"Hey," someone says.

I start, my breath catching in my throat. Color rushes to my cheeks when I see Liam standing there. I clear my throat. "Hey."

"What're you doing here?" Liam says, taking a couple of steps toward me.

"Nothing."

Liam's eyebrows rise, and he looks suspiciously like he's smiling at me. "Nothing? So you weren't stroking that copy of *Robespierre and the French Revolution* like it's a purring cat?"

I definitely was stroking the spine of *Robespierre and the French Revolution* like it's a purring cat. I snatch my hand back and wipe it on the skirt of my uniform as though I just got caught doing something perverted. "Just—you know—wanted to feel what the cover material was."

"Through the library's plastic covering?"

For a moment, I wonder if I should press on. But why bother fighting the Crazy Kiki label? The more time that goes by, the more I'm starting to wonder if perhaps Jonas was right all along, if maybe I *am* crazy and I simply never knew. My shoulders sag, and I sigh. "Yeah, okay, I was stroking books. I swear I'm not doing it in a creepy way, if there is indeed a non-creepy way to stroke books. I just—I don't know why, but it's comforting?"

"Hey, I'm not judging. You know what I love doing?" Liam picks out a random book and opens it. He lifts it to his face and takes a deep inhale. "Ahhh." Then he coughs. "Okay, this one's a bit dusty." He puts the book back on the shelf and gives me that cute, boyish grin of his. "I like smelling books."

It dawns on me slowly, gently, like a sun peeking over the horizon, making the shadows melt away: Liam isn't making fun of me. He's smiling, yes, but it's a bashful smile, not a sardonic smirk. No, I shouldn't hope for a friend, not after the terrible, shitty way that everyone else has smacked me down. God, the memory of Jeremiah's sneer makes me wince even now.

"Are you okay?" Liam says.

I was all prepared to say yes, of course, and shut this conversation down, but when I open my mouth, what comes out is "Not really." What the hell? Why did I say that? I shake my head and add, "But who's ever really okay, right?" I punctuate it with a weak laugh that sounds desperate.

"Um, so . . ." Liam licks his lips. "I have a confession to make: I followed you here."

That makes my breath hitch. I have to remind myself to keep my tone casual. "Now who's being creepy?"

Liam raises his hands. "Okay, I know how it sounds, but I swear I'm not being creepy. I just wanted to apologize."

My eyebrows knit together. "I don't get it. Apologize for what?"

Liam's breath comes out in a sigh. "God, where do I even begin? I'm sorry about how everyone's treating you, for one thing. I knew that people here don't like anyone who's different, but I really didn't think they'd be so . . . well, so fucking horrible to you."

Oh god. My nose is tingling and my eyes are misting up and gahhh, lord help me if I cry in front of this boy, I swear. "It's not your fault," I mutter.

"It kind of is. I should've spoken out sooner. I mean, your first day, I tried warning you, but . . ."

Warning me? So that's what he was trying to do. I dismissed it as Liam trying to threaten me.

"I was wrong. I shouldn't have warned you. I should've just addressed the cause: Jonas. He's such an asshole, I swear."

"He is!" I cry, relief pounding through me at the realization that here, finally, is someone who feels the same way I do.

"I've never liked him," Liam says. "I've always kept my head down and gone along with everything he said because I thought that's the only way to survive here." He runs his fingers through his hair and sighs again. "But now I realize that it's the cowardly option. I hate it. I hate pretending that everything Jonas says is great. I hate pretending that his ideas are awesome."

I'm holding my breath, because I sense it coming, and I don't want anything, not even breathing, to get in the way.

And then Liam says it. The beautiful words I have been longing to hear. "I fucking hate his ideas for our group project."

My squeal is so loud that someone a few shelves away shushes me. I clamp a hand over my mouth and hiss-shout, "*Yessss.*"

Liam laughs. "They are *so* bad."

"*So* bad!"

"Like a completely unoriginal copy of *Lara Croft*," Liam says.

"Her boobs are bigger than her head," I add.

"And the guns!"

"Don't knock the guns. They're 'feminist.'"

I don't realize how hard we're both laughing until one of the librarians storms over to us and hisses, "If you two can't be quiet, you'll have to leave the premises."

We apologize to her and scurry out of the library like guilty children. Outside, we double over laughing, and it feels so good. It feels like I'm waking up after a deep sleep, my dulled senses coming back to life. And when I finally straighten up and meet Liam's eyes, I know that I've finally found my first real friend at Xingfa.

"So I'm sorry," Liam says, still half laughing. "But I promise you that from now on, I'm not going to be such a coward. I'll stand up to Jonas."

That makes me laugh, because it sounds so dramatic. "You don't have to." Why did I say that? I want him to. But my instinctive reaction is to say no, because . . . part of me doesn't think I'm worth standing up for.

"I do. Everyone should be doing it, actually. If everyone did it, we wouldn't have a bullying problem. I don't wanna be part of that problem. And you don't deserve to be treated like that."

My chin trembles so hard I have to bite down on my lower lip to keep from bawling. I manage a nod, not trusting myself to speak. I *don't* deserve to be treated like that. I don't. When did I lose sight of it? In such a short time, I've gone from loving myself to wanting to disappear, and it's scary to think of how quickly it all happened. But not anymore. Now that I have an ally, I've got some of my fight back.

We chat easily all the way back to class, and for the first time, I don't get a surge of terror when I see our classroom and the label YEAR ELEVEN PURITY above it.

The first thing I hear when we go inside is Jonas's cronies, Elon and Tristan, bitching to each other about how shitty Jonas is.

"He got owned by Angelus last night, can you freaking believe it?" Elon says.

"Uh. Seriously? A healer? What was he playing as?"

"Titanimus! He should've been able to one-shot Angelus, but nope. She killed him three freaking times. Our entire team was, like, Dude, what the fuck?"

I have to fight hard to hide my smile. This is glorious. Last night, after Sourdawg logged off, I stayed on, found Jonas, and this time, I killed him while playing as a healer. I don't know if it's clear just how humiliating this is for Jonas. Healers are designed to, well, heal. Healing characters tend to be pretty weak in terms of health and armor; they have to be well-protected by their teammates so that they can go around casting healing spells on everyone. The healer I chose, Angelus, only has a sad little hammer as her weapon. Jonas was playing as Titanimus. There shouldn't be any way in hell that my character could have killed his, but there you go, that's just how crappy a player Jonas is. While he flailed in a panic, I used my tiny hammer to bludgeon his stupid head in before dancing over his fading corpse. Then I camped out at the respawn site and did it twice more before his buddies came to his aid and drove me away. Definitely something that sparks joy.

"It's embarrassing! I think we need to—"

Elon nudges him and the two turn to look at the doorway, where Jonas has just arrived. They stop talking and give him a nod. Jonas approaches, and he's obviously in a crappy mood. He immediately zeroes in on Elon.

"What the hell was that about last night?"

Elon glances at Tristan, who shrugs. "Uh, what do you mean?"

"You guys left me alone. Where was the team support while I was getting griefed by that fucking Dudebro troll?"

"Uh . . ." Elon side-eyes Tristan with obvious uneasiness. "Um, we were trying to capture the flag, which was, you know, kind of the mission? And, I mean, you were playing as Titanimus, and Dudebro was playing as Angelus. You shouldn't have been able to be defeated by a healer, so . . ."

"He was obviously cheating!" Jonas snaps. "Don't be putting this on me, Elon. Just because you're a shitty team player. You guys should've had my back! You know this asshole's been after me for days now."

"Well, yeah, but . . ."

Heh-heh. I grin at Liam as we settle into our seats.

"Sounds like Jonas is having a hard time on *Warfront*," Liam mutters under his breath.

"Yeah," I giggle. Then stop. I stare at Liam.

"What?" He stops short, his eyes widening ever so slightly. "Do I have something on my face?"

"No, it's just . . . how did you know they were talking about *Warfront Heroes*?" They'd only mentioned the characters' names, not the actual game.

"Oh." Liam lowers his voice so I have to lean closer to hear him. We're so close to each other now that I can see the curve of his eyelashes. My heart thumps so hard I can feel it in my neck. "I play too. But don't tell anyone, because Jonas has been trying to get me to join his gaming crew for ages."

My throat is so dry I can barely get the next few words out. "Wha-what's your *Warfront* name?"

Liam frowns at me. "Sourdawg, why?"

Is it possible to black out for half a second? Because that's exactly what happens to me. The world falls away, and in that split second, everything is pitch-dark and silent. All I can hear is the sound of my breath and the roar of blood rushing through my head.

I've found him. Sourdawg. It's Liam.

"—okay? Hey."

I'm snatched back to the present moment. I blink. Liam is staring at me, and his hand is on my arm. *Sourdawg's* hand is on my arm. My real arm, not my in-game character's arm. I jerk up at the what-the-hellness of it all, and Liam must have thought I was reacting to his hand on my arm, because he says, "Sorry!" and pulls his hand away.

The teacher walks in then, and for the first time, I'm thankful that he has chosen this very moment to arrive in class, because WHAT THE HELL?! I turn to face the front of the classroom and stare at the blackboard with laser eyes, refusing to even glance at Liam, because, have I mentioned, WHAT THE HELL?! My hands are bunched into fists on my lap, and the whole period, I have to keep from screaming, "SOURDAWG?! IT'S MEEE! YOUR ONLINE BESTIE! DUDEBRO!"

Oh god. Dudebro. My online male persona. How would Liam react if he were to find out that Dudebro is actually a girl in real life? I swear my rib cage hasn't just tightened; each rib has turned into a snake, and now they're all writhing about and squeezing my lungs, and okay, maybe that's a weird metaphor, but holy shit, I'm sitting next to Sourdawg.

The moment class ends, I choke out, "Bathroom!" and rush out of there, pausing outside the classroom to grab my phone from the basket. I sprint all the way to the bathroom and slam myself into the farthest cubicle.

Kiki: Aaaa! AAAHH!!!
Sharlot: Omg what?
Cassie: Wkt?

I guess Cassie's typing in class again, which means she's typing while staring ahead so she doesn't get caught doing it.

Kiki: I found out who Sourdawg is!!!!!!

Cassie: OMJ!!!

Sharlot: Ahh!! Who??

Kiki: LIAM! The guy who sits next to me!!

Sharlot: !!!

Cassie: !! The hot juy?? He's hot, tight?

Kiki: Ew, 'tight'?

Cassie: I meant "right"

Kiki: You need to stop typing in class, you're gonna get caught

Sharlot: Did you tell him who you are?

Kiki: What?! Of course not! He thinks my online persona is a GUY, remember?

Cassie: Oh god, that's right, DUDEBRO

Kiki: What should I do???

Cassie: Act normal@@@

Kiki: Should I just tell him the truth?

Sharlot: Definitely not right now. You're in the middle of the school day, right? I think for now, just act normal. We'll come up with a better way to expose yourself later

Cassie: Expose herself, huh?

Kiki: CASSIE

Sharlot: CASSIE

Despite everything, I snort a little at Cassie's comment. That's so Cassie. The thought brings about a whole wave of sadness. I wish we were still in the same school. We'd be going to the bathroom together, gripping each other and squealing over the revelation of Sourdawg's identity. Oh god, Sourdawg.

Aka Liam. Oh, lordy lordy lordy. I take a deep breath. Ew, gross. One definitely should not do any deep breathing in a school bathroom. I breathe out through my mouth.

I can handle this. I mean, as far Sourdawg candidates go, Liam's pretty freaking amazing. He's kind, he hasn't bought into the whole "Crazy Kiki" thing, and he's just promised that he's going to start standing up to Jonas. The memory of that makes guilt lance through my gut. Liam is a decent person. He doesn't deserve to have me lying to him. But then I think of all the conversations we've had online and how honest he's been about his parents' divorce and, god, I feel like total and utter crap at the thought of Liam sitting behind the screen, typing earnestly to Dudebro. Dudebro, who he thinks is a dude. This is the worst.

Cassie and Sharlot are right, I can't possibly let him know who I really am. Not now, at least. I'll have to come up with a way to—uh, expose myself (damn Sharlot for putting those words in my head!) as gently as possible. Yes, good plan.

With another deep breath—ugh, big mistake—I brush down my skirt and make my way out of the bathroom. I can do this. I can totally act normal with Liam.

Dudebro10: Hey, so you mentioned that there's a new kid sitting next to you?

Okay, so I can't, in fact, act normal with Liam. But hey, can anyone really blame me? I mean, okay, yes, they totally can, but I bet anyone in my shoes would be totally digging for information.

> **Sourdawg:** Did I? I think there are a couple of new kids in
>   my class this year
> **Dudebro10:** Yeah, I think you mentioned in passing

Oh god, oh god, I am *sweating.*

> **Sourdawg:** Oh OK. Yeah I'm sitting next to a new girl
> **Dudebro10:** Cool. Is she hot?

My soul folds into itself over and over until it's a tiny, dense wad screaming into the void. I can't believe I just straight out asked Liam if I'm hot. I'm fishing for compliments, I know, but it's been a rough week. The universe owes me this one.

> **Sourdawg:** She's cute. But kind of grumpy. You know
>   Grumpy Cat?

He did not just compare me to Grumpy-freaking-CAT.

> **Dudebro10:** Yeah . . . ?
> **Sourdawg:** Yep. She's got that pissed-off expression
>   down. Exactly like Grumpy Cat
> **Dudebro10:** Maybe she's pissed off because people are
>   bullying her?
> **Sourdawg:** Yeah, maybe. I did apologize to her for not
>   standing up to those assholes. TBH, I was kinda talking

abt it with my therapist and she was, like, "How does it make you feel to watch this girl get bullied?" and welp, feels like shit. So I'm gonna say something next time

Dudebro10: I bet she'll rly appreciate it

Sourdawg: Maybe. Should've done it a lot sooner. Anyway, enough about me. What abt you, bro? Seeing anyone?

Dudebro10: Sure

Sourdawg: That's cool. You never mentioned your gf. Or bf

Dudebro10: Oh, nonono. I don't have one of those. I just take it easy, you know. Not rly a one-woman kind of guy

Oh my god what am I even saying?! Stop typing, fingers!

Sourdawg: Ah

Dudebro10: Sorry, that came out rly wrong and douchey. I don't know why I said that. I'm not seeing anyone. No one's rly into me at school, lol

Sourdawg: Hah, saaame

I almost type "I find that hard to believe, given you're about as hot as the center of an active volcano," but manage to stop myself in time.

Sourdawg: I think I'm starting to like someone, though

Dudebro10: Oh?

Oh my god?! My fingers hover over the keyboard. What do I say? Should I ask him who? No, that'd be weird, because

I'm not supposed to know anyone at his school, so the "who" shouldn't matter to me. He could say "Jane" or "Mary" and it'd be all the same to me, his anonymous online buddy. Right. Gah!

Dudebro10: Someone in your class?

I watch as the three dots appear next to his name. But just then, the screen changes and the chat disappears. We're out of the waiting room and being logged on to an actual battleground.

"NO!" I shout at my computer. This is the first time in my life that I've been so enraged about being let into the game. By the time the battleground loads, the chat window is overloaded with new teammates saying hi and discussing strategy. I scroll up frantically, hoping against hope that Sourdawg had time to reply, but nope. The chat looks like this:

Dudebro10: Someone in your class?
[Warfront Heroes]: Guns at the ready! Loading Silmerrov Gulch.
[Warfront Heroes]: Heroes, assemble! 30 seconds before the gates open. Time to meet your teammates and talk strategy!
Firestar202: Hey, guys. I'm gonna flank from the temple side
Darksak: Dude, you're playing Doringa. You're not strong enough to flank FFS
Sourdawg: You can flank, but you need a tank in front of you to take damage. Dudebro, can you go ahead of Fire?

Sourdawg: Dudebro

Firestar202: I don't need to hide behind a tank

Darksak: Yes you do. DUDEBRO, wake the f*** up, man!
Omg is our tank AFK?

Oops. I spent so long trying to locate my private chat with Sourdawg that I missed all the drama. I quickly type: "OK" and hit Enter just as the gates open and the battle begins. The round ends up being a tragedy. I fail to hold up my shield properly and get sniped in the head within the first five seconds. While I wait to respawn, the rest of my team is taken out. Curses flood the chat window, but I don't even care. My heart isn't in the game at all.

Sourdawg likes someone. And I can't ask him about it. It would come off so weird. I'll have to figure out who it is some other way.

Not that I care. Because I don't. I force myself to take a deep breath. It's none of my business who Liam likes. The only thing that matters is that Liam has promised that he'll stand up for me. No matter who he has a crush on, things are going to look up from here on out, I just know it.

CHAPTER 10

I can't believe this, but things don't actually look up. They leap up. They soar up. They are positively hurled up into the glittering sky.

Okay, maybe that's kind of dramatic. But is it really? Somehow, within just one day, it feels like things have completely changed for me, and it's all thanks to Liam sticking to his word. Today, when we're told to go into our groups and work on our projects, I get the now-familiar feeling of my stomach lurching and my chest tightening, making it harder to breathe. I hate these sessions so much. I hate Jonas's obnoxious I'm-in-charge-of-this attitude and Peishan's indifference and Liam's silence. But as we put our books away, Liam meets my eye and gives me the tiniest nod. The tightness in my chest loosens, just a little.

"Great news, guys," Jonas says. "That illustrator I was telling you about agreed to illustrate our game's cover!"

What the hell? I stare at him. There's so much wrong with his statement I don't even know where to begin. Have I zoned out so much over the past few days that I've completely missed all the stupid crap Jonas has been up to?

"Hang on, what illustrator?" I say. "Are we even supposed to hire professional illustrators? Doesn't that kind of go against the whole point of a school project?"

Jonas rolls his eyes and keeps talking, as though I haven't said anything. "He costs quite a bit, like three thousand US dollars, but it's fine, guys, don't worry about it, I've got it covered."

"Actually," Liam says, straightening up in his seat, "Kiki made a good point. First off, I don't think we're supposed to be hiring anyone. We're supposed to do everything ourselves."

"Dude," Jonas groans. "Come on, this is gonna count toward our final grades. It's not the time to be all virtuous and shit, okay?"

"Who's the artist?" Peishan says.

Jonas brightens up and turns on his iPad. "You guys are gonna freak out when you see his work. He did the concept art for the latest *Tomb Raider,* and *Metal Gear Solid,* and . . ."

The more he talks, the more I want to groan, because I know the character designs for these games, and the female characters are known for—

"See?" Jonas says, holding up his iPad. And yep, just as I thought, it's a collage of illustrations of female characters with melon-sized boobs and tiny waists, dressed in outfits so tight that I wonder how they move without everything squeaking.

I can't help snorting. "Seriously, Jonas? I mean, this is worse even than what I was expecting, and trust me, my expectations were already at rock bottom."

"Gamers have a very specific art style, okay, Crazy Kiki?" Jonas snaps. "Just because you don't understand it—"

"Um, actually, I don't like them either," Liam says. "They're too . . . I don't think the school would approve. And can we cool it with the whole 'Crazy Kiki' thing?"

Golden light floods my chest, flowing all the way down my arms, warming my cheeks. I thought that I didn't need anyone standing up for me. And I don't; I'm more than able to stand up for myself. But still, when Liam tells Jonas to back off from the "Crazy Kiki" thing, I feel as though he's just reached down into a very dark tunnel and pulled me out. I try not to stare at Liam, but I'll admit it, it's a challenge.

"Obviously, we would ask him to tone it down for our project, make it more school-appropriate," Jonas says slowly, as though we're particularly stupid, completely ignoring the "Crazy Kiki" comment.

"Why not just do it ourselves to begin with, so we don't have to mess around with this . . . this mess?" I say.

Jonas narrows his eyes at me. "Oh, you can draw this well, can you?"

Admittedly, ignoring the humongous boobs and hyper-arched backs, this artist is gifted. His drawings are well-rendered, light and shadow painted on meaningfully to bring them to life. I mean, he's a pro. There's no way I would be able to draw as well as he does.

"That's the point: none of us are pros," Liam says. "What you're proposing is actually cheating, and I'm not prepared to risk flunking the whole project because you don't want to do the work."

Oooh, snap.

"Yeah, I don't really wanna cheat either," Peishan mutters. "Sorry, but if anyone ever found out, we'd be expelled."

"They won't find out unless one of you squeals," Jonas hisses.

"Oh, shut up, Jonas. And your design sucks, okay? All of this?" I gesture at the collage of cartoon women. "It's all really sexist, and I'm over it. Vote to scrap it all and start over?"

"Aye," Liam says immediately, raising his hand. "Agreed, it's sexist and I have faith we can come up with something better."

There's a moment of shocked silence. Everything inside me is fighting against meeting Peishan's eye, but when I finally do, I see that there's some sort of internal battle raging behind her placid features. Liam looks at her and nods, and Peishan's features soften. Sighing, she nods. "Aye. I agree, I'd like us to come up with something that's less . . . booby."

Oh my god. I can't believe it. It's as though golden light is spearing down into me, bringing everything back to life. I smirk at Jonas. "The ayes have it. We're starting over."

Okay, so maybe that was somewhat obnoxious, but hey, can anyone blame me?

Jonas snaps his mouth shut and looks like he's grinding his teeth for a moment. Then he forces a smile. "Sure, okay. Whatever you guys want. I'm a team player." Like hell he is. In school and on *Warfront Heroes*, I know he's the opposite of a team player. But it doesn't even matter, because there are three of us and only one of him.

When the recess bell goes off, I automatically start heading for the library. A few steps outside of the classroom, I sense a presence next to me. I look up and do a double take, because Liam is walking beside me. He smiles at me and my insides go all gooey. God, I thought Liam was cute before, but after what just happened in class, he's gone from cute to absolutely edible, and I'm not prepared to deal with it.

"This is not the way to the canteen," I say.

Liam nods slowly. "Believe it or not, after spending the last ten years here, I'm aware of that."

"So why are you headed this way? Are you following me? Is this a Joe Goldberg situation?"

Liam raises his eyebrows. "Okay, first of all, I've been going to the library during break a lot longer than you have. Second of all, are you kidding me? I am *not* setting foot in the canteen after that showdown with Jonas."

"Are you scared?" I tease.

"Uh, yeah? I was practically shitting my pants back there."

I'm so caught off guard by his honesty that I double over laughing.

"Like you weren't scared too?" Liam cries.

"I very definitely was. I mean, I of all people know what Jonas is capable of. I just—" I take a breath between laughter. "I guess I was expecting you to be, like, 'I am man, I not scared of anything.'"

"Oh, right." Liam puffs out his chest. "Well, obviously I am very manly and not scared of anything. Except privileged billionaires who can make my life a living hell. And cockroaches."

"Cockroaches?" I shake my head in disbelief. "You realize

we live in Jakarta? The big durian? I see a roach literally every day."

Liam shrugs, his cheeks turning adorably pink. "They creep me out, what can I say?"

"Fair enough. I—"

"Ci Kiki!"

"Oh god," I hiss, "don't move!"

"Are you hiding behind me?" Liam says.

"Don't move, I said!"

"Ci Kiki!" Eleanor Roosevelt calls out again, and this time, she sounds closer.

"You know we can see you hiding behind the hot guy," Sarah Jessica Parker says flatly.

"Thank you," Liam says.

With a sigh, I slink out from behind Liam's back (noting for a second how broad his shoulders are). "Hey, girls. How's it going?"

"We should be asking you that," Eleanor Roosevelt cries. "We've sent you fourteen messages in total, and you've ignored every single one of them."

"According to the contract you signed, you are obligated to check in with us after each Lil' Aunties date to give a detailed report of the date."

My mouth falls open. I gape at them, then at Liam, who's openly staring at us, and back at them. "It's not really—uh—I'll update you later."

"Are you two loan sharks?" Liam says.

Eleanor Roosevelt frowns at him. "What? Obviously, we're entrepreneurs."

"Pretty sure that's what loan sharks call themselves nowadays too. I'm just saying, I'm getting a somewhat threatening vibe from you."

"Thank you." Eleanor Roosevelt preens.

"It's not a compliment," I say, but it seems that I've been forgotten for the moment, because suddenly Eleanor Roosevelt and Sarah Jessica's attention is riveted on Liam. Sensing their interest, Liam takes a hesitant step back.

"What's your name?" Eleanor Roosevelt asks.

"Uh. Liam?"

"Year Eleven?" Sarah Jessica says.

"Um, yes?"

They exchange a look and nod. "Okay, you're in."

"In what, exactly?"

"In our highly sought-after matchmaking program," Eleanor Roosevelt says. "Congratulations. We do have a waiting list, but since you're such a fine specimen of a Year Eleven boy, we'll let you in. I'll forward the contract and NDA to you by the end of the workday."

"An NDA?"

"It stands for nondisclosure agreement," Sarah Jessica says.

"I was going to ask why you need me to sign an NDA," Liam says, "but you know what? A matchmaking service that requires an NDA sounds like exactly the kind of thing I would regret not joining."

We all gape at him. "You might want to think it through first," I whisper to him.

"We do not condone slander," Sarah Jessica says, narrowing her eyes at me.

Eleanor Roosevelt nods. "Yeah, Ci Kiki, I love you, but slander is an actionable offense. And you should be actively marketing our product, given you have shares in the company."

I pinch the bridge of my nose. These kids, I swear.

"I'm in," Liam says with way too much confidence.

Eleanor Roosevelt and Sarah Jessica grin at each other. Their grins say: *Ha, what a sucker.* Poor Liam has no idea what he's in for.

But then an idea surfaces. Maybe I could use this to my advantage. I could—hmm—ah! I could help fill out Liam's Lil' Aunties profile, which would give me the chance to find out just who it is he has a crush on. Mwahaha!

"I'll help you," I blurt out. They all stare at me. "Um, you guys are right. I have a vested interest in the company. I'll help you fill out your profile. That'll expedite the process." I give the world's most innocent smile to the girls.

Both Eleanor Roosevelt and Sarah Jessica look somewhat dubious, but then Eleanor Roosevelt shrugs and says, "Okay. Make sure he signs the NDA before you start building his profile, though."

These kids are way too into their NDA. "Just out of curiosity," Liam says, "how many profiles do you have in your database?"

At this, Eleanor Roosevelt and Sarah Jessica look shifty-eyed. "Only a handful," Eleanor Roosevelt says.

One corner of Liam's mouth crooks up into a small smile. He looks utterly adorable. "Only a handful, huh? But you two are confident that you'll be able to find me a perfect match within such a small pool?"

The shifty looks intensify. "Never you mind that," Eleanor Roosevelt says cryptically.

"Eleanor Roosevelt, can I just remind you that George asked me to keep you out of trouble?" I say.

Both Eleanor Roosevelt and Sarah Jessica give me this look, like, *Who are you kidding, lady?* and I can't say I blame them. Pretty sure that nobody, not even a seasoned CIA agent or marine captain, could keep these two out of trouble.

Sarah Jessica pats my arm. "The less you know, the better. Plausible deniability."

"Oh for god's sake," I groan. "It was awful, okay? He took one look at me and noped out of there because he didn't want to go on a date with, and I quote, 'Crazy Kiki.' And that's that. Date over."

Eleanor Roosevelt and Sarah Jessica Parker look so horrified that, for a second, I actually feel bad for them. They look so young and innocent, and though they knew that the date hadn't gone well, they probably had no idea just how badly it had gone.

"That's so messed up," Liam says.

"Did Jeremiah not tell you that part?" I say in a gentler voice.

The girls shake their heads. "He only said that we should've told him who the date was going to be with," Eleanor Roosevelt says.

"And then he quit the service," Sarah Jessica adds.

"He quit? In your texts, you made it sound like you kicked him out," I say.

The two girls look down guiltily at their feet. But of course, since this is Eleanor Roosevelt we're talking about, the guilt doesn't keep her down for long. In the next moment, she grins up at me and says, "But don't you worry, Ci, we'll make it up to you."

Sarah Jessica nods.

"Uh, no need, I'm totally fine. I think it's better if I lie low. . . ."

"I insist," Eleanor Roosevelt says, beaming. "Don't you worry about a thing. We've got it all under control."

And with that, they march off, leaving Liam and me gaping after them.

"What just happened?" Liam says. "Why do I feel like I've just been drafted into something bordering on illegal?"

I bite back my smile. "You're probably not way off there."

Liam nods slowly. "Should I be scared?"

"Yes," I say without hesitation, then I can't help but laugh, and it feels good to laugh in school. To laugh non-ironically, to laugh and have it be not about laughing to hide my hurt or sadness or shame. To laugh purely because I find the situation funny. To laugh with . . . a friend. It hits me then how long it's been since I could laugh like this with someone at school.

That was the first day of change. The next project meeting we have, Liam and Peishan start speaking up more. What about a puzzle game? Or a gentle farming game? Or, sure, an FPS, but one that's meant for everyone and not just for a very specific subsection of the audience? Jonas becomes increasingly quiet and more sullen, and while his grumpy silence makes things somewhat awkward, I'm really good at ignoring his presence.

Even though the change is great, I still retain my nickname of Crazy Kiki. I guess it'll take more than just our little group changing its dynamics to get rid of the nickname, but you know what? I can live with it.

A handful of days go by, and Liam and I no longer feel the need to spend recess hiding away in the library. We start going to the canteen for food, where Liam slurps at his soto ayam. I'm not sure how he makes eating chicken soup noisily adorable. "Argh." He looks down in dismay at the yellow spatters on his shirt.

I can't help but laugh. In addition to being kind of a noisy eater, he's also really messy. At the end of every meal, his plate or bowl is surrounded by little spatters of food, which he's considerate enough to clean up. He glances at my clean eating space and goes, "How do you manage that?" and it's so cute I could just die.

"I came prepared." I whip out a packet of baby wipes and hand one to him.

"Thanks." Liam scrubs at his uniform, and the stains get wider.

"No, not like that." I grab the wipe from him and dab at his shirt. "See, gently, like this, so you're not spreading the stain everywhere."

It strikes me then that I'm touching him. With my hands. My hands, which are on his body.

My head explodes like a watermelon. Or at least that's

what it feels like. And now that I've realized this, I can't un-perceive it. My hands! Are on his chest! I can feel his pecs! Ooh, his pecs. They are very . . . pec-y. My tongue darts out and licks my dry lips. It's official: I am a pervert. I jerk back as though touching him has burned me. I can't even look him in the eye. My fingertips are tingling where they touched his pecs. I give him the wipe and mutter something like "I think you get the gist."

Liam takes it from me, his fingers brushing the back of my hand, leaving a tingling line, and dabs at his shirt.

All right, time for me to start Operation Find Out Who's Liam's Crush. I clear my throat. "So Eleanor Roosevelt told me that you've signed the contract and NDA for the Lil' Aunties?"

"Oh yeah." Liam shakes his head. "I really wasn't expect-ing a twenty-page contract. I showed it to my dad, who's a lawyer, and he was very impressed. And concerned. But I as-sured him it was for a good cause."

I have to bite back my smile at the image of Liam convinc-ing his dad to let him join Lil' Aunties. "So now that you're officially in, we should start building your profile."

"Okay," Liam says easily. He pushes his bowl aside and leans forward, resting his elbows on the table. Surely, he must know how irresistible he is. He must.

I take out my phone so I can take notes. Also so I have something else to stare at besides Liam's annoyingly hand-some face. "Okay, first question: What are you looking for in an SO?"

He shrugs. Is it just me or do his eyes seem to soften as he looks at me? It feels like he's looking at an old friend. There's a soft, familiar comfort in his expression, and I wonder if he's going to realize that I am Dudebro10. "Someone who's into the same stuff I am, I guess."

"*Warfront Heroes?*" The moment the words fall out of my mouth, I wish I could grab them and cram them back inside.

He smiles. "Yeah, I would love to play with my girlfriend."

Oh my god. The thought of playing together with Liam, and not as Dudebro10 but as his *girlfriend,* fries my insides to a crisp. I would kill to do that. Oh yeah.

"Girl gamer, got it." *It meeee,* my insides squeak. "Anything else?"

"I mean, I'm into making breads, but that's a me-thing, so I don't feel the need to be doing that with anyone else. Would be great if she's into eating them, though." He takes a sip of his drink. "I would love to be able to bake for her."

My muscles all turn into goo. This is impossible. A guy who wants to bake for his girlfriend? I want to shake my fist at the universe and scream, *What are you doing to me?* I nod and make a big show of typing everything on my phone. "I think you're going to be quite popular."

"Really? I don't know, my breads might actually suck."

"Oh, right." Somehow, I never even gave that any thought as a possibility.

"What about you? You must've gotten the same questionnaire?"

"I didn't, actually. I guess because Eleanor Roosevelt knows me already. She knows most of the stuff I'm into."

"Like what?" Liam says.

"Uh . . ." *Like* Warfront Heroes*!!* my mind yells. But no. I can't possibly say that to him. He's going to ask me all sorts of awkward questions, like my gamer tag. "Like hanging out with my friends." God, that sounds so meh. "And . . ." Do I really not have any hobbies other than *Warfront Heroes* and hanging out with Cassie and Sharlot? Good grief. "Anyway, let's focus on your profile. What would be your ideal date?"

Liam thinks for a bit. "Exploring a new place together— maybe it's a new hiking trail or a new restaurant."

"Pretty run-of-the-mill stuff," I say with an eyeroll.

"Excuse me? Are you saying I'm boring?"

"No, it's just the kind of answer anyone would give, isn't it."

He makes a mock-offended face. "Nuh-uh! The part about the places being unknown is the rare bit. Not many people like to explore, you know. My dad is always, like, 'Let's just go to the restaurant we already know has good food.' Which is how we've ended up going to the same place every weekend for the last five years."

"True, I guess. Okay, adventurous. I'll give you that. Ooh, have you hiked up to the waterfalls at Sentul?"

"Yes! I love it there. I've been wanting to hike up Mount Bro—"

"Mount Bromo?" I squeak. "Yes, me too!"

"Okay, we've got to go over summer break."

He says this so casually that I know it's just a throwaway comment. By the time recess is over, he will have forgotten this, but I won't, and *gah*, Universe, why must you torture me so?

Just then, Liam's school-sanctioned iPad, which he's put on the seat next to him, *boops*. So do a few other iPads around the canteen. He picks it up with a quizzical look. "Well, that's interesting."

"What is it?"

He turns the iPad to face me and points to an icon. I recognize it as the Lil' Aunties icon. "That wasn't there before," he muses.

I look around the canteen and see that those who have brought their iPads here are looking very confusedly at their screens, pointing and murmuring.

"What the hell is Lil' Aunties?" someone says.

"Is this spam?"

"Don't open it, it's gotta be a scam."

My iPad is back at my classroom, so I have no idea if the Lil' Aunties app has mysteriously appeared on it as well, but it seems a safe bet that it has. I think back to our last interaction with Eleanor Roosevelt and Sarah Jessica and how they so cryptically said not to worry about their not having a large enough pool of profiles to matchmake. "Oh god," I groan. So this was their plan all along, to hack into the school-issued iPads and force every machine to download their app.

Liam's expression is torn between disbelief and admiration. "Did those kids just do what I think they did?"

I nod glumly, thinking of how disappointed George Clooney will be when he finds out that I've failed so completely at keeping Eleanor Roosevelt in check.

Liam slides the iPad to the middle of the table so we can both see the screen. He taps on the Lil' Aunties icon, and a notice appears:

Welcome to the Lil' Aunties Know Best matchmaking
service! This is for COOL PEOPLE only. If you are an
uncool snitch, then simply do nothing and the app will
be uninstalled in under one minute. If you are COOL and
AWESOME, please scroll down to read our terms and
conditions. Clicking Agree means you are legally bound
by our contract and NDA. If you break our NDA, we will
know. Join to find your soulmate today!

Liam and I look at each other, and the utter disbelief on his
face makes me burst out laughing. I mean, *oh my god, Eleanor
Roosevelt!* What has she done? Even as we sit there cracking
up, another notice appears. It says: "App will be uninstalled in
ten seconds unless you click Agree."

Our eyes meet once more, and an unspoken agreement
crosses between us. Liam taps Agree. The app opens to an
empty profile page. He raises an eyebrow at me. "I mean . . .
gotta admire their entrepreneurial spirit, right?"

"How much you wanna bet they've installed some spyware
in the app as well?" I say dryly.

"Oh, totally. I would be disappointed if they haven't
thought to do that."

I wasn't sure what I expected would happen after Eleanor Roosevelt and Sarah Jessica's stunt. Part of me feared
that people would report it to the teachers and they'd get
dragged to Principal Lin's office by their ears. Or that they'd

become the laughingstock of the school. Or something else equally dire.

But what actually happens is . . . nothing. People talk about it, some roll their eyes, others laugh and join, but most seem to assume it's spam and immediately delete it from their iPad. And no one tells the teachers, at least that I know of. I guess even in a school as strict as Xingfa, it doesn't pay to be known as a snitch. By the time recess is over and we all shuffle back to our respective classrooms, it seems as though the Lil' Aunties app has been largely forgotten.

In the car on my way home from school, I open the app. After clicking Agree, I fill out my profile page as quickly as I can and enter it into the system. I was expecting the app to load a directory of profiles for me to swipe through, but instead, I get a message that says: "Thank you for filling out your profile! All our members are kept strictly confidential. Matches are made at our discretion. You will be notified once we identify the perfect match for you."

Ah. Okay, that makes sense. If everyone knew who's on the app, it'd be way too easy for someone to snitch. This way, most people won't know who's joined or who's running the app. Genius. Despite myself, I'm having to hold back my laughter. Amazing how Eleanor Roosevelt and Sarah Jessica really have thought of everything.

The rest of the day passes peacefully, but my peace is short lived, because that evening, Sourdawg asks Dudebro:

So at some point we should totally meet up in person, right? Or is that creepy?

Oh, Liam. What I wouldn't give to meet up with you in person and come clean to you. My hands open and close as I try to come up with a viable excuse for not meeting up in person.

Dudebro10: Oh no. Not creepy. But I'm just going through a lot of stuff right now
Sourdawg: Oh, shit. I'm sorry to hear that. Anything I can help with?
Dudebro10: No, it's just some family stuff
Sourdawg: Do you wanna talk abt it?

I'm so overcome by guilt that I feel compelled to give him something that holds at least a shred of truth.

Dudebro10: It's just . . . I'm having a lot of resentment toward my parents for sending me to this fucking school
Dudebro10: Sorry, I know that makes me sound like a total douche
Sourdawg: No, not at all. I have a lot of resentment toward my parents too. I've been doing a lot of work on it with my therapist. Do you want me to share some of what I've learned?

Guilt pinches harder. Liam is opening up about his secrets, because he thinks I'm someone else. This is so wrong. I should tell him to stop.

Dudebro10: Sure

Sourdawg: Okay, so, like, first off, it's rly important to have an open line of communication with your parents. You can start off with the parent you trust more. For me, that's my dad, obviously. And it's going to be rly hard to begin with, but it gets easier. Obviously, like, your parents have to be receptive to it. You need to identify, like, your triggers and when you feel defensive and try to avoid them or acknowledge them. I used to get into these huge fights with my dad, and I finally realized that I was just feeling rly vulnerable and that I should tell him that I'm feeling that way. Since I did, he's been a lot more open when we talk. Does that make sense? Sorry, I kinda wrote a whole essay there, lol

Dudebro10: No, that makes perfect sense

I can't imagine having an open conversation with Papi or Mami, though. I'm just so mad at them, and no doubt they'd just dig their heels in and insist on what an amazing school Xingfa is and how I can't possibly be having a bad time there because it's so amazing.

Dudebro10: Yeah, anyway. Things have been improving a lot lately. In school, I mean. At home it's still pretty hectic

Sourdawg: :(

Dudebro10: What about you? How's everything at sch?

Sourdawg: Remember that grumpy chick I told you abt?

Dudebro10: The one sitting next to you? Yeah

Sourdawg: She's pretty cool, actually. Heh, because of
her, I had to join this, like, matchmaking thing, so I'm
abt to go on plenty of dates

Dudebro10: Haha, that sounds cool

Is it just me or does Liam sound a tad too excited about being set up with other people?

Sourdawg: Yeah. I'll be really impressed if I'm matched
with someone who's a good fit

Okay, so he *is* excited about being set up with other girls. Of course it would've been too good to be true if he were into me.

CHAPTER 11

Four days. That's how long it takes for Jonas to report me to the principal for "being disruptive and making it impossible to work in a group environment." Does the principal bother talking to me to find out how I'm supposedly being disruptive? No, of course not. Not when the complaint is coming from Jonas, the school's golden boy. When I'm asked to report to Principal Lin's office during recess, Liam goes with me for moral support.

I sit outside Principal Lin's office and stare at my hands, my throat sticking each time I try to swallow. I'm nervous, but it's not because I'm about to be reprimanded. No, I'm nervous because the chairs outside the office are placed right up against each other, so Liam and I are sitting really, really close to each other. There's only one lonely inch between our forearms, and my body is so aware of his that the hairs on my arms are standing straight up, as though they're straining to touch him. I swear, if my arm hair grazes his arm, I am going to die. But I don't want to move my arms away, because I don't want him to think I'm not into him.

When my name is called, I stand on shaky legs.

"Hey," Liam whispers.

I turn to look at him, and he winks at me, which is so adorable I could just die. "You'll be fine," he says. "Good luck."

And as it turns out, I needed it. Mr. Lin crooks his index finger, summoning me inside, and with a knotted stomach, I follow. The door isn't even closed when Mr. Lin slumps into his chair with a huge, dramatic sigh and rests his chin on his steepled fingers.

"Well, Kristabella, here we are again."

"Uh. Hi, sir."

"What are we going to do with you?"

My gaze skitters around the room. What am I supposed to say to that? "Um."

"I'm very disappointed to receive this report from your classmate about you disrupting classes, especially the group project you're supposed to be working on as a team. I'd hoped you'd settle into our school's culture and community by now."

I think Principal Lin fully believes that he's conveying concern for my well-being when he says this. Problem is, he's also getting his information from Jonas, dirtbag of the year. I take a breath before replying, reminding myself not to get shrill or indignant. "I feel that you've been misinformed about what's been going on. I've been bullied since I got here—remember I told you how I was called Crazy Kiki? I reported that to you, and—"

Principal Lin sighs. "That's not a big deal, is it?"

I want to scream at him. "Honestly, sir, it kind of is—"

He snorts, giving a single shake of his head like a tired horse. "Look, you need to be less sensitive, ya? You're so . . . you kids nowadays, you need to toughen up. Get thicker skin. Who cares if you're called crazy? It's not even a bad word. Now, if you said someone called you an actual slur, that would be a problem. The student would be reprimanded. But 'crazy'? We use that all the time, and sometimes in positive ways. 'Wow, this ice-cream is crazy good!' or 'That new Batman movie was crazy!'" He leans back with a satisfied smile, obviously happy with his own reasoning.

"Well—" My insides are climbing up my rib cage, spitting with anger. "Sure, it's not necessarily a slur, but I can assure you they're not using it with me in a positive way. They're using it as a—"

Mr. Lin waves his hand at me again, and this time his magnanimous smile is gone. He looks impatient. "Enough of this. You are so sensitive, it's ridiculous. Or, some might even say, crazy." He chuckles at his own joke, and I wish fleetingly that he played *Warfront Heroes* so I could kill him over and over again like I did Jonas. "Now, we're here to discuss your inappropriate behavior in class."

"My inappropriate behavior? This is ridiculous, you're only taking Jonas's word as evidence? Jonas is full of shit, he—"

His hand slams down on the desk. Within the small office, it's as loud as a thunderclap, and I immediately shut up. I'm so shocked by the sudden turn that a lump forms in my throat. Principal Lin looks furious. He points a finger at me.

"Stop. Interrupting. Me," he hisses. "My god, I've never

come across such a rude girl. I've been trying to be patient with you. I've reminded you time and again to respect your elders, but no. You push and you push. Haven't your parents taught you *RESPECT*?" The last word is barked out with such ferocity that tears immediately flood my eyes.

I can't believe this is happening. My head buzzes. *Stop it,* I scold myself mentally. *Do not cry. Don't give him the satisfaction of making you cry.*

Principal Lin isn't done with me. "You'll no longer be disruptive in your group discussions, do you understand? None of this"—he gestures at me—"this disagreeable attitude you have. Is that clear?"

No! What in the hell? It's the furthest thing from clear.

"Is. That. Clear?" He repeats in a dangerous tone. "Expulsion won't look good on your college applications."

Expulsion? I want to jump up and shout at him, but my voice is gone. This can't be real. What I've done—disagreeing with Jonas and coming up with a new idea with my group—that's nowhere near bad enough to warrant expulsion, surely? And let's not forget that I'm not the only one asking the hard questions! What about Liam? What about Peishan? They disagreed with Jonas too!

As though reading my mind, Principal Lin says, "It's your word against his, a model student who's done nothing but excel over the many years he's been enrolled here. And I've been told that you were the first one who started disrupting the discussions. And you're influencing other students—students who have had no previous record of misbehavior—to do the same. I'm being generous by giving you a second chance, but no more trouble out of you, mengerti?"

I stare at him dumbly until he widens his eyes and raises his eyebrows, clearly expecting an answer. And somehow, I manage a small nod.

"Good. Now you can go."

It feels as though my feet aren't mine. They barely understand the messages that my brain is sending them. It takes a while for them to get it, then they start marching, and before I know it, I'm out of the office and blinking in a dazed way at my surroundings.

"Hey, how did it go?"

Liam stands and walks toward me. Seeing him makes the vice around my chest release its painful grip. I feel as though I can finally breathe once more. Still, I don't trust myself to talk just yet. If I did, I'm sure my voice would crack and the tears would start flowing, and that would be that. So I just shrug and walk out of the admin office.

In the hallway, I release some of my frustration in a long, heavy sigh.

"Wow, that bad, huh?"

"He threatened to expel me." My voice comes out leaden, dropping out of my mouth lifelessly.

"What?!" Liam moves closer and leans forward so he can look at my downturned face.

"Yeah, he said I was behaving 'inappropriately'—" My voice does crack, so I quickly stop talking.

"Wow. That's such BS. I can't believe it. Or, rather, I can

believe it, because what the hell else is new? I don't know why I expected better." He shakes his head, then his eyes turn tender. "You okay?"

I shrug. "It is what it is."

"No, don't say that. You shouldn't have to accept this. I'll go and talk to him. I'll explain what's been going on."

"No way." I turn away so I don't have to look at Liam. Somehow, the earnest look on his handsome face is grating on me right now. "No. I don't want you to do that."

"But I could tell him everything, about how Jonas has been bullying you and basically steamrolls over everyone during group discussions."

"It doesn't matter. He'll just—I don't know—he'll shift the blame onto me somehow. Or maybe he'll expel both of us. What's that gonna achieve? Jonas is untouchable. He's too well loved, and what with his parents owning an entire media conglomerate . . . forget it." I can't remember the last time I felt so defeated. So exhausted. And as I slump down the hallway back toward my classroom, it hits me that I don't just feel tired, I feel really freaking stupid too. Because I've watched so many Netflix shows where the schools are progressive and the counselors and teachers and principals are receptive to the students' needs, and I've been in a school like that, and so I thought—stupidly—that most schools are like that. And now, here at Xingfa, one of the biggest, most sought-after, prestigious schools in the country, I'm realizing that things haven't really changed that much. The patriarchy is very far from being smashed. In fact, maybe they're even a little bit worse, because we pretend that the patriarchy is done and we're in a society with gender equality, so we can't even fight it because the fight's over.

How do I fight something that's already playing dead but is still very much alive behind closed doors?

By the time recess rolls around, I'm still in a crappy mood. I tell Liam I'm having period cramps, because I'm done pandering to guys and have run out of fucks to give. To his credit, he doesn't cringe or look like he's searching for the nearest exit. In fact, he says, "That sounds shitty. Do you want me to pop down to the nurse's office to get you some paracetamol?"

His kindness is like a knife that's being stabbed into my belly over and over again. It's all too much. Principal Lin threatening to expel me, Liam being the absolute nicest person about it, and meanwhile, there's me, lying to his face, pretending online to be someone I'm not. I shake my head, not trusting myself to speak, and go to the bathroom.

I splash some water on my face and am drying my cheeks with a tissue when someone clears her throat. I turn to see two girls behind me, Peishan and another of our classmates, named Zoelle. Uh-oh. My mind immediately spits out a warning based on the countless mean-girl situations that have dominated teen movies since the eighties. Is this where I find out what being dunked headfirst into the toilet is like? At the very least, the toilets at Xingfa are sparkling clean, like an ad for toilet bleach or something. Still, I don't really want to be dunked into one. I straighten up, planting my feet firmly and preparing to—I don't know—fight or take flight?

"Hey, Kiki," Peishan says, and something about it makes the tight knots in my shoulders release, just a little.

"Hey," I say, still somewhat wary.

Peishan and Zoelle glance at each other. "We heard that you were called to the principal's office," Zoelle says.

My breath releases in an angry *whoosh*. "Yeah, I get it. I'm an embarrassment to your precious school's reputation—"

"No!" Peishan cries. "Sorry. No, I mean—we're angry about it. At the principal, I mean. Not angry at you."

The rest of what I was about to say dissipates. "Really?" I can't believe what I'm hearing. The past few weeks play across my mind. I recall how my classmates are so studious, so respectful, and so, so obedient. I shake my head. "No, that can't be right. I didn't earn the nickname 'Crazy Kiki' because people here like it when I stand up for myself."

Peishan winces and wrings her hands. "Yeah, I—we're really sorry about that. It's just—" She sighs. "Zoey and I have been here since Year One. That's, like, over ten years of strict Xingfa education."

Zoelle does a grimace-smile. "And the entire time, we've been taught the same things over and over: Protect the school's image. Don't make a fuss. Don't ask questions. Never talk back to your elders."

Listening to them is depressing as hell, and I still don't get why they're telling me this.

"Then you came," Zoelle says. "And you were, like, 'Why

are things this way? Why this? Why that?' And . . . we relate to that. To your anger, I mean."

"Well," Peishan adds, "to be honest, it was kind of annoying at first."

"Thanks," I mutter without much venom, because what they're saying is kind of blowing my mind. I recall my conversation with Peishan where she told me I was krill, and I feel the ghost of a smile tugging at the corners of my mouth. I don't know why. I guess this is giving me some context, at least.

"The reason it was annoying," Peishan continues, "is because it reminded us of our own shit. All the crap we've learned to put up with over the years . . ."

"Did you know, for example, that the boys' swim team is given preference over the girls' team?" Zoelle says. "Every year, the boys' team gets to choose which day and time they want to practice for the year. The girls never get first pick. And if they have an upcoming swim meet, they get to kick us out of the pool for extra practice, but if we have an upcoming meet, we're not allowed to book extra time at the pool."

"Seriously?" I gape at her.

"Yep. And a couple years ago, the school started a robotics club and they—like, I wouldn't say they discouraged girls from joining—but they were very definitely prioritizing the boys. Mr. Tan was in charge of setting up the club, and he'd be, like, 'Boys, this is a really exciting opportunity. It'll look so good on your college apps, et cetera.'" Peishan scowls. "I put up my hand and was, like, 'Teacher, is it open to girls as well?' And he looked so surprised. He was, like, 'Oh! Yes.' But he didn't say anything more about it. Then, later on, I found out he formed an email chain personally inviting a bunch of boys to join the robotics team."

"Wow." I shake my head, unable to find the words to convey just how enraging it is to listen to this.

"Yep, and you know what makes everything so much worse?" Zoelle says. "It's their hypocrisy. They're always, like, 'We're a progressive school! We're raising feminists! World-class leaders of both genders!' But it's all just a front."

"To be fair, they might believe in their own bullshit," Pei-shan says. "They might genuinely think they're progressive, but their own internal biases keep getting in the way."

"Doesn't matter if they mean to be misogynistic or not. The end result is the same," Zoelle grumbles.

We all nod, and it dawns on me that although I feel enraged, I also feel much better. The whole reason why I was infuriated was because of Principal Lin and how differently he'd treated me and Liam. But now, knowing that I'm not the only one going through this, that I haven't actually imagined it, that I wasn't just being "sensitive," it's so affirming that I actually choke up.

"We watched *Moxie* when it came out on Netflix—have you seen that?" Zoelle asks.

I nod. Ironically, when I watched *Moxie,* I thought it was unrealistic how sexist a school could be. Ha. Little did I know.

"And you're, like, a real-life Moxie."

A shocked laugh escapes me. "What?"

"Okay, maybe that's going a bit far," Zoelle says. "I mean, you kind of gave up."

I gape at her. "Uh, I gave up? You guys all bullied me into giving up!"

Peishan holds up her hands. "Whoa, for the record, we never joined in with the others. We never called you names."

"Okay, so you stood by and watched as I was bullied. Good for you."

Peishan and Zoelle exchange guilty looks. "I know. We suck. I'm sorry," Peishan says. She reaches out and gives my arm an awkward pat. "That's why we're reaching out to you now." She takes a deep breath. "I—I'm grateful that you've been speaking up during group discussions. I thought Jonas's idea was . . ." She grimaces.

"Shitty?" I suggest. "Sexist as hell? Tired? Unoriginal?"

She gives me a reluctant smile. "Yes, all that. But I didn't dare say anything—I mean, contradict Jonas Arifin? Are you kidding? But you did it, and I think what we're coming up with now is so much better. I'm actually kind of excited to present it to everyone. So thank you for—you know—being different."

Being different. What a strange concept that is. I wasn't different at Mingyang. I blended in. I didn't like standing out, but now I'm being thanked for it, and I don't know what to say to that. I clear my throat. "Well, it doesn't matter. Principal Lin told me that if I continue 'disrupting the group discussions,' I'll be expelled."

Zoelle and Peishan gape at me. "Seriously?" Peishan hisses in outrage. "He can't do that!"

"Uh, well, he's the principal of this school, so I think it means he can, in fact, do that."

Peishan's mouth flattens into a thin line. "Don't worry. I'll be the disruptive one during group discussions."

I swallow. I'm not sure how I feel about this. "I don't want to get you in trouble. . . ."

"What's he going to do, expel both of us?" Peishan snorts.

There's silence. "Uh," I say, "yes?"

"Well, there's Liam too," Peishan argues. "He doesn't like Jonas's ideas either."

"Yeah, except he's a guy, so I doubt he'd get in the same kind of trouble for disagreeing," I say. This makes me feel slightly guilty, like I'm betraying Liam somehow, so I add, "It's not his fault, but I don't think Liam's being held to the same standards we are."

"Of course not," Peishan says. "When girls do it, we're being disrespectful. When boys do it, they're being independent thinkers."

"Leaders of tomorrow," Zoelle adds.

"Thinking outside the box," I say.

By now, we're all smiling wryly at one another, and despite everything, I actually feel better. "Thanks for trying," I say. "But really, I'd rather just lie low. I've had enough drama to last me the rest of the year."

They give me sympathetic smiles. "Hey, speaking of which," Peishan says, "what's going on between you and Liam?"

My mouth snaps shut.

"Aww, look, she's blushing," Zoelle teases.

"I am not!" I snap. "There's nothing going on between us. In fact, we're both in a matchmaking scheme. To be matched with other people." As soon as I blurt that out, I wish I could grab my words and shove them back into my big fat mouth.

They both frown at me. "A matchmaking scheme?" Peishan says, then she gasps. "Oh my god! Is that the weird app that suddenly showed up on all our iPads?"

"Um. Yes?" Oh lord, how I wish the floor would crack open and spout lava and burn all of us to a crisp. Or something less deadly.

"That's a real thing?" Peishan says. "I thought it was a prank. I deleted the app."

"I signed up for it," Zoelle says.

Peishan stares at her. "What the hell, Zoey?"

"What?"

"Dude, it could've been malware! Or spyware!"

"But it's not." Zoelle turns to me. "It's not, right?"

"Uh." I consider this. "It's not malware. But no promises that it doesn't contain spyware."

"Who's behind it?" Peishan says.

I hesitate. "I don't know if I can say."

They both narrow their eyes at me. "But it's legit, right?" Zoelle says.

"I guess? I can't guarantee anything."

"But you and Liam joined it." Peishan is looking very intense right now.

I nod.

"See?" Zoelle says.

Peishan side-eyes her.

"You're gonna be left out, girl," Zoelle cries. "Half the girls' swim team joined already, and the whole of the gymnastics team, both the boys and girls. And the drama club too. All the cool kids are joining!"

"Wow, really?" I say. I assumed that most people deleted the app.

"Yeah, dude, you're underestimating how horny most of us are," Zoelle says. "We would've joined anything that promises us dates."

I laugh at that.

"And now we know that Liam's also a member," Zoelle says, elbowing Peishan. "She has a little crush on him."

My stomach sinks. Of course she does.

"Zoey wants to be matched with Klodiya," Peishan stage-whispers.

Zoelle elbows her.

"Klodiya?" I gape at Zoelle, forgetting Liam for the moment. Klodiya is in our class, but she mostly keeps to herself and seems to be so different from the kind of person I would guess someone as outgoing as Zoelle would be into.

She shrugs. "You got something against that?"

"No!" I say quickly. "I just—she's so . . ."

"Stuck up?" Peishan says. "Uncool? Walks around like she's got a stick up her butt?"

I nod. "Yeah, and you seem so chill and . . . the exact opposite of everything she is. But," I add before Zoelle can reply, "opposites attract, right? Um, well, this is really cool." Is it? I'm beginning to realize that all these people signing up means—oh god—a larger pool of girls for Liam to be matched with. Not that it matters. *Look on the bright side*, I tell myself. *It seems like I've made new friends here!* Wow, okay, that sounded very juvenile. But still! I'm excited to finally make some friends, even though one of them is interested in Liam. Which is totally fine. I don't have a problem with that at all. Liam's just a friend. A friend I'm lying to online, so. Probably best that nothing ever happens between us in real life. Not that I want anything to happen between us in real life anyway.

CHAPTER 12

Kiki: Hey, aunties, I heard that you got a ton of new sign-ups thanks to your hack

Eleanor Roosevelt: 👀

Kiki: I don't know whether I should be congratulating you or telling you off for hacking into everyone's iPad

Eleanor Roosevelt: What can we say? We're scrappy!

SJP: Resourceful. Outside-the-box thinkers

Kiki: Rule breakers. Some might even call it delinquent behavior

Eleanor Roosevelt: Ci Kiki! I thought you of all people would appreciate ingenuity!

I chuckle and shake my head at my phone. I glance up at my computer, where I'm waiting to be logged on to *WH*. It loads then, and I click on my Friends list, cackling evilly when I see that Jonas is online. Mwahaha!

Kiki: Hey, aunties, I've got one new sign-up for you.

Eleanor Roosevelt: Who?

Kiki: My classmate Peishan Tjoeng. And I met with Zoelle Tanady and she said she signed up already.

SJP: Yes she did! Zoelle Tanady is a STAR! She played Juliet in last year's play. She was sooo good

Wow, okay, did not know that, but now that I do, I can totally see Zoelle shining on the stage.

Kiki: Cool! Well, they both really wanna be set up. Zoelle wants to be set up with Klodiya Febina

Eleanor Roosevelt: Done

Kiki: That was fast. Is Klodiya one of your customers?

SJP: They're clients, not customers

Kiki: Okaaay, is Klodiya a client?

Eleanor Roosevelt: Not yet, but she will be

Kiki: I have a feeling I don't wanna know how you're planning to achieve that

SJP: No, you don't. And what about Peishan? Does she have someone in mind?

An hour later, I've managed to kill Jonas about seven times on three different battlefields. Each time, he's raged at me and threatened to, (1) Report me to the mods, (2) Hunt me down IRL, and (3) Beat the shit out of my scrawny loser's ass. Oh, Jonas. He's nothing if not predictable.

I log off, still wearing my villainous smile. Then I check the notifications on my phone, and my smile falls off my face.

Peishan: Hey, come out for coffee. We're setting up my matchmaking profile.

Technically, Peishan has done nothing wrong. In fact, she's turning out to be pretty cool. But I can't ignore the fact that she wants to be matched with Liam. The idea of Liam being set up with Peishan is making me want to curl up in a dark corner and inject chocolate straight into my veins while listening to emo music. But I know I'm just being selfish. There's nothing between Liam and me, and there can never be anything more than being friends. And it's all my fault. It's all because I've been so deceitful. Maybe I could've come clean to him the moment I found out that he's Sourdawg, but now it's way past the acceptable window of time where I could be, like, "Guess what? I'm your online bestie, Dudebro!" and not have it be massively weird.

Zoelle: Come to Kopi-Kopi. You live in Senayan, right? It should be abt 5 min from ur house

Whaaa? I'm about to say no when I realize that this is exactly what I've been aching for. A group of girlfriends I can hang out with after school. It's just that it's happening so quickly I have no idea how to react. No, wait, I know exactly how to react. By behaving like a normal person and saying yes! To hell with Liam. I need girlfriends more than I need my online crush. I type out a quick "OK" and change into my jeans and a shirt in record time. As I rush down the stairs, Mami's head pops out from the kitchen.

"Oh, Kiki! I didn't even realize you were home. Where are you off to?" There's a vinegary smell from the kitchen, which tells me she's making kombucha again.

"To see some friends from school." She looks surprised before she smiles, and anger leaps in my chest, because she doesn't get to be happy that I finally have friends again. None of this was her doing. I duck my head and make my way to the door.

"Have a good time!" she calls out.

I ignore her and make sure to close the front door extra hard on the way out.

When I get to Kopi-Kopi, I find not just Peishan and Zoelle but Trissilla, another classmate, and a girl I don't recognize.

"This is Renata. She's from Eleven Diligence," Zoelle says. "She wants to sign up too."

Renata rubs her palms together. "Oh yeah, I'm ready to be matched up with all the hotties!"

That gets a laugh out of me. I sit across from them.

"Kiki here has all the inside intel about this app," Zoelle says, putting an arm around my shoulders and squeezing me. "You're going to help us make our profiles appeal to whoever's running the app, right?"

"Um . . ." I hesitate, because it sounds like they think the people behind the app are seasoned pros instead of two thirteen-year-old kids. I want to tell them who's behind it, but I also don't want to risk getting Eleanor Roosevelt and Sarah

Jessica into trouble. The more people that know who the Lil' Aunties are, the higher the chances of the school finding out. "I'll help. Although I'm sure you guys have everything under control. And the matchmaking app is definitely not foolproof. I was set up on a date with Jeremiah, and he could not get out of there fast enough."

Zoelle's mouth drops open. "Wait, what happened with Jeremiah? And are we talking about Jeremiah Riady?"

"Yeah. And nothing happened. We were . . ." My voice trails away, and I hesitate. "Wait, I signed an NDA. That means I can't talk about the date."

They all stare at me. I shrug. "It's contractually binding!"

"We won't tell," Peishan says. "Come on, spill."

I sigh. "Okay, but if anyone decides to press charges, you guys are gonna have to pay for my lawyer."

Zoelle laughs. "Done."

"Okay, so Jeremiah showed up, took one look at me, and said, 'I'm not going on a date with Crazy Kiki.' And that was it. He left right away."

They all look horrified. After a stunned silence, Trissilla says, "What the fucking fuck?"

"Triss!" Renata says.

Trissilla glares at her. "No, but seriously! What a little ass-hole. He's one of my twin's best friends. I can't believe he's such a jerk. Next time he comes over to our place, I'm going to . . ." She narrows her eyes. "I don't know what I'm gonna do, but it's not going to be good."

"Okaaay," Renata says.

Peishan chews on her lip as she watches me. Then, in a small voice, she says, "I'm sorry."

"Huh? What for?"

Her mouth purses. "I was there the whole time, in class, watching the whole 'Crazy Kiki' thing catching fire, and I never did anything to stop it. I just sat there and sort of . . . hoped it would go away on its own. I'm sorry."

"I'm sorry too," Zoelle says. "We should've said something."

"We should've," Triss says. "We were all too chickenshit to say anything."

My throat closes up with tears, and I have to suck in a breath very slowly through my mouth. I swallow hard. "It's okay," I say thickly. And it really is. I mean, being called Crazy Kiki is definitely not okay, but sitting here and hearing these girls say they're sorry is so healing, a large part of me wants to cry and cling to them. I clear my throat. "Anyway, so how can I help with your profiles?"

"Well, given there are so many new sign-ups, we want to make sure ours will stand out," Peishan says.

"She wants to make sure she's matched with Liam," Zoelle says.

"Ahem, me too," Triss says.

Peishan glares at her, and the two of them narrow their eyes at each other for a few moments before they both double over laughing.

"You two are such dorks," Renata says.

"Hey, it's not a crime to be into the same guy," Triss says.

I shrug, my cheeks turning warm. I don't know how to feel about them liking Liam, but it's really cool to see that Triss and Peishan are still friends regardless of their feelings for Liam. I need to follow in their footsteps and be as gracious as they're being. "Okay," I say. "Honestly, I don't really know what would appeal to the people running the app, but we can at least make sure your answers are really interesting."

"Yay!" Triss claps. "Okay, can we start?"

A server arrives with trays of iced coffees with palm sugar syrup and plates piled high with croffles.

"We ordered the same drink for everyone," Zoelle says. She glances at me. "You drink coffee, right?"

"Of course!" I grab one of the cups and take a sip of the rich, strong coffee. Happiness blooms inside me, a warm flower. Good coffee and warm pastries and a tableful of giggly girls. I never want this afternoon to end.

We spend over two hours there, taking our time to pick out the most flattering photos of Triss, Peishan, and Renata for their profiles. Then we go through each question, and the proposed answers start off serious but soon morph into jokey ones, which have us all cackling.

Q: What do you look for in a match?

Triss: Liam.

Peishan: Hey! You can't just say "Liam"! You need to come up with a description!

Triss: Okay, however you want to describe Liam, that's what I'm looking for in a match.

Zoelle: Sooo desperate. Me, I want hip dips.

Everyone: Hip dips??

Zoelle: I have a thing for them! Stop being so judgey!

Q: What is the most interesting thing about you?

Renata: I'm into scuba diving.

Me: Ooh, that's really cool!

Renata: Yeah, my family and I go to Bali once a month to dive. I'm competing in—

Triss: Okay, okay. If you let her, she'll spend the whole day talking about diving. Just write down "Diver." And that's enough.

Me: Haha, okay. But I would love to hear more about it some other time! What about you, Triss? What's the most interesting thing about you?

Renata: Triss is a true Crazy Rich Asian.

Me: Ooh. Really?

Triss: No, not—

Peishan: Yes, really. Her parents own the Kwangtang Zipper. Check your jeans' zip.

Me: Oh my god, it says KWT! That's your family company? But these jeans are from Zara.

Triss: Yeah, Zara, GAP, etc. They all buy zippers from my family company.

Me: Incredible!

Zoelle: She seems sweet, but she's rich enough to hire hitmen if her date is bad.

Me: . . . You're kidding, right?

Triss: Oh my god, don't listen to them! Of course I wouldn't!

Everyone: She would.

Triss: I would not!

Me: Uh-huh. "Make sure date is fun and awesome." Got it.

Before I know it, it's fully dark outside. I'm exhausted but in a really good way. Playing *WH* and killing Jonas and chatting with Liam is great, but there's just something about having a good group of girlfriends to laugh with that feeds my withered, jaded soul. And I would do practically anything to keep this going, which means that tomorrow, I will let the Lil' Aunties know that Liam has got two girls who want to date him.

"A match?" Liam blinks at Eleanor Roosevelt like she's just started speaking Russian to him.

The Lil' Aunties ambushed Liam and me right outside our classroom at recess time and told Liam proudly (in low voices, since they don't want the entire world overhearing) that they're setting him up on his first date.

"Yeah," Sarah Jessica says. "It's kind of the whole point of running a matchmaking business?"

"And it's a really good match," I add. Ugh, saying these words to him feels like gargling scalding water. I spot Triss walking out of the classroom with Zoelle, and my gut clenches. They smile at me as they pass us, and Triss glances shyly at Liam before looking away, and *gahhh*. But it's fine! It's not like I can date Liam myself, not after the lie that our friendship has been built on.

"Yeah, I'm sure it's a good match. I just"—Liam gives me an indecipherable look—"I didn't think it would be this fast. So, like, you two are done putting together my profile?" He glances at me again.

Why is he looking at me like that? He shouldn't be allowed to look at me like that. It's too open, too tender, too everything!

I drop my gaze as Eleanor Roosevelt grins and says, "Yep! Your profile is done and it's awesome, and there are at least two really great matches we've lined up for you."

Liam nods hesitantly. "Cool. And these girls—uh—they know they're being matched with me? And they're okay with it?"

Eleanor Roosevelt laughs. "Where's your confidence? Of course they do! And they're up for it. So, this Saturday, you've got a date with the lovely Trissilla."

"Oh, okay."

"Is that a happy 'oh' or, like, an 'oh no' oh?" Sarah Jessica asks.

I stare at Liam hard enough that I can practically see, through his skull, the thoughts swirling around in his brain. My emotions are a mess. I don't want Liam to be happy about it, but I also don't want him to be mean about it if he's not interested in Triss. Bwaaah! Why must humaning be so hard?

"It's just a . . ." Liam chews on his lower lip for a second, increasing my heart rate by about 60 percent. "It's an—'oh, cool' sort of 'oh.'" He pauses, giving me that look that leaps through the windows of my soul (i.e., my eyes) and reads my innermost thoughts. "Are you . . . cool?"

"Me?" I squeak. Eleanor Roosevelt and Sarah Jessica stare at me, and oh my god, these two kids are legit terrifying. I force a laugh. "Why're you asking if *I'm* cool? Of course I am. I couldn't be cooler about it. I'm, like, subzero. Anyway, any thoughts on where you might take her?"

Liam's mouth snaps shut. "Cool. Well, we could probably go for a coffee."

My stomach sinks. I don't know why it does, because "go for a coffee" sounds pretty generic as far as first dates go, and I should've been expecting it, but just hearing the words from his mouth makes this impending date way too real. Somehow, my mouth manages to move and make the word "Cool" plop out like a dead rat. I simply cannot with this moment anymore, so I tell him I have to go.

"What? Go where? I thought we were going to eat together."

I glance, panic-eyed, at Eleanor Roosevelt, who's most definitely smirking now. "Yeah, I forgot that I haven't finished my . . . calculus homework, and you know how Miss Tian is about it, haha. Okay, see you later!" I hurry away down the hallway, feeling his eyes on my back the entire time.

When I get to the bathroom, it's blessedly empty. I go to the last cubicle, lock myself inside, and rest my head against the wall. Immediately, the conversation with Liam replays itself in my head. Had he looked secretly glad? No, he just looked shocked. Or maybe slightly disappointed? Ha, I wish. My phone suddenly buzzes. I take it out of my pocket to find a Discord notification. Endorphins bubble through me the way they always do at the familiar sight of the icon, because I know there's only one person it could be from.

Sourdawg: So I guess I'm about to have my first date
Dudebro10: Ooo0Ooo0Oooo

I wince. Is that something a teenage boy would say? Or did that just come off really weird and creepy?

Sourdawg: Oh hey! Wasn't expecting a reply. Aren't you in
     school?

Oh shit. I stare at the screen for a beat, wondering what to say to him.

Dudebro10: Yeah, I am. But it's recess time right now

Belatedly, I realize this makes Dudebro10 sound like an absolute loser who doesn't have anyone to sit with during recess and therefore spends the time on his phone. Oh well.

Sourdawg: Oh cool, yeah, same here
Dudebro10: So tell me abt the upcoming date! Who's it
     with? You excited?

Is that too many questions? Do I sound like a nosy parent?

Sourdawg: Haha, IDK if I'm excited. It's with someone
     nice, at least
Dudebro10: Niiice

Okay, that definitely sounded creepy.

Sourdawg: I'm actually rly glad to go on a date. Things at
home have been pretty bad. My parents' divorce isn't
so much amicable as it is scorched earth, haha
Dudebro10: Oh shit. I'm so sorry to hear that

I bite down on my lip, hating myself in the moment.
Here I am, holding a grudge against my parents just because
they made me switch schools, and meanwhile, Liam's going
through something a million times worse. I shouldn't even be
worrying about my stupid crush on him. If I were a true friend,
I would want him to have a great time on his date. He deserves
that. I release my breath in a defeated *whoosh*. Well, Triss is
awesome, so I have no doubt they'll have a wonderful time.

CHAPTER 13

"I hate this," I wail for the millionth time.

"Okay, Whiney McWhinerson," Cassie says very unsympathetically.

"Whine, whiiiine."

Cassie levels her gaze at me through her charcoal face mask. "I don't know that whining consists of you actually saying 'whine, whine.'"

"Oh yes, it definitely does." I sigh and plop back down on my bed. "Argh, shoot!" I quickly get up again, but it's too late: a bit of my charcoal mud mask has smudged off onto my pillowcase. Mami is going to flay me alive. Well, never mind. I've had to deal with all this unnecessary drama in my life thanks to her, so she can very well deal with a stained pillowcase.

"Come here and have more of this coconut cake," Cassie calls from where she's sensibly sitting on the floor.

"I don't deserve you."

"No, you don't. And yet here I am anyway."

I can't help but smile as I hop off the bed onto the rug,

where Cassie has laid out in a pile all the goodies she brought over. I truly do not deserve her. She came bearing all sorts of snacks: little coconut rice cakes filled with warm, caramelized palm sugar; crunchy, salty cassava chips; salted egg crispy fish skin; and chocolate-covered local coffee beans. The last one might have been a mistake, though, because after popping half a dozen of them into my mouth, my heart feels like a wild horse that's just been released from its stable. She's also brought the mud masks and a pedicure set, but I told her to trust me—she really does not want to come anywhere near my naked feet.

"Why don't you ask the Lil' Aunties to match you with Liam?" Cassie picks out a particularly large piece of crispy fish skin and nibbles on it, careful not to get any crumbs on her face mask.

I flail at her. I seem to be doing a lot of flailing recently. "Because! Haven't you been listening? I lied to him about—"

"Who you are online, sure, whatever. Everybody does."

"It's different. It's not like editing your online profile pic to look more presentable. He thinks I'm a guy."

"So what? You don't have to tell him that you're Dudebro. You can just be your own person."

I gawk at her. "And continue chatting with him online as Dudebro in the meantime? No, I can't do that. That feels really slimy. We don't just play together. He tells me a lot of things online. Like, private stuff about his family."

Cassie sighs. The mask around her mouth is now covered in flakes of salted egg. If I weren't so down about Liam being out on a date with Triss, I would've laughed at the sight of both of us covered in black masks and crumbs.

"I bet they're hitting it off," I moan. I almost flop over dramatically but catch myself in time before I smush charcoal mud all over my rug. Damn it, these masks were a terrible idea. I need to be able to do my melodramatic flops.

Cassie glances at her watch. "They've been out, what, an hour? That's a pretty long coffee date."

I glare at her. "You're not helping."

"Have more coconut cake." She picks one up and literally pops it in my mouth.

"I bet they're making out." Since my mouth is filled with delicious cake and syrup, it comes out as "Oomfh oomph mff."

"Making out?" I have no idea how Cassie understood that, but now she's staring at me like I've just sprouted tentacles from my head. "You seriously think they might be making out on their first date? Their first date, which, might I add, is taking place at a café."

I shrug forlornly. "Okay, so it sounds a bit unlikely when you put it that way, but please tell that to my asshole brain, because it won't stop conjuring up images of Liam and Triss kissing and slurping at each other."

"Kissing . . . and slurping?" Cassie cackles. "Tell me you've never made out with anyone without telling me you've never made out with anyone."

I narrow my eyes at her. "Clearly, I have made out with plenty of guys."

"And all this making out involved slurping?" Cassie makes

a face, which makes her mask crack. "See, this is why I'm thankful that I'm not into guys."

"Okay, not specifically slurping. But, you know, there was a lot of tongue involved."

"Too late, you said 'slurping.' You can't take it back."

"How do girls make out?"

"Well, it's very hot and very sexy, and there is definitely no slurping."

By now, despite everything, I'm finding it hard not to laugh. Cassie joins me, and as we laugh, our face masks crack and flake to the floor, which makes us laugh even harder.

A beep interrupts our laughter. It shoots straight through my consciousness and lights up a Liam-shaped area of my brain, because *ah!* It's the alert from Discord. I leap up so abruptly from the floor that Cassie goes, "What the hell?" but I don't respond as I pounce on my phone and open up the app.

Sourdawg: U there?
Dudebro10: YES—

I delete that and type in "yes," no caps, like a normal person would.

Sourdawg: Wanna do a battleground?

I stare at my phone as though the message were in German. "What is it?" Cassie asks.

I turn to her with a frown. "Liam's asking me—well, Dudebro—if I want to play *Warfront Heroes.*"

Cassie shrugs. "Why not?"

"Well, he just came home from a date with a really pretty, really smart girl. And the first thing he does is play *Warfront Heroes*?"

"Sounds pretty normal for a hetero male. You do realize they are very inferior creatures, right? What did you expect, a heart-to-heart conversation breaking down every detail of the date?"

Yeah, actually. But it did sound stupid when Cassie put it that way.

"Go play with him. I'm gonna raid your closet."

I type out "OK" and go to my desk to fire up my laptop. Behind me, Cassie stays true to her word and starts rooting around my closet with abandon. We get in a queue for the next available battleground.

Dudebro10: So how did your coffee thing go?

Is that casual enough? Is it something a guy would say to his totally platonic guy friend?

Sourdawg: Haha, can't believe you remembered!

My sweet Liam, I have been obsessing over it for the past two days, since I was cursed into signing the girls up with the Lil' Aunties.

Dudebro10: Haha, yeah, I just randomly thought of it
Sourdawg: It was OK

Okay? *Okay?!* What does that mean? Luckily, I'm spared from digging for more details, because Liam continues typing.

Sourdawg: She's rly pretty

Kill me now.

Dudebro10: Haha, cool! What did you guys do?
Sourdawg: Had coffee, chatted, the usual
Dudebro10: That sounds awesome!

Argh, that was probably way too strong.

Sourdawg: Yeah, it was great. She's a rly cool person

I'm nearly overwhelmed by a sudden surge of resentment toward poor Triss, who has been nothing but kind to me. *Stop it, self.* I don't want to be the kind of person who sees other girls as competition. Deep breath in. Triss has done nothing wrong, aside from being her usual awesome self. I'm the one who's a dirty liar who's lied and keeps on lying to her supposed best online friend.

Dudebro10: I'm glad to hear it!

I type that through teeth gritted so hard I can hear my molars crack. Of course, the message comes out stilted and awkward and not at all sounding like something a teen boy would say. Or a teen girl, for that matter. I've somehow morphed into business-speak. Next, I'll start saying stuff like "I hope this finds you well," and then he'll think I'm some ancient millennial.

Just as I'm about to log off and quietly have an emotional crisis, Sourdawg sends another DM.

> **Sourdawg:** But I don't know if there was much chemistry there, to be honest

My heart grows to the size of a basketball. Never mind, that doesn't sound good. It swells, is what I'm trying to say. It swells and swells, and I swear I've never felt this happy.

> **Dudebro10:** Oh?

The most loaded "Oh?" in the history of "Ohs."

> **Sourdawg:** Yeah, it's weird, right? Because I liked everything about her. She's pretty, she's so smart, and she's rly funny too

Come on, let's get to the "but"!

> **Sourdawg:** But . . .

Yesss.

> **Sourdawg:** IDK. It's just weird. I'm being weird, right? There is literally nothing wrong with her. She's awesome

Dudebro10: I mean, if you're not into her, you're not into
   her. You can't help how you feel about someone
Sourdawg: Very wise, Confucius
Dudebro10: That's me all right

Just then, we're let into a game, so the conversation is, thankfully, put to rest. Phew. Of course, I can hardly focus on the battle, because my mind is at odds with itself, flinging back and forth from relief (*yay, he's not into her!*) to dread (*ugh, this means I'm going to have to set him up with someone else*). I swear, this whole matchmaking thing is going to age me twenty years.

Hmm. An idea forms, blobby and vague at first, then slowly coming into focus. Why don't I use the matchmaking thing to my advantage? Once the round ends, I tell Sourdawg that I have to go afk for a bit, then swivel my chair around.

Cassie sees my expression. "Uh-oh. What is it?"

"Do you think . . ." I bite my lip, feeling out the idea in my mind before plunging forward. "Would it be entirely terrible if I asked the Lil' Aunties to—I don't know—set me up on a double date that just so happens to have Liam in it?" Argh, now that I've said it out loud, that sounds bad.

"Not terrible, but why bother with a double date? Like I said, you should ask them to set you up with him."

"And I already told you why I can't do that. But a double date feels less bad, at least. I don't know." I sigh. "It's probably a bad idea."

"God," Cassie groans. "You are so into Liam, it's kind of sad."

"Thanks."

Cassie smirks at me. "I think it's a great idea. I mean, it's not as good as going on a solo date with him, but hey, beggars and choice. Go for it. This way, you'll be able to interact with him outside of your dystopian school, and who knows? Maybe sparks will *fly!*"

"Really?" I hate how hopeful my voice comes out.

Cassie grabs my phone and shoves it at me. "Yes. Talk to the Lil' Aunties now. They'll go for it, I'm sure."

I stare at the phone for ages, wondering what to write to the Lil' Aunties. Finally, Cassie snatches the phone out of my hands and starts typing.

> **Kiki:** Hey, girls, I've got a great idea. Instead of boring coffee dates, what about something exciting, like mushroom foraging or hiking up a waterfall? You could set up more than one couple at a time on these dates

I grab the phone back from Cassie, glaring at her. "I can't believe you just said that." Technically, I realize Cassie hasn't actually said anything terrible, but still! She's typing as me; she should be a tad more careful.

> **Eleanor Roosevelt:** Love it!
> **Sarah Jessica Parker:** Good idea. And we just got one more guy sign up, so we can now set up a double date
> **Eleanor Roosevelt:** Yeah, we were actually just about to message you, ci
> **Kiki:** Oh? Why?

Sarah Jessica Parker: The guy who signed up specifically asked to be matched with you

Heat floods my cheeks. Cassie, who's reading over my shoulder, goes, "Oooh!" She grins at me. "Someone's got a crush on you."

It's hard to keep the smile off my face. I mean, I'm so very into Liam it's gone into uncool territory, but still, finding out that someone's into me is nice. "Shut up," I say to Cassie, biting my cheek to keep from smiling too hard. I'm still fighting back a huge-ass grin as I type a carefully nonchalant reply to the Lil' Aunties.

Kiki: Oh? Cool. Who is it?

Cassie and I both hold our breath as three little dots appear next to Eleanor Roosevelt. My mind flicks through all the guys I've interacted with at Xingfa. Not many of them, to be fair. Maybe that guy who said hi to me that time at the canteen? Or maybe the guy I bumped into on the way to chem lab? Or maybe . . .

Eleanor Roosevelt: Jonas Arifin

Or maybe it's the last person I would've guessed. And the last person I would ever, ever go out with. My jaw thumps to the floor. I stare at Cassie, who's looking as shocked as I feel. We speak at the same time. "What the hell?"

CHAPTER 14

I don't know what I was expecting when I picked up the phone, scrolled through our class group chat, and texted Jonas: "WTF?" but his reply was definitely not it.

> **Jonas:** Ah, I was wondering when you'd message :)
>
> **Kiki:** Srsly Jonas, WTF? A date with me?
>
> **Jonas:** I'll explain in person. This isn't the kind of conversation you have over WhatsApp ;)
>
> **Kiki:** What???
>
> **Jonas:** I'll come over
>
> **Kiki:** Wait, what??
>
> **Jonas:** See you in twenty min
>
> **Kiki:** Wait
>
> **Kiki:** JONAS
>
> **Kiki:** FFS

"He's coming over," I say, and my voice feels like it's coming from a very faraway place.

"What? Like, over here? Right now?" Cassie says.

"Sounds like it."

"Let me see that." Cassie plucks my phone out of my hand and scrolls through my chat with Jonas. "What the hell? This douche is something else. How does he even know where you live?"

"I don't—" I shake my head, feeling dazed. "I don't know. Maybe it's on the class register or something?"

"What're you gonna do?"

"Uh, I don't— What should I do?"

Cassie gnaws on her bottom lip for a while, then sighs. "Well, you need to talk to him anyway, right? So I guess that's what you do."

"But. Here?" The thought of having Jonas in my house, of all places, is horrifying.

For a second, Cassie frowns, but then the frown suddenly melts away and is replaced with a smirk. "You could talk on the front porch? That could be a real power move, not letting him inside your house."

I nod slowly. "I guess . . ."

"That sends the right message," Cassie says. "So you stand right outside your door, at the top of the front steps, hands folded in front of your chest, and go, 'You can talk from there.' And you'd be, like, three steps above him, so you'd be looking down at him. Perfect."

I run through this scenario in my head and find that I don't hate it. "Okay, I guess that could work. . . ."

"But first, let's put some makeup on you and turn you into a bad bitch."

"I'm not putting on makeup for Jonas freaking Arifin."

"Think of it as war paint. It's not to impress him, it's to intimidate the ever-living shit out of him."

It's clear that Cassie isn't going to take no for an answer, so reluctantly, I let her lead me to my vanity and start dabbing BB cream onto my face. As she works on my makeup, she goes through lines like "I'm not really seeing your point, Jonas," and "I think you're full of shit, Jonas," and so on.

Barely ten minutes have passed when all of a sudden, Mami calls up the stairs for me. "Kristabellaaa!"

I startle, and Cassie very nearly pokes my eye out with eyeliner.

"Damn it," Cassie groans. "Look what you did."

I glance at the mirror and find a stray black line going up across my right eyelid. I rub at it, but instead of erasing the line, it merely smudges it. I quickly grab a tissue and wipe it off.

"KRISTABELLAAA!"

What is going on? Then cold realization seeps down my spine. Mami's got that tone of voice, the one she puts on when we have guests at the house. It's high and smooth, with an extra generous helping of British accent.

"Oh god," I murmur. "I think he's here already. And Mami must've let him in."

Cassie stares at me in horror. "But. So fast?!"

I stand, brushing lint off my pants, my mind a scrambled mess. In a doomed daze, I walk to the door and down the stairs.

"You've got this!" Cassie hisses from my room.

I walk down the curving staircase and find the worst sight awaiting me down in the living room. Jonas Arifin is sitting on my sofa, holding a saucer with a cup of tea, looking downright at home. He beams up at me.

I blink. I blink again. The apparition remains there, on my sofa, smiling politely. Well, it looks like a polite smile, but I've known Jonas long enough now to know when he's really smirking. But—how did he get here so fast? My mind is short-circuiting. I can't even form complete thoughts. How did I miss the doorbell? How did—

"Hi, Kiki," he says in a genial tone, putting the saucer down gently.

"It's Jonas Arifin," Mami hisses, as though I didn't already recognize the snake sitting there. "Why didn't you tell me that you're friends with an Arifin?" Her eyes are glowing with the fierce fire of Asian ambition. Great. As much as I love my mom, she's also a shameless social climber. She's going to crow for ages about having an Arifin in our house.

"How'd you get here so fast? Speed all the way here in one of your fancy cars, did you?" The words blurt out of me without warning, as ugly as a burp.

Mami's mouth drops open in shock. "Kiki! Is this how you greet your friend who's been so nice and so polite? He even brought us gifts!" She gestures to an obnoxiously huge hamper that's taller than she is. It's filled with artisanal cakes and cookies and exotic orchids. The sight of it only makes me even more suspicious, because if Jonas is coming to my house bearing gifts, then he must have an ulterior motive. It's like Satan offering up something: you just know he's going to want your soul in return.

"Truly, Jonas, you shouldn't have," Mami is saying.

"Yes, you shouldn't have," I say flatly.

"Kiki!" Mami snaps. "What has gotten into you?"

"No worries, Tante." Jonas gives an easy laugh that's so fake my insides seize. "Kiki and I are always messing around with each other like this. We like to give each other a hard time, but it's all in good fun. For example, she likes to kill me over and over again in the game that we play online." He turns his full attention to me then, and his smile grows wider, showing more teeth. "Don't you, Kiki? Or should I say, Dudebro10?"

The floor gives way under me. I would've fallen if I hadn't caught hold of the back of a nearby chair to keep me standing. This can't be real. No, he didn't just call me—

"Dude . . . what?" Mami says, laughing uncertainly.

"Dudebro10." Jonas's eyes are still on mine. "It's her gamer tag—the nickname she uses in-game."

Mami waves her hand and laughs. "Oh, you kids and your ever-evolving lingo. I can't keep up with you."

Jonas opens his mouth, but I quickly bite out, "Mami, can I speak with Jonas alone? Please," I add.

Mami dithers, hesitating. She looks wholly torn. On one hand, she disapproves of me dating anyone while I'm still in high school. On the other hand, this is an Arifin, and if there's anything that can break her no-dating rule, it's the likes of Jonas. After all, it's one of the real reasons she moved me to Xingfa in the first place. She only did so after finding out that George Clooney goes there, and she's hoping that I'll make friends like George, and now here is Jonas Arifin. After a few long, torturous seconds, she nods. "Okay, you may go into the study. But leave the door cracked open."

"You can trust me, Tante," Jonas says. "I won't disrespect your daughter."

What little bit of tension there was on Mami's face melts away at this. Gag. I can't believe how easily she fell for that.

I lead Jonas from the living room to the study. After my bedroom, the study is my favorite room in the house. It's far enough away from the living room to be quiet, and there's a large picture window that looks out into a corner of the backyard, washing the whole room with gentle sunlight. The walls are covered with warm wood panels, and it feels so safe and cozy in here.

Well, usually it feels safe and cozy, but for the first time, with Jonas in it, I feel the furthest thing away from safe or cozy. As soon as we're inside, I push the door so it's only a crack open, then I take a deep breath and turn to face him.

"How did—"

"I find you?" Jonas cocks his head to one side. "Did you not hear your mom repeatedly say I'm an Arifin?"

I grit my teeth. "Yes, Jonas, I know who you are. Big freaking deal. I don't see what that has to do with—"

"My family owns TalkCo."

"Yes, Jonas, we all know your family owns the nation's leading internet and cell phone service provider, big freaking deal. Wooow, can I please have your autograph?"

Jonas snickers. "I wasn't saying that to show off. Okay, maybe a little." He winks in what he probably thinks is a very adorable way. "But basically, it's really quite simple. First, all I had to do was ask one of my employees to look up Dudebro10's IP address, then all they had to do was trace the IP to your home address, and . . ." He leans back in his seat, smirking. "Here I am."

"*What?*" For a few moments, all I can do is gape at him. "What the shit?" I cry. "Jonas, that is such a breach of privacy. You've broken pretty much every freaking privacy law there is, not to mention betrayed the trust of your customer!"

Jonas rolls his eyes. "Methinks someone's been watching too many American shows. You know the rules are different here."

And as much as I hate to admit it, I do know. I can rant on and on about Jonas breaching privacy laws, but am I actually sure that such laws exist? Or, rather, they probably do exist, but am I certain that our internet contract didn't come with fine print that says the provider can use our IP address to track us down? And even if the law were on my side, am I really going to take on someone as rich and powerful as Jonas Arifin? His family won't just have a lawyer, they'll have a whole entire legal team, and they'd probably countersue or something and we'd end up being buried under legal fees for years to come.

I gape at him wordlessly, taking in his smug expression, the way he's sitting so relaxed in Papi's chair. He knows he's won. He knows there's not a damn thing I can do about him being here. All I can do is . . . what? What *can* I do? I shove all that aside and try to focus on why I contacted him in the first place. "Okay, so . . . but why have you asked the Lil' Aunties to match us with each other?"

"Ah." Jonas leans forward, putting his fingertips together, and says, "Keep an open mind, because I actually have an amazing proposition to offer you."

I almost blurt out that I'd rather eat my own foot than enter into any kind of agreement with him, but I remind myself that he has the upper hand, so I should at least hear him out.

Jonas raises an eyebrow at me, and I can just tell that he thinks he's so damn cute. "The reason I asked those kids to match us with each other is . . . I want you to be my girlfriend."

I swear the entire universe implodes right then. All forms of logic and reasoning shatter into a billion meaningless pieces of rubble, leaving nothing behind but this most nonsensical of situations. Jonas freaking Arifin, asshat who has tormented me ever since I arrived at Xingfa, asking me to be his girl-friend. Do I cry or do I laugh?

"You can go right to hell" is what hisses through my lips.

Jonas places his palms on his chest dramatically. "Kiki, you wound me."

"Well, the answer's no, so you can fuck right off now."

"Hear me out. I have to admit, when I first went looking for Dudebro, all I wanted to do was take revenge. I thought it was some asshole dude—" He snorts, shaking his head. "A literal dude bro! Great job with the name, by the way. None of us even suspected it was a girl. Why did you play as a dude?"

"To avoid getting hit on or threatened by assholes like you," I mumble.

Jonas frowns. "Wow, Kiki. I would never."

"No, all you did was gaslight and bully me in person. So much better than bullying me online." I can barely keep my voice at a reasonable volume, I'm so incensed.

Jonas sighs. "Maybe we got off on the wrong foot at school. Anyway, where was I? See, my employees all guessed that

Dudebro must be someone I knew in real life, because why else would he be so invested in griefing me continuously in-game? I thought it was Andre from Charity, or Tommy Hilfiger from Kindness. Those two losers have had it out for me since day one."

"Oh? Did they also not take kindly to your gaslighting and bullying them?"

Jonas only gives me one of his bashful, winning smiles. It doesn't win anything with me, except maybe the almost overwhelming urge to punch him right in the face. "Anyway, imagine my surprise when they traced the IP address to your house!" He chuckles. "I was so certain it would be a guy that it took an embarrassingly long time to figure out it was you, even after I saw that the account holder is Siregar. I was, like, this surname sounds familiar, but I can't think of any guy at school with this last name! Then one of my employees said, 'Maybe it's not a guy?' and it clicked into place. Kiki Siregar." He gazes at me, shaking his head slowly. "You are amazing."

"What the hell are you smoking? You just told me that you found out I'm your online troll. Well, good for you." I raise my arms wide before letting them fall back down. "Here I am. I bet you hate my guts even more now. So. Yes, you're right. I am Dudebro10. Yes, I took pleasure in killing you over and over in *Warfront Heroes*. I wish I could tell you I'm sorry, but . . ."

Jonas laughs again. "Kiki, no! I don't need you to apologize. I just—god, how do I even describe it? When I found out it was you, it was like . . ." He rakes his fingers through his hair. "It's so unbelievably romantic, right?"

"What?" I must be dreaming right now. This has all the

hallmarks of a dream—sudden plot twists that make zero sense, me being stuck and powerless to do anything.

"Do you know how boring it is to be me?"

At this, my mouth quirks into a smile. "I do, actually. Probably mind-numbingly boring."

Jonas rolls his eyes. "You know I didn't mean it that way. I mean, like, being me . . . there's not much that's a challenge. Every girl would kill to date an Arifin. All of them so eager to please me."

"Poor you, life is so tough."

Jonas points at me. "See? This attitude right here, that's what I like about you, Kiki. You're not like all the other girls."

Not like all the other girls. I'd like to find the asshole who normalized "Not like other girls" as a compliment and grind his stupid head into the dirt.

"You're so strong and stubborn," Jonas continues. "You don't care about offending me. It's so refreshing. You're exactly the kind of girl I need in my life. And it's pretty romantic, don't you think? Classic enemies to lovers. You're this strong, stubborn girl. I was your enemy, and you killed me in-game every night. But why were we always fighting? Because there are so many feelings simmering underneath."

"The only feeling I have for you is revulsion, you privileged asshole!"

Jonas's eyes narrow. "I don't believe that. You don't spend hours killing someone in-game over and over again unless you have some serious feelings for him."

"Yeah, those feelings are called hate," I cry. "And I don't

get it, Jonas. All this time, you've been calling me Crazy Kiki, and now you suddenly want to date me? I just—I don't get it!"

"Really?" He looks genuinely confused. "How can you not get it? Isn't it obvious?"

"Isn't what obvious?"

"You know how when we were kids and if a boy liked a girl, he would pull her pigtails?" Jonas raises his eyebrows at me. There's a moment of expectant silence as I gape at him.

"You're saying . . ." I hesitate. "That this whole time, you . . . liked me?" The words sound so alien and wrong that I'm pretty sure I'm hallucinating.

Jonas shrugs. "Yeah, why not? You're pretty cute, and I did find you intriguing, yes. I told you, before you, no one dared to ever question me. You're refreshing."

"You tormented me this whole time because you thought I was cute?" My words come out as a shocked whisper.

"Aww, Kiki, come on, I wouldn't call it 'tormenting.' It was just a bit of teasing. Flirting, you could even call it."

"I don't think—no." I take a deep breath. "Look, I don't give a shit what your explanation is. The answer is still no."

The warmth leaches out of Jonas's face, but only for a moment, before a slow smile spreads across it. "Don't you think the other kids would find it interesting that you, Crazy Kiki, have been bullying me online while disguised as a guy? I mean, if that isn't crazy, I don't know what is."

My mouth falls open. "But I—" Nothing else comes out, because what else is there to say? I have no idea how to defend myself, because yes, it sounds absolutely ridiculous. It sounds so bad when he puts it like that, and even if I were to convince myself that I wouldn't care what the whole school thought of me, I care a lot what Liam would think. If he found out that I'm Dudebro10 from Jonas, it would look a thousand times worse than it is.

Jonas's smile wanes a little at my horrified expression. "Hey," he says quickly, "don't look so terrified. Jesus, Kiki. I'm not a total asshole, okay?"

He is so completely in love with the image of himself as the hero of the story that he can't see what a huge asshole he's being. I very nearly snort out loud at him.

"Come on, just give me a chance. You'll see that I'm a nice guy. You know how many girls would kill to have me as a boyfriend?"

"Said like a true nice guy," I mutter with obvious resentment.

Jonas laughs. "See? This is what I like about you! So feisty. So sassy."

"So patronizing. I don't understand what's in this for you. You said it yourself: girls are falling over themselves to date you. Why go for me?"

Jonas shrugs. "I like a challenge. Also, everyone at school basically worships me, and having you there obviously hating me is kind of a bummer, you know?"

That's probably the realest reason he has for wanting to date me. I'm pretty sure I've never been so angry or disgusted by anyone before. "I'm not 'a challenge,' Jonas, I'm an actual living human."

Jonas makes a *tch* sound. "You know what I mean. And I never shy away from challenges."

A revolted shudder trembles through my entire body. I want to violently gag at him. But I know when I'm beat. I can't have him tell everyone that I'm Dudebro, especially not Liam. For a moment, I squeeze my eyes shut, willing this day to end. I feel so utterly defeated, not a single atom inside me has any fight left. No way out. I can't believe it, but I am going to have to enter into this deal with the devil. "No touching," I manage to force out. "Absolutely nothing physical." If I were forced to kiss Jonas, I would vomit all my organs right into his stupid face.

Jonas mimes a stab wound to his heart. Oh, if only it were a real stab wound. "Ye of little faith," he moans. "Do you really think I would kiss a girl who isn't into me?"

"Yes, actually."

He pouts at me. "Okay, well, you're wrong. I'm not like that. No physical contact, deal."

I'm releasing a sigh of relief when he holds up his index finger.

"Except hand-holding."

My head immediately whips back and forth. Ugh, the thought of having to hold his slimy hand . . .

"Hand-holding, because we are going to be a couple, and that's only expected. And I've got great hand-holding skills. I don't get sweaty palms, I've got huge hands. . . ." He wiggles his eyebrows. Oh lord, kill me now. He holds out a hand toward me.

"Jonas, I'd rather chop off my right hand than have to hold yours."

He grins. "See? And they say romance is dead." Then he nods at his hand. "Take it."

"Nope."

"Seriously, Kiki. Unless you want everyone to know the truth about Dudebro."

It's truly amazing how quickly this sociopath switches from grinning romantic fool to coldhearted mercenary. My insides recoil as I reach for his hand, but I have to hand it—haha, hand it—to Jonas: he's right about having decent hands to hold. Not that it makes this situation any less bad, but at least holding his hand doesn't feel like I'm holding a frog. Then he gives my hand a friendly squeeze, and I instinctively yank it back. So gross. God, I hate everything about this. "And there needs to be a deadline. One week, then we're done."

"Two. Until the Spring Dance."

Two weeks of dating Jonas Arifin. I squeeze my eyes shut. I can do this, to keep my online identity a secret. To keep my friendship with Liam from being destroyed. I nod.

"Cool," Jonas says easily. "Well, I'll get out of your way. I'll pick you up for school Monday morning." For one horrifying second, he starts to lean forward, as though he's about to plant a kiss on my cheek, but at the last moment he catches himself with a laugh. "Sorry! Force of habit." He raises his hands in an exaggerated I'm-so-harmless way and winks at me before sauntering out of the study. I hear Mami ask him why he's leaving so soon, and he tells her he needs to study as she clucks over him, happiness bursting out of her every word.

Dear god, what the hell just happened?

CHAPTER 15

Cassie stares at me open-mouthed the whole time I tell her about Jonas's proposition. When I'm done, she doesn't react, just continues staring at me, unblinking, until I wave my hand in front of her face. She starts, then blinks at me.

"So . . ." She shakes her head. "Sorry, I must've misheard."

"Which part?"

"All of it?!" Cassie gestures wildly. "Jonas Arifin, son of a billionaire family, who's dated literal supermodels and celebrities, wants to date . . . you?"

I narrow my eyes at her. "*That's* your takeaway?"

"Kiki!" Cassie cries. "Don't you think that's at least a tiny bit ridiculous?"

"Yes. Very much so!" I cry back. "This is why I'm telling you, my best friend, about it. In the hopes that you come up with some good idea that would magically make all of this disappear."

Cassie's eyes are still barely blinking as she continues shaking her head at me. "Magically make Jonas Arifin disappear?

Like, take him out into the woods and bury him, that sort of 'disappear'?"

I groan. "No. I don't know, like somehow make his threat go away. Without murder."

Cassie sighs. "Okay, let's think." She closes her eyes and rubs her chin. "Right, so to solve any problem, we need to look at the root of the issue. Solve the cause, not the symptom."

I nod eagerly. "Yes, you're right. Exactly."

"So the root here is . . . what is it? Why does Jonas want to date you?"

"He gave me a bunch of reasons. He said that we're like enemies to lovers in real life and it's really romantic. He thinks I must have feelings for him, because I've been so 'obsessed' with killing him over and over in-game. I mean . . ." I shrug. "Who knows?"

"Hmm." Cassie rubs her chin again. "Okay, I'm seeing a pattern here. My theory is that Jonas is so used to everyone kissing his ass that he thinks he's genuinely amazing. And then you come along and you make him realize that he actually kind of sucks, and I think it's shaken him to his core. I think he's trying to prove to himself, more than anyone else, that he is lovable, and the way he's trying to do that is to make the one person who hates him love him. It's all about fixing his tattered self-confidence."

"Oh god," I groan. "I think you're right. I really did hurt this stupid baby's feelings, didn't I? I didn't know being honest about how much he sucks would affect him like this." I rub my hands across my face. "Okay, so how do I fix this?"

"I don't know. He's feeling shitty about himself—rightfully

so, because he sounds pretty shitty—but if you don't want to deal with it, then maybe you could somehow reassure this baby that he's awesome?"

The thought of affirming Jonas about his repugnant self is too much to bear. "I can't. The last thing this asshole needs is yet another person telling him he's great."

"Yeah." Cassie winces. "Even telling you to reassure him gave me the ick. No, you should definitely stand up to him. I think maybe there isn't much you can do aside from sucking it up and going out with him until the Spring Dance. Oh, and you could be the worst-ever girlfriend in the meantime. Maybe he'll get so annoyed that he'll break up with you before then." She glances at her watch. "Oh shoot, I have to go. It's almost dinnertime. You got this."

My stomach churns as I watch Cassie leave. I do not have this. Not even close. This is a nightmare scenario. With a groan, I flop onto my seat and log back on to *Warfront Heroes*. But when the theme song starts up, the familiar, dramatic notes remind me of how Jonas knows about me and *Warfront Heroes*. A choked cry of frustration burbles up my throat, and I slam my laptop shut. I can't believe Jonas has ruined not just school for me but *Warfront Heroes* too.

My phone beeps with a message from Discord.

Sourdawg: Hey, did I see you log on to *WH* for a second and then log off? Everything OK?

For the first time ever, reading a message from Sourdawg doesn't make me feel good. In fact, it makes me feel like crying.

True to his promise—or, rather, his threat—Jonas picks me up from my house on Monday morning. Mami practically squeals and claps with excitement when she sees his flashy Aston Martin outside our house.

"Aren't you afraid that he might speed and we might get into an accident?" I point out helpfully.

Mami gives me a look. "Where, pray tell, can you speed in Jakarta?"

I hate to admit it, but she's right. Jakarta traffic is notoriously bad. Most streets have stop-and-go traffic. Even if Jonas wanted to, there's no way he can go over twenty-five miles an hour unless he goes outside the city.

I can only watch helplessly as Mami steps out of the house. Jonas climbs out of his ridiculous car and saunters up our driveway, waving at us. When he reaches the doorstep, he gives us a winning smile and hands Mami a box.

"Hi, Tante. Mami says to give you this. It's macarons, straight from Pierre Hermé in Paris. She had it ordered especially for you when she heard that Kiki and I are"—he pauses for a second to give a bashful smile—"going out."

Mami practically swoons at that. She grabs the box and clasps it to her chest. "Oh, you are such a good child! What a polite Chinese boy you are! Jonas, have you had breakfast? Can I get you anything?"

"We're going to be late," I say flatly, pushing past Mami, keeping my glare locked on Jonas and his smarmy face.

"Kiki!" Mami snaps.

"She's right, Tante," Jonas says with an easygoing shrug. "We should get to school."

"Have a wonderful day!" Mami says. "And please thank your mami for the macarons." I know she's already frantically scouring her mental list of patisseries to find the perfect thank-you gift for Jonas's mom. It's going to be an ongoing battle where they are stuck in this hellish loop, each one sourcing more expensive gifts for the other until they realize they just dropped five grand on a cream puff and call a truce.

"Great job sucking up to my mom." I refuse to meet his eye as he opens the passenger door for me.

"It's called having manners. You might want to try it sometime." He lets me in with a flourish and gives one last wave to Mami, who's still standing on our doorstep like some 1950s housewife seeing her husband off as he leaves for Wall Street.

Jonas is a surprisingly good driver. I fully expected him to be a complete douche on the road, bullying everyone like he does in person, but he carefully maneuvers the car and doesn't speed. Then I realize he's so careful because he doesn't want to accidentally nick his precious car, because of course. I bet he's one of those jerks who call their cars their baby and make kissy noises at them as they wash them with gentle caresses.

He glances at me. "How was your weekend?"

"Oh god, no."

"No what?" He actually looks confused.

"No, let's not do small talk." I maintain eye contact with him and give him a defiant smile as I put on my headphones.

"So rude." He laughs. Then he reaches over and actually pulls off my headphones. He does so gently, but it's still so shocking, an actual violation of my personal space. When my mouth drops open, he gives me a look. "Come on, Kiki. Let's not behave like toddlers."

I grind my teeth. I have never in my life wanted to hit someone as much as I want to hit Jonas Arifin. How long do I have to keep this up? The answer floats up like a bubble of toxic gas from a swamp. Until he gets bored of me. Yes, of course. And he will, no doubt about that, because privileged rich kids like Jonas have one thing in common: they get bored very easily. They can't help it. They grew up getting anything they wanted. When you have access to all the toys the world has to offer, it doesn't take long for you to get bored with the ones you have and move on to the next thing. And to Jonas, I'm nothing more than a toy.

Okay, new strategy: I am going to bore the hell out of Jonas. I'm going to be such an uninteresting, droning, tedious girlfriend that he's going to beg me to leave him alone. *Good plan, self.*

I turn to Jonas and smile. "I had a great weekend, actually."

"Oh?" He brightens up, and I nearly laugh in his face. This asshole thinks I'm actually about to share how my weekend went with him because I want to.

"Yeah, so I spent it . . ." I consider topics that he might find boring. Knitting? Gardening? "Scrapbooking."

"Really? I didn't think you'd be into that sort of thing." The disdain in his voice comes through loud and clear.

"Oh yeah. I'm really into scrapbooking. I've got an entire desk full of scrapbooking supplies. Let me tell you what they are. So first, I've got my scrapbook, of course." My mind flies ahead, trying to remember everything I know about scrap-booking. "Then I've got about twenty different kinds of washi tape. Do you know what washi tape is?" I tell him anyway, without waiting for an answer. "My favorite one has pine-apples on it, and a blue background. And my second favorite is a rainbow-colored one. Now, my third favorite is a draw between . . ."

"Babe."

Oh god, did he just call me babe? A repulsed shudder shivers up my spine, and I have to actively stop myself from gagging.

Jonas quirks up the corners of his mouth at me. "C'mon, you can't seriously be into that stuff."

Ugh, could he be more of a jerk? I mean, yes, I'm not actu-ally into it, but I could be.

"That's for old, sad women who own way too many cats for their own good," he continues. "You're way better than that. You should be into . . ." He waves a hand flippantly. "I don't know, like, snowboarding, or deep-sea fishing. Oh hey, speaking of fishing—"

We weren't speaking of fishing, I want to snap.

"My dad bought a new yacht. We should take it for a spin, huh? Go out to one of the islands and see if we can catch a shark." He glances at me with wide, eager eyes and an expect-ant smile, probably expecting me to be hopping with excite-ment at the suggestion.

"Why the hell would I want to catch a shark?"

Jonas lets out a short, affronted breath. "Okay, don't be appreciative of my awesome suggestion. Doesn't matter, I already told the Lil' Aunties about my yacht. They love the idea of setting up a double date on the yacht."

Good grief. I could practically hear the excitement in Eleanor Roosevelt's and SJP's voices. If word got out that the Lil' Aunties hooked their customers—I mean, clients—up for a yacht date, they would get so many new sign-ups.

"Fine, whatever. We'll go on your stupid yacht."

"You know, most girls would die to get on a yacht with me."

"So they can throw themselves overboard, probably," I mutter.

"Kiki," Jonas sighs, "a little bit of sass is cute. But now you're just being rude, which is honestly really unattractive."

Anger lurches up my chest, and I have to fight to keep myself from exploding at him. Who the hell cares what Jonas finds attractive or not? Fortunately, we arrive at the school, so I don't have to listen to Jonas telling me how to behave. I don't even wait for him to turn off the engine; as soon as he's parked, I open the door and jump out of the car like it's about to catch fire. Thank god. I wouldn't be able to stand another minute in there without hitting Jonas in the—

"Kiki?"

I glance up and oh god. Nooo!

Liam is standing there, one hand resting on the strap of his messenger bag. He's looking really, really confused, especially as Jonas chooses this very moment to climb out of his stupid Aston Martin.

"Did you just—did you guys drive here together?" Liam looks back and forth at us with a puzzled frown.

"No, it's not like—" I struggle for the right words, but let's face it. In a situation like this, there are no right words. "I mean, yes, but—"

"My man!" Jonas says, lifting his fist for Liam to bump. Liam hesitates for a moment before bumping it. "How's it going?"

Liam pushes his hair away from his face. "Uh, good. Did you guys get here together?"

Jonas grins. "Yeah, of course."

No, no, no!

The confused frown on Liam's face deepens. "Oh, why 'of course'? Are you neighbors or something?"

"No!" I cry, and at the same time, Jonas laughs and says, "No, but we are dating, so."

"Wait, no—"

"Don't make a big deal out of it, though, okay? 'Cause you know, school rules and all that," Jonas says, then—oh god—he winks.

My mouth opens and closes like a fish drowning on land. Liam turns to look at me, and I've never seen this expression on his face before. It tears through my skin and burns up my insides. It's disappointment and hurt and surprise all rolled together, and there's nothing I want more in this moment than to grab him and explain everything.

"That's . . . cool," he says after an eternity. "I'm happy for you guys."

"It was a long time coming," Jonas says. "Right, Kiki? We've been flirting for weeks now, and over the weekend we finally made things official."

"Flirting for weeks, huh?" Liam's eyes meet mine, and I

stare back soundlessly, a world of emotions warring inside me. *Look at me and see the truth,* I plead silently. *You've got to know that Jonas is spouting bullshit.*

Jonas finally senses the weird vibe between Liam and me. He glances at Liam, then at me, and his eyes narrow a little. Okay, maybe now he'll end this conversation and put me out of my misery.

But of course, that isn't what happens, because Jonas is an agent of chaos. When he senses something off, he doesn't avoid it; instead, he jumps headlong into it. I see the moment of decision, the glint in his eye, far too late.

"How was your date? You had one, like, a week ago, right?" Jonas laughs. "I love how whoever's running that app thinks an NDA would shut anyone up. Pretty sure the entire school knows who's going out with whom."

"Uh, right. It was okay." Liam's gaze burns through me before he drops it.

"Well, don't worry about it, mate. I already asked the Lil' Aunties to set us up on a double date."

Both Liam and I snap our heads around and stare at Jonas, mouths agape. Oh my god. I did say that I wanted to go on a double date with Liam recently. But things have changed massively now that I'm "dating" Jonas. I would rather chew off my own arm than go on a double date with Liam, with Jonas as my date. Well, maybe not my own arm, but I would definitely rather chew off *an* arm than do that.

Jonas grins at us. "They think it's a great idea. It'll be on my new yacht, by the way. You're gonna love it. Kiki's excited about going on it, aren't you, babe?"

Acidic words claw themselves up my throat and then die halfway up, because seriously, what the hell can I say to that?

Liam shoves his hands into his pockets, not meeting my eye. "Cool," he mumbles.

"You're all gonna love my new yacht, I promise."

Not even eight in the morning and Jonas has said "yacht" about seventeen times. And I can't believe I'm going to have to go on a double date with him as my boyfriend while Liam goes out with another girl. How did my life take such a disastrous turn?

CHAPTER 16

Sourdawg: So something REALLY weird happened
Dudebro10: Yeah?
Sourdawg: You know that girl sitting next to me
Dudebro10: Yeah
Sourdawg: So I found out today that she's dating this guy
who's been straight-up bullying her and calling her
crazy
Dudebro10: Huh.

Huh is right. What else can I say to that? My entire
face—hell, my entire body—feels like it's on fire. I swear my
scalp has shrunk until it's squeezing my skull. There's so much
I want to tell Liam. But there's nothing I can say. Nothing
aside from "Huh."

Sourdawg: That's weird, right? Like, why would you date
someone who's been such an asshole to you?
Dudebro10: Yeah, it's super fucked up

Super fucked up's right. I squeeze my eyes shut until the urge to bawl passes.

Sourdawg: Sorry, I know I'm kind of hung up on it, but it's just kind of really frustrating to watch
Dudebro10: Yeah, totally. I get what you mean

Trust me, Liam, I empathize so much more than you think.

Sourdawg: I mean, you've come across all those stereotypes too, right? You know, the ones that are about how girls just want to be mistreated? And I've always believed they're BS, but IDK anymore
Dudebro10: OK, well, first of all, this one girl isn't representative of every girl in the world, so . . .
Sourdawg: Yeah, you're right
Dudebro10: And second of all, maybe there's something going on that you don't know about?
Sourdawg: Huh.
Sourdawg: You mean like . . . maybe the guy isn't such a douche toward her in private? I guess. Yeah, that makes sense. Maybe this whole time, him calling her crazy was an inside joke or something . . .

No. *No!* That wasn't what I meant, Liam! Of course Jonas is as much of a douche to me in private as he is in public. And of course calling me crazy isn't some cute inside joke! Damn it, Liam.

Dudebro10: I meant, like, maybe she has other reasons for wanting to date him

Sourdawg: Hmm. Well, the guy is apparently one of the richest people in the country, so maybe that's why

Wait, *nooo!* Oh my god, now he thinks I'm some gold digger.

Dudebro10: No, I didn't mean that. I mean, like . . .

What did I mean to say? Well, what I really want to say is: *Maybe there are other reasons she has to date him, like maybe he's blackmailing her.* But of course I can't say that. So after an excruciating eternity, I simply type: "Nvm. Yeah, I have no idea why she might want to date him" and leave it at that.

Life as Jonas's girlfriend is so much worse in a myriad of ways I didn't foresee. I thought, foolishly, that at least a silver lining in this whole farce would be that Jonas would stop bullying me and I would cease to be the school pariah. Jonas did stop bullying me, but it's not as easy to erase weeks of my Crazy Kiki reputation.

When people found out that we're supposedly dating, the reactions ranged from vitriol from his diehard fans to confusion from the newfound, tentative friends I made in the last couple of weeks. The latter makes me want to sob. On Tuesday afternoon, the girls once again invite me for coffee.

"Are you and Jonas really an item?" Zoelle asks.

I focus on stirring my iced latte so I can avoid looking at her and the other girls. There's no good explanation I can give them, especially Peishan, who happily accepted the offer of a double date with Liam. After a while, I say, "It just happened."

"Are you going with him to the Spring Dance?" Peishan asks.

I shrug. Technically, that was our deal. I'm still holding out hope that Jonas will dump me by then, but who knows?

Looks are exchanged around the table. These girls don't like Jonas, and god, I would give my left arm to be able to say that I despise him too. But now that I'm his girlfriend, they don't know how to relate to me. They probably think something is seriously wrong with me, that I'm one of those jerks who's into Jonas because he's an Arifin.

That's the last time they ask me out for coffee.

Online, there are a bunch posts discussing how unworthy I am of Jonas. On Wednesday, I see the words DIE, LOSER carved with ferocity into my desk. Tears blur my vision, and I wonder if I should report this, but the thought of having to speak with Principal Lin exhausts me, so I just slam my folder onto my desk, obscuring the hateful message.

Liam glances over with a start. "Hey. You okay?"

No. Not even a little bit. I force a small smile, but I feel it wobble on my lips. Liam's face creases with concern, and he scoots his chair over so it's right next to mine. His arm brushes mine, light as a feather, and goose bumps erupt across my skin. "What's going on?" he murmurs, his voice low and soothing. Why is he still so nice to me? I know he's no longer interested in me, but he's still so caring, and I hate it. I don't know how to deal with it.

I can't bear to answer, so I just shift my folder to one side and nod at my desk. Liam's expression darkens as he reads the words that have been cut into the wooden surface.

"What the fuck. That's messed up. Let's report this."

"No." The answer comes out too harshly, too abruptly, but I can't be bothered to soften my tone. "Principal Lin is not exactly my biggest fan. And this is just a prank. I just have to ignore it, and they'll get tired and move on."

"If it is a prank, it's a really . . . aggressive one," Liam says. "Are you sure you don't want to report it? I'll come with you."

"Stop being so nice to me. I'm Jonas's girlfriend, remember?" I spit out with venom. I wish I could grab the words, take them back, cram them into my mouth, and pretend they were never said. The way Liam's face changes, hurt slashing across it, breaks me. Why did I say that? I just couldn't bear it. Liam's gentle concern, the way he's been so wary around me ever since Monday, the way our conversations have become so stilted. And he thanked Dudebro10 for stopping him from making a fool of himself. I wanted to scream at the screen: *You are not the one who made a fool of yourself. It was me. All me. All this mess that has spun so far out of my control has been my fault, my cowardice. And now I'm paying for it. As I should be.* Maybe having to be Jonas's girlfriend is a fitting punishment. Karma and all that.

Liam's face shuts down, and he nods. "Yeah, you're right. Sorry, I should get used to you dating Jonas." And with that, he scoots his chair away from me and pores over his notebook, effectively shutting me out. I deserve this. I wanted this—it's so much more bearable than having Liam be so kind to me. But even as I think that, I know that I have never been more miserable in my life.

Jonas's new yacht is just about as revoltingly huge as I expected. A towering monstrosity that is a fuck-you to the environment, it bobs on the water, its sides gleaming, and Jonas stands on the prow and waves at me. He's wearing an actual captain's hat, and I marvel at the surprising capacity I have in me to hate one single human. I stand on the pier as Jonas walks down the yacht and across the plank with both arms spread out.

"Huh?" he says. "Right? Didn't I say my new yacht slaps?"

I can barely hide the distaste in my expression. I'm spared having to reply when someone calls out to us. Not just any someone. I would recognize that voice in my dreams. I turn around and, sure enough, Liam is here. With Peishan. Who he's holding hands with.

Kill. Me. Now.

Bile burns its way up my throat as the two of them walk down the pier toward us, smiling and waving. And holding hands; I've mentioned that already, right? I mean, what gives? Where are our strict Chinese Indo parents when we need them? Why isn't a random auntie popping out of the bushes to tell us that holding hands leads to teen pregnancies?

And to make matters worse, Liam and Peishan look

straight-up fire. He's in casual wear, his off-white linen shirt showing off his biceps, and she's in a peach-colored sundress that grazes the tops of her knees, and they look like they belong in an Instagram ad. I curse myself for choosing to go with denim shorts. What was I thinking? I'm ridiculously underdressed. Liam's eyes flick toward me before he abruptly looks away. My skin is already burning, and it has nothing to do with the blinding sunlight.

Jonas holds up a champagne bottle with dramatic flair, and I resist the urge to remind him that, (1) We are underage, and (2) It's barely ten in the morning. I mean, I really, really want to remind him of that, but I don't know where Liam falls when it comes to drinking, and I don't want to seem uncoo—

What the hell is wrong with me? Who gives a shit what anyone thinks? I shouldn't care. What's happened to me? The old me, the one from Mingyang, wouldn't even have hesitated before telling Jonas to put down the stupid bottle of champagne.

The realization of how much I've changed and how there is so little about myself that I like now hits like a sack of cement swung into my chest. I swallow the lump that's formed in my throat and force a smile at Liam and Peishan.

"Looking good, guys!" Jonas calls out. "Please, climb on board the *Catalina*. Sexy name for a sexy ship."

Liam and Peishan laugh at this, though I'm not quite sure if Liam's laugh is a cringey one or if he's just grimacing because of the blinding sunlight reflecting off the water and the incredibly shiny yacht.

"How's it going?" Peishan asks me.

I shrug. "Good." I don't dislike Peishan, I really don't, but she's just a reminder of this shitty thing I've done. She's done nothing wrong aside from being an A-plus human. "I'm good." I force a smile and try not to notice how, as Liam walks past me, he completely avoids my gaze. *That's okay, Liam. You're not the only one who has a hard time looking at me.* I can no longer look at myself too long in the mirror either. Ever since transferring to Xingfa, I'm liking myself less and less each day.

We walk across the plank onto the yacht, and as we're climbing on board, Jonas hoots and swings the champagne bottle against the side of the yacht. Instead of shattering, the bottle hits the polished surface with a surprisingly loud *thunk* and leaves a mark on the shiny white polish before bouncing out of Jonas's grip and falling into the ocean.

My hand flies up to my mouth, but not before a shocked laugh coughs out. It is nearly physically impossible to keep the smile from taking over my face. I'm biting my lower lip so hard that I swear my teeth are about to meet. I turn away so Jonas won't see my smile, and I catch Liam looking at me, one eyebrow up and his mouth looking suspiciously close to stretching into a smile as well.

Jonas moans. "Oh no. My parents are gonna kill me."

Right. I should be feeling bad for my supposed boyfriend. I reach out and pat him gingerly on the arm. "There, there. It'll be okay." That's what a girlfriend who isn't secretly repulsed by her boyfriend is supposed to do, right?

Jonas gives me a baleful glare. "It's going to cost thousands to repair this."

"Then maybe you should've thought twice before smashing a champagne bottle into it," I snap.

Jonas is about to retort when Liam claps him on the shoulder. "It'll be fine," Liam says. "I'm sure we can google some way of, like, rubbing it out or something."

Grumbling, Jonas nods, and the two of them lead the way inside the yacht. I hesitate, wishing I were anywhere else but here.

"Come on," Peishan says, linking her arm through mine. "He'll get over it soon, I'm sure." She gives me a kind, supportive smile, which sears even more guilt into my gut.

Inside the yacht, we're greeted by a blast of cold AC and a surprisingly spacious room decked out with beautiful leather furniture and a fully stocked bar. There's even a bartender, shaking a mixer with gusto. Next to the bar is a table laden with canapés. Jonas seems to have recovered from his battle with the champagne bottle and is waving his arms and saying, "Nice, huh? Help yourselves. Only the best for my friends and my girlfriend. Isro here is making margaritas."

"I'll have mine virgin," Liam says.

"Me too," I say quickly.

Jonas frowns. "Seriously? You guys are lame. Peishan?"

She shrugs. "I'll have one cocktail, but that's it."

Jonas grins and raises his eyebrows at her. Gross—is he hitting on her right in front of me and Liam? Not that I'm jealous or anything, god forbid, but it's just such a maximum slime thing to do. Liam doesn't seem to notice, though. He's looking through the array of canapés with interest.

The yacht starts moving as the drinks are served. I look out of the windows and marvel at the land behind us getting smaller and smaller, wishing that I could jump into the water and swim back to shore. I sip my virgin margarita, which is really very good, and try to tune out Jonas, who's telling everyone about the huge swordfish he caught last week with his dad. Liam eats the food appreciatively and chats with Peishan, and the silence between me and Jonas is almost physically painful. The yacht slices across the waves with speedy ease, and before long, we're surrounded by nothing but blue sea.

Jonas tells us it's time to start fishing, so we all clamber out of the room, blinking in the bright sunlight. We move to the side of the yacht, where a row of fishing rods has been prepared for us. The baits are even attached already, so we don't have to get our hands dirty. Jonas picks up one of the rods.

"Okay, so this is how you fish properly—watch closely, guys. Look!"

Ugh, I swear this kid can't get enough attention. I'm so glad I put on my oversized sunglasses so I don't feel the need to hide my disdain toward him. I take another gulp of my drink and bend down to pick up a rod but sway with the movement of the boat and nearly fall over. A strong hand shoots out and grabs my arm just in time to keep me from face-planting, and I look up to see Liam frowning down at me with concern.

"You okay?" he says as he pulls me up.

"Yeah, just need to get my sea legs, I guess." I put my drink down and focus on the fishing rod so I can avoid looking at Liam. Whenever I look at him, I see everything he's typed to Dudebro10 flashing before me. All the stuff he was vulnerable enough to share with Dudebro10. And I can't risk Liam seeing the truth in my eyes. "Cool rod." Oh god, did that come out as an innuendo? Argh!

Liam gives me one of his lopsided grins, and my stomach flip-flops. He picks up another rod and tests its weight. "Watch and learn, kid." With that, he swings the rod, but instead of unreeling, the bait only swings around and around, splashing all of us with spatters of raw fish guts.

"What the hell?" Jonas cries. "Dude, watch it!"

Peishan just looks wordlessly down at her pretty sundress, now speckled with dark red spots. She tries halfheartedly to brush off the spots but only manages to smear them across her dress. Liam grimaces, and he looks so lost and sorry that I can't help snorting.

"It's fine," Peishan says as Liam hands her a wet wipe. "I expected to get dirty while fishing."

"Nice," Jonas says. "You're not squeamish like most girls, huh?"

What is up with this douche and his endless "not like other girls" comments? I bite back my retort and focus on my fishing rod. Let's see, how do I . . .

"C'mere, let me show you." And before I know it, Jonas is behind me, both his arms around me, his hands grasping the rod over my hands. Oh my god. My entire body goes rigid. "Chillax," he says, guiding my hands to the right before swinging the rod out.

The line unravels with a smooth whir, and with a satisfying *plop*, the bait breaks the surface of the water. "See?" Jonas says, and I can almost hear the smirk in his voice. He steps back before I can shove him away, and I release my breath, wanting to peel off my skin so I can forget the feeling of his body pressed up against mine.

I'm still standing there, white-knuckling the rod, when Liam steps up beside me. "Hey, uh, I hate to keep asking you this, but . . . you okay?"

I give him a terse nod. "Just a bit seasick, but I'll be fine."

Liam nods, his expression unconvinced. "Cool. Let me know if you need anything."

"Hey, don't worry about it, I got my girl." Jonas pops out of nowhere, carrying two fresh glasses of margaritas, which he pushes at me and Liam. "Two virgins." I bet he thinks he's real witty.

I slip the rod into a holder and take the fresh drink from Jonas. I wonder if I'm going to manage to see the end of this cursed day without shoving Jonas overboard. Fortunately, he goes to help Peishan with her rod. I notice that he does the exact same thing with her, putting his arms around her like they're in a bad ad for sexy golfing or something. Sexy golfing? Where did that thought come from? Liam watches with a bemused expression, though he doesn't say anything. Peishan doesn't seem to give a crap one way or another and swings her fishing rod casually.

Just then, Liam's rod twitches in its holder, and I jump so fast that I slosh half my drink on my legs. "You got a catch!" I shout.

Liam quickly grabs hold of the rod and yanks up.

"No!" Jonas cries. "Don't do that, you'll break it." He

snatches the rod from Liam and begins to reel the fish in with expert ease. I hate to admit it, but Jonas seems to know what he's doing. Before long, we can see white froth on the surface of the sea as the fish is pulled farther up. Then a silvery fin breaks the water, and suddenly the fish is out and it's thrashing and light catches its scales in a mesmerizing dance. We all can't help but cheer as Jonas pulls it into the boat and drops it into a bucket. It's a medium-sized fish with dark silver stripes going down its length.

"Cakalang!" Liam says. "Wow." He looks up, beaming. "Can I cook it?"

"Really?" Jonas's eyebrows knit together. "I have a chef here."

"Yeah, I've always wanted to clean and cook my own food from start to finish."

Jonas raises his hands. "That's really sick, but whatever, dude."

"Do you wanna come with me?" Liam says to Peishan, but she shakes her head.

"If I see that poor fish being gutted and cleaned, I'm not going to want to eat it."

I remember Sourdawg telling Dudebro10 that he believes we should all try to butcher and clean and cook our own meals at least once in our lifetime so we're more aware of what it takes to put food, especially meat, on the table. He reasoned that we only mostly see animals in the form of neatly packaged meat in the supermarkets, and that if we were responsible for rearing or catching the animals ourselves, we would be a lot more respectful about our consumption. And now, Jonas and

Peishan have just proven his point. They're okay with eating the fish as long as it's presented nicely to them and they don't have to deal with the reality of killing and cleaning it. To be honest, I'm feeling a bit queasy at the thought myself, but I raise my hand. "I'll come with you." And before Jonas can say anything, I get up and follow Liam off the deck and into the yacht's galley.

Liam glances behind his shoulder at me as we make our way indoors, and I could swear he's about to say something—I can practically feel him trying to form the words—but the bartender spots us and says, "Can I offer you another drink?"

Liam shakes his head. "We're looking for the kitchen?"

"Ah. You can pass me the fish you've caught and I'll have the chef—"

"No, we want to do it ourselves."

My chest expands at the word "we," which is probably really pathetic, but hey, chests are gonna expand when they want.

"Of course." The bartender leaves the bar and leads us to a side door. Opening it, he steps aside and ushers us in.

The kitchen is small and nowhere near as impressive as the rest of the yacht. Instead of polished wood and warm yellow lights, it's all about being functional: bright halogen, steel countertops, ceramic floors. There's a man inside, presumably the chef, who jumps to attention when we enter.

"They want to cook the fish themselves," the bartender calls out from behind us.

"Sure, just give it here for me to clean," the chef says, but Liam shakes his head.

"Is it okay if we clean it ourselves?"

The chef hesitates. "Are you sure? It'll be a dirty job."

Liam shrugs. "Yeah, if that's okay? I don't want to create more work for you."

"Not a problem!" The chef quickly opens cupboards, taking out various tools before setting them on the countertop. "Do you need me to stay and help with anything?"

This time, I'm the one who speaks up, and I do it before I even realize what I'm saying. "No."

They all look at me, making me squirm. That was way too eager, wasn't it?

"Thank you," Liam says to the chef, who nods and leaves us alone in the tiny kitchen. Liam turns back to me. "Ready?"

"Please. I was born ready." Wow, that was so clichéd. Where is this cheesiness coming from?

"Right. Let's put these on . . ." Liam tosses an apron at me before deftly putting one on himself. I'm still struggling to tie mine behind my back by the time he's done. "Here, let me help you with that."

I almost say no—it's my habit to turn down any offers of help—but I clearly need someone to tie the apron behind me. My fingers have turned into sausages, probably from nerves. Wordlessly, I nod and turn my back to him. Liam tugs at the apron strings. There is slight pressure from the front as he tightens the strings, and suddenly, my heartbeat and my breath sound super loud in the enclosed space. His knuckles brush against the small of my back for just a split second, but it's enough to set off a line of flame coursing up my back. I'm sure my neck and ears have turned red now. I swallow, the gulp deafening in the silence. I bite my lip. Is he aware that he touched me, and what kind of effect his touch had on me? Is he blushing as well? He's so close to me that I feel his breath, his warm exhale, caressing my neck. Just when I'm about to lose it and whip back around to grab his face in both hands and give him the world's hottest kiss, he says, "Done."

It takes a second before I gather myself enough to turn around and face him, and even then, I keep my eyes on the floor, because I don't trust that I won't pounce on him if I look at his hotness right now. "Thanks," I mumble. Is it just me or is Liam lingering just a touch longer than normal? There's only about an inch separating us, his nearness an ache I need to resolve. Then he clears his throat and takes a step away from me, and that single step is enough to break the spell.

"Okay, let's do this." He rubs his palms together. I chance a glance at him and am both relieved and disappointed that he's not looking at me. He crouches next to the bucket, takes a deep inhale, and reaches in for the fish. "Argh, argh. Oh god, this feels so weird." He lifts, and we both squawk when the fish thrashes in his hands, panic reviving it from its temporary snooze. Droplets of water splash here and there from the silver blur in Liam's hands. "Help!"

I rush forward and reach out as well, but all my instincts are telling me to stay away from the flailing thing, and I have to consciously make myself grab the fish. My fingers brush against it, and I squawk and fall backward. My shoes slip on the floor, and before I know it, the room is swinging and I fall. My brain hasn't even had time to register the pain—it's still dazed from the fall—when there's a loud *splat* and a wet, flip-flopping, writhing mass smacks right next to my head. The fish's tail slaps my forehead as it wriggles frantically, and I half scream, half laugh.

"Oh god! Oh god, oh god—" Liam lunges for the fish, catches it, loses his grip, and the fish lands a foot away from me before he catches it once more and throws it back in the bucket. He crouches next to me, out of breath. "Are you okay?"

I can only blink in confusion.

"Come here, let me help you up." He holds out his hand and I accept it, noting even in my daze how big it is and how gentle his grip is. I let him pull me up, but just then, the yacht dips to one side and I end up falling straight into his arms. "Oof!"

"Sorry!" Already I'm pushing away, but his arms only tighten around me. I glance up, surprised, a question almost out of my mouth when I realize how close our faces are to each other's. So close that I can see a tiny freckle just under his left eye. So close that I can feel his heart beating against my chest. Or maybe it's my own heart, thumping against my rib cage hard enough to crack it.

Liam's expression is unreadable, his gaze soft as it takes me in, a world of sweetness swirling behind it. "Kiki," he murmurs, his eyes dipping to my lips.

The door bursts open and the chef rushes in. "Is everything oka—" His mouth hangs open as he takes in the small space, Liam and I caught in an embrace, and, now I'm realizing, the kitchen covered in spatters of sea water. "Oh no," the chef moans. "My kitchen! This is so unhygienic. Please, let me clean up." He scuttles around, moving pots and pans with a lot more noise than necessary, clearly as a hint for us to get the hell out of here.

Liam and I break apart guiltily. I can't even look anyone in the eye. "Sorry."

"So sorry. We'll get out of your way." Liam hesitates with the bucket. "Uh, the fish—"

"I'll take care of it." With that, the chef practically pushes us out the door.

We're barely out of the kitchen when the door slams shut. Welp. We glance at each other, and there's so much in our gazes that I immediately break the eye contact.

"Kiki." His voice is so heavy with emotion that it pulls me back to him. I look up into his eyes. "I just wanted to—"

"Yo, you guys done with the fish-icide yet?"

For the second time, Liam and I break apart in a guilty rush. Jonas is here, with Peishan behind him. He's carrying a bucket with something thrashing inside. When he sees me looking, he grins and lifts the bucket. "Caught a baby shark."

I can't even muster up the energy to smile. It's too much, all of it. The moment with Liam, the disastrous attempt at killing and cleaning our own catch. I duck to one side, muttering, "I need some air," and hurry outside.

I vaguely hear Jonas say, "Wow, that gruesome, huh? Told you to let the chef do it."

Once I step outside, the sunlight pierces my eyes and I grimace, shielding my face with my hands. I lower my sunglasses from my hair and sigh, heading for the lounge chairs on the deck. I'm pretty sure I'm the most miserable person there ever was on a fancy yacht. I slump onto a lounge chair and rest my gaze on the endless horizon. I love being surrounded by nothing but the waves. The vastness of the ocean is a reminder of how minuscule I am and how my problems don't actually matter in the big scheme of the world. Well, usually it's a comforting thought, but right now, it doesn't do me any good. All I want is . . .

Liam.

I want Liam.

The thought surfaces with such clarity, such force, that it shocks a gasp out of me. I can't lie to myself any longer, can't pretend that there's nothing between us. That moment inside the kitchen should have been the least romantic moment ever. I mean, we were literally covered in fish water. But just thinking about it gives me goose bumps, because it's Liam, and he could make any situation incredibly hot. I just need to find a way to break things off with Jonas without pissing him off, then I'll somehow find a way to come clean to Liam.

Easier said than done.

CHAPTER 17

Dudebro10: So how was the yacht date today? Anything
interesting happen?

Was that too obvious? It was probably too obvious, wasn't
it? No, surely it's natural between friends to ask about a date,
especially a yacht date. Right? Just to be safe, I type out another message.

Dudebro10: What was the yacht like? I've always wanted
to be on one

Ha, that's totally normal and not at all suspicious. Go me.

Sourdawg: It was fine

What? Just "fine"? I almost type out: "Just fine?? What
about that hot moment you had with me in the kitchen,

Liam?!" but through a heroic effort of self-restraint, I manage to stop myself.

Dudebro10: Cool. Did you hit it off with your date?
Sourdawg: No. Wanna know something rly stupid?

I smile bitterly. Nothing could be stupider than this predicament I'm in.

Dudebro10: What?
Sourdawg: The real reason I couldn't get into either of my dates is because . . . I'm really into Kiki
Sourdawg: Kiki's the Grumpy Cat girl, btw

A sound that falls somewhere between a squeak and a laugh and a hoarse yelp burps out of my mouth. I'm squeezing my mouse so hard that it almost cracks. I blink several times at my screen, rereading the last message from Sourdawg. Oh god. What is this mess I'm feeling? Am I happy? Yes, yes! So much yes. So happy that my blood is roaring in my ears and I want to shriek out my window: *LIAM LIKES MEEEE!* I can't believe this is happening. My head is completely scrambled, every neuron in my brain misfiring, or maybe firing everywhere all at once. When he told me there's someone he likes, that was *me*?

More than anything, I wish I could tell Liam the truth. But how can I, especially now that I'm fake-dating Jonas? And let's not forget how I've been lying to Liam this whole time. Even now, he's telling me something I shouldn't have access to. It's such a huge betrayal to our friendship, to him. As quickly as the euphoria comes, it evaporates, leaving me crushed under the weight of my reality.

> **Sourdawg:** It's so stupid, right? We've been hanging out all this time and I was working up the courage to tell her how I feel, and then . . . suddenly she's dating Jonas
>
> **Sourdawg:** Hey, dude. U still there?
>
> **Dudebro10:** Yeah
>
> **Sourdawg:** I just—I really can't shake off the feeling that she's into me too. Do you think I should talk to her about it?
>
> **Sourdawg:** Ugh, that's probably a dick move, huh?

God, what fresh hell am I in? What do I say to him? Can I just shout: *I AM REALLY INTO YOU TOO!!!*

I force myself to lean back, taking my fingers off the keyboard, and take a deep breath. What is the ideal outcome here? Well, the ideal outcome is that Jonas magically stops existing so Liam and I can skip together hand in hand into the sunset.

Okay, and how do we get there?

My mind goes, "Insert blank space here."

I give a cry of frustration, burying my face in both hands. There is no way out. I would give everything to be able to have a heart-to-heart with Liam in person, but I know he's going to be furious, and I can't stomach the thought of it. First things first: I need to end things with Jonas. Then I can focus on Liam. But before that, I need to buy myself some time. I can't have Liam telling me his feelings in person, not before I get rid of Jonas.

I lean forward, my hands hovering above the keyboard. After a shaky breath, I start typing, and each letter fights back, as though my keyboard were battling this message. I will myself to keep going despite the anguish that every click brings.

> **Dudebro10:** Yeah bro, I don't think you should bring it up with her
>
> **Sourdawg:** Yeah. I think I just got a bit carried away there
>
> **Dudebro10:** Yeah, and if she were into you, I think she'd say. Sorry, just being real
>
> **Sourdawg:** You think so? We've been having rly great conversations, though
>
> **Dudebro10:** Well, they were probably great because she sees you as a friend
>
> **Sourdawg:** Huh. I guess so . . .
>
> **Sourdawg:** Good thing I got you to talk some sense into me, huh? Lol! I would've made such a fool of myself
>
> **Dudebro10:** Haha, np

For a few moments, I can't type because tears have blurred my vision. I swipe an arm across my face savagely, wiping them off, before typing out a quick "GTG, TTYL!" I slam my laptop screen shut and flop onto my bed, burying my face in my duvet. I wish I could burn the events of the day from my memory. One thing is clear: I need to break things off with Jonas, and I need to do it fast.

"Looking good as usual, my queen," Jonas says as I slide inside his Aston Martin on Monday morning.

"Do you just memorize cheesy pickup lines from rappers or something?"

He grins at me and puts the car into gear. "I'm just saying, you're looking fine."

I close my eyes for a second. Deep breaths, Kiki. Stay calm. "Anyway, I don't think things are working out between us."

Jonas doesn't even spare me a glance as he joins the traffic.

"Did you hear me, Jonas? I don't think we should see each other anymore."

He gives me a look.

"What?" I feel strangely defensive. Jonas just has that effect on me.

"I don't think you've given us a fair chance. I've been nothing but nice to you. I even invited you to my yacht!"

Oh lord. I resist the almost overwhelming urge to roll my eyes. Can this dude be any more obnoxious? I mean, seriously, his big plea to show his sincerity is the fact that he let my peasant ass on his ridiculous yacht? It's a fight to keep my voice even as I respond. "Well, I really appreciate that, Jonas, but I just don't feel any chemistry between us, do you?" Before he can answer, I quickly add, "And there are so many better candidates than me who are just dying to date you."

Jonas groans. "Yeah, that's exactly the problem. They're dying to get with me. Do you know how tiresome that is?"

Poor little rich boy, I want to snap, but by some superhuman effort, I manage to keep my mouth shut.

"The last girl I dated had about as much personality as Siri." He snorts, turning the wheel and going around a corner. "I would be, like, 'Where do you wanna go for dinner?' and she'd be, like, 'I want to go wherever you want to go.' I'd ask, 'What do you wanna do on Saturday?' and she'd go, 'Whatever you want to do.'" He rolls his eyes.

I sigh. "Okay, that does sound tiring. But you realize it was probably because she liked you so much that she wanted to please you?"

"Yeah, but it's boring. They're all like that."

I bristle at that. "Yes, yes, all girls are the same. There is no space for individualism in your misogynistic perception of the female species." I should stop talking; none of this is going to get through to him.

"No, it's just that the ones I keep dating seem to only want to be with me because of my money or my family name."

"Yeah, because that's all you offer!" I snap.

Jonas's mouth parts slightly, but he doesn't say anything. He looks stunned.

"I'm not saying that that's all you *have* to offer—" Well, to be fair, I don't know that he does have anything else to offer. "But, like, for example, even with us, you were just all about showing off your wealth. Like you so proudly pointed out just now, you took me on your yacht. *You* feel that the only thing you have to offer is wealth, so you can't blame your exes for being attracted to you for your wealth. Why don't you offer them something else? Good conversation. Banter. Ask them about themselves, show some interest in them instead of yourself."

There's a moment of choked silence. I can practically hear my words being digested by Jonas. Maybe I was too harsh. But then again, maybe that was exactly what he needed to hear to drop me as a girlfriend.

Then he sighs. "See? That's what I like about you. You're so intuitive. And you tell it to me like it is." He smiles ruefully at me. "Come on, the Spring Dance isn't that far off. If by then you haven't developed feelings for me, we're done. That was the deal, right?"

I release my breath in a long, heavy sigh. The Spring Dance is this Saturday. Jonas is right that it isn't far off, though in this moment it feels like an eternity. On one hand, I'm sad because, of course, a small part of me had been secretly hoping that Liam would ask me. Not that there was any chance of that ever happening, but try telling that to the stubborn little thing called hope. On the other hand, that means I only have six days left as Jonas's girlfriend. I can just about manage that. Having an end date in sight is such a relief that I nod quickly. "Okay," I say before he can change his mind. "Deal."

"But you have to promise to keep an open mind," Jonas continues. "You've gotta actually give me a chance for this whole thing to work."

The idea of giving Jonas an actual chance is unthinkable. I don't even know what that would be like. I'm about to just nod and go along with it, but then I think, maybe he deserves the truth. "You were tormenting me from the very first day I got here and dared to disagree with you. I honestly don't know how to 'keep an open mind' with you."

Jonas sighs. "Doesn't the fact that I'm no longer teasing you count for anything? And I told you, I only teased you because I like you."

I keep quiet then. I don't see the point in prolonging the discussion. Best thing I can do is go along with it for the rest of the week. Be as pliant and boring as I can be and call it quits right after the Spring Dance.

Of course, as soon as we get to school, it hits me just how hard another week as Jonas's girlfriend is. We're walking with each other, with Jonas right in my personal space. It signals to everyone that we're an item. He even insists on carrying my laptop bag, which is a dead giveaway. Eyes brush over us, take in my bright teal laptop bag slung over one shoulder, and stop, widening. Whispers fly like wind rushing through the trees. I have no idea what to do with my hands, so I white-knuckle it from the entrance of the vast school all the way to class.

Liam glances up when I walk through the doorway, his eyebrows lifting, but Jonas is right behind me, and when he sees Jonas, the light in Liam's eyes wanes a little. My stomach flips. God, I want so badly to tell Liam the truth. I can't stop sneaking glances at him as Jonas makes a show of handing me my laptop bag and saying loudly, for the benefit of others, "I'll see you later, yeah?"

I manage a curt nod before hurrying to my desk, reminding myself to be grateful that Xingfa has such strict rules surrounding dating. No touching allowed on school premises. So

Jonas is limited to loudly proclaiming to everyone that we're going to have lunch together. I should be thankful for every small blessing, really.

"Hey," I say softly to Liam after I settle into my seat. Should I ask him how his Sunday went? Maybe ask him what he's reading? I sneak a glance without moving my head but can't quite see the book title.

"Hey." Liam straightens up and tugs lightly at the collar of his uniform. He clears his throat. "Do anything fun over the weekend?"

I have to bite my cheeks to keep from grinning wide. "Well, you know. Tried to murder a fish. Failed."

A smile appears, and god, how is it possible for a guy to be this cute?

"Well, you know, those small fish, they're known for being deadly."

"Oh yeah." I nod solemnly. "Very deadly. It wasn't small, really. It was big and strong. A real monster."

"Uh-huh, exactly." Liam grins at me, and it's so sweet and sincere that I almost blurt out everything to him.

Is he going to bring up that incredible moment we had on the yacht? Where I was so sure that he was about to kiss me? But for the next few seconds, we just smile at each other expectantly, the moment growing more and more awkward until I clear my throat. "Anyway, how was the rest of your weekend?"

He shrugs. "It was fine. I spent Sunday with my dad. We watched a movie. Sat in Velvet Class."

"Oh, fancy. Velvet Class is the one with beds instead of

seats, right?" I nod solemnly at him. "Yeah, definitely the place to go with your dad."

Liam bursts out laughing. "We had no idea the cinema would have beds instead of seats! I mean, what the hell? And when we bought the tickets, they didn't even bother telling us. My dad and I ended up perched on opposite sides of the bed. I had one leg hanging off the side."

By now, we're both laughing like mad. "To be fair, the ticket person was probably quietly judging you guys for being weird," I say.

"Thanks for that insight. Very helpful."

I give a mock bow. "I try."

I love the banter I have with Liam, but I'm also smarting at the thought that this is the only kind of conversation I can have with him in person. Only surface-level stuff and nothing more. I can't talk to him about all the stuff with his mom, his going to see a therapist, or anything meaningful like that. I can't even talk to him about our real hobby, *Warfront Heroes.* So I guess that's that. I'm just going to have to be patient and wait until Jonas and I are officially over before sorting out the mess with Liam.

When Mr. Tan walks in and tells us to go into our respective groups, things become even more awkward. The first thing Jonas says once we're settled into our groups is "Look at that, two happy couples working together on a bomb-ass project."

Liam, Peishan, and I glance at each other. I have no idea what's going through Peishan's head, but she looks as uncomfortable as I feel, which makes me feel even more shitty, because none of this is her fault. She has a crush on Liam, and she doesn't know that I have one on him as well and—and—god this is all a mess.

Liam clears his throat. "Uh, anyway. I really like the direction our project is headed." He gives me a quick smile, and though it lasts for about a second, it conveys so much.

It takes a moment for me to recall where we left off in our last meeting, and when I do, my spirits lift. Because last group meeting, we outvoted Jonas and settled on a game set in outer space. The main character crash-lands on an alien planet and has to scavenge for parts to try to rebuild a working spaceship. It's basically a gathering/engineering game with a female main character who's fully covered in a spacesuit, no in-your-face boobs or butt. Jonas whined that it was boring and had no clear target audience, but Peishan made a case that, actually, farming/gathering games are a huge subgenre, and the engineering aspect would make it popular among parents.

We spend the hour coming up with the game's poster and overall logistics, and I'm surprised to find Jonas actually participating instead of sitting back and sulking. He still makes remarks like "Can the spacesuit be tighter?" and "What about having the main character be a guy so it would appeal to everyone?" but other than that, he's not actively trying to impinge on our progress, so I'm taking this as a win.

By the time the period ends, I'm actually in high spirits. I believe in our game design. I'm proud of it. I can't wait to share it with my classmates.

"Great job, everyone," Liam says.

Peishan beams at him. I try not to grin as widely as she does. I feel like I'm intruding on a moment between the two of them. Jonas wiggles his eyebrows at me, and my smile disappears. God, Saturday cannot come fast enough.

The rest of the week is barely bearable, and only because I am constantly reminding myself that I have just six more days to endure as Jonas's girlfriend. Then it's five more days, then four. The girls invite me to go dress shopping, which is a huge surprise because they'd stopped inviting me for coffee. I would've said no, because I don't find the prospect of dolling myself up for Jonas appealing, but Cassie reminds me that Liam is also going to be at the dance, so I might as well look gorgeous.

We go to a local boutique that specializes in gowns. The whole store is luxe, with crystal chandeliers hanging from the high ceilings, illuminating satiny gowns and soft chiffon dresses. Triss and Zoelle squeal and immediately start going through the racks. I linger behind, because even the sight of these beautiful dresses isn't enough to take my mind off the fact that my date is—ugh—Jonas. I notice that Peishan isn't diving in either. In fact, she's looking at me and biting her lower lip. Uh-oh.

"Hey, Kiki," she says.

I immediately start sweating. "Yeah?" Did that come out as easygoing as I hope it did?

"Um, I just wanted to apologize again for how I treated you when you first moved to Xingfa." Her mouth presses into a thin line for a second. "I was kind of a bitch to you."

"What? No, you weren't."

"Kind of. But you turned out to be pretty cool, and a great friend. And thanks to you, we came up with a project I actually like."

"You mean you weren't into Jonas's big-boobed, gun-toting main character?" I joke.

Peishan laughs. "It was awful! But see, I questioned myself too much. I thought—well, I don't play games. Jonas does. So he'd know better what the audience wants. But now I know to trust my instincts more. And I have you to thank for that. So. Thanks."

I manage to choke out, "No worries." Guilt and gratitude fight for space in my gut. On one hand, I'm so happy that we're sharing this moment. On the other hand, I feel so freaking guilty, because we like the same guy and she doesn't know it. I can't deal with the guilt, so I break eye contact abruptly and take her hand, leading her to the nearest rack. I grab an emerald-green dress, almost at random, and say, "I think this would look amazing on you." Fortunately, the dress turns out to actually be really great—a knee-length satin number in a rich shade of green that contrasts beautifully with Peishan's creamy pale skin.

Peishan's eyes widen. "Ooh, that is gorgeous." She sighs happily. "I'm so excited. This is the first year my parents are actually letting me go. The past few years, they said I was too young to go to a dance with"—she lowers her voice dramatically—"boys."

I place my hand over my heart in mock horror. "With boys! What next?"

"I know, right?" She laughs. "They're always, like, 'Next

thing you know, you're a pregnant teen and have made all of us lose face!' I do love that they have so little faith in me."

"I wouldn't take it personally. They sound like every Chinese Indo parent I know."

"Yeah." She sighs. "Anyway, have you found a dress yet?"

I shrug. Now that I'm actually talking to Peishan, it feels slimy to want a pretty dress to charm Liam. "I'll probably just borrow something from my mom."

"Does she have an entire closet full of custom-made dresses that she wore once for a wedding and then never wore again?"

"Yes! Exactly." Mami's closet is bursting with beautiful, expensive gowns that she can never wear again because being seen in the same dress twice would make us lose face.

"Well, you're going to look amazing, I'm sure," Peishan says. "Jonas is going to die."

"If only," I mutter. Then I feel bad for being so evil. "I mean, figuratively."

She laughs, then hesitates. "Um, what's going on with that, by the way? I mean, I totally respect your dating choices, but how did you and Jonas get together?"

My breath releases in a hiss. Oh god, how do I explain this? I give her a stupid little smile and say, "It was just one of those things, haha." Lord, do I ever hate this situation that I'm in.

Luckily, Peishan just nods and moves on. "Come on, I'm gonna try this on. You'll have to tell me if it looks good or not."

I smile weakly, feeling like the world's biggest shit. Just three more days, I remind myself. Then, even if I can't bring myself to tell Liam how I feel, I would at least shake off Jonas, which is definitely not nothing.

CHAPTER 18

Mami insists on taking eight billion pictures of me and Jonas, clucking over how "dashing" and "princely" he looks in his tux. I mean, I would have to be blind not to admit that Jonas does look really good in a tux. His hair is slicked back, and the tux highlights his broad shoulders and strong jaw. It's kind of hard not to admire the whole effect. Not that it changes the snake he is underneath the good looks and the expensive outfit.

When I came down the stairs in Mami's black mermaid dress and Ferragamo heels, Jonas gave this approving nod, his chin jutting out in a smug smirk, and I had to fight the urge to punch him. I wonder if the number of times I've had to hold myself back from punching him is indicative of an anger issue. Or maybe it's something that people commonly feel, should they be unfortunate enough to cross paths with Jonas. I wanted to scream, *I didn't dress up for you!* But I bit my tongue.

"Have fun this evening," Papi says. He claps a hand on Jonas's shoulder. "I'm trusting you to look after Kiki."

Oh god, kill me now. I had more faith in Papi than this clichéd show of patriarchy. "I can look after myself just fine," I hiss through my teeth.

"Kiki," Mami scolds, though she does so without her usual bite, probably so she doesn't scare Jonas, "Papi is just showing that he cares about you."

"Well, considering the number one concern that women have when they're on a date is that their date might rape and kill them, isn't it weird that we keep expecting our dates to 'look after' us?"

"*Kiki!*" Mami snaps.

I press my mouth into a flat line. My stomach feels tight, and it has nothing to do with the unforgiving corset that's sewn into the dress. "Sorry," I mumble to Jonas. "Didn't mean to imply that you're a rapist-slash-killer." Just an asshole, I mentally add, though I wisely decide to keep that thought to myself.

"It's all cool." Jonas laughs. "It's what I've always liked about your daughter, Om, Tante," he says, addressing Papi and Mami like I'm not there. "She always speaks her mind, no matter who she might offend. I find it refreshing. I love girls who can challenge me."

Mami and Papi beam, lapping up every piece of bullshit he's feeding them. On the surface, it sounds good. But if one were to scrutinize his words, they'd know that Jonas is as sexist as they come. He likes "girls who challenge him," as though my having my own opinions and not being afraid to voice them is purely for his entertainment; when he gets tired of it, he'll expect me to stop being "sassy" or "feisty" and expect me to be pliant and agreeable.

"Well, have a wonderful time!" Mami calls out as Jonas escorts me out of the house.

He's opted to leave the Aston at home today, going instead for a chauffeured Rolls-Royce. He makes a big show of opening the door for me, and I can hear Mami sighing happily from the front door. All her dreams are coming true; her daughter is going to a ball with a member of the highest echelon of society. I know that she's been dreaming of this happening to me ever since Sharlot got together with George Clooney; she hasn't stopped bitching about why Sharlot was able to do that and I wasn't, and how if I had any wits about me, I would do as Sharlot did and bag myself a billionaire.

Whatever it is that Jonas has up his sleeve, he's obviously very excited about it. He rubs his palms together. "You're in for the night of your life." His eyes shine and he fidgets in his seat.

I somehow doubt it, I almost say, but since it's our last day as a couple, I've decided not to be a raging asshole about anything. Instead, I give him my blandest smile and gaze out the window. The charade is almost over. After tonight, I can call it quits with Jonas and come clean to Liam. My heart rate quickens as I daydream about life as not-Jonas's-girlfriend.

Jonas chatters about various uninteresting things the whole way to school—or maybe they are interesting, just not interesting coming from him. Either way, I keep zoning out and nodding once in a while and going, "Mm-hmm," and he doesn't seem to realize that he's basically having a conversation with himself. When we arrive, I can't help but notice that he doesn't open the door for me; his chauffeur does. Not that I needed Jonas to open my door, but it's just funny that he made such a big show of opening the door for me at my house, in front of my parents. He stands a few paces away, holding out his elbow, his chin proudly up. Do I really have to take his arm?

Benign and boring, I remind myself. We're almost at the finish line! I take a deep breath and link my hand through Jonas's arm. I even manage to keep myself from wrinkling my nose or sneering with open revulsion, so go me!

We ascend the front steps together and make our way toward the gymnasium. As we walk down the hallway, music spills from the gym and a handful of students all dressed to the nines are scattered here and there. Jonas waves to them, and I take the chance to pull my hand away, but he catches it and pats it. He probably thinks he's being reassuring, but to me, it only comes off as patronizing.

"Hey man! You look great!" some guy I recognize from Year Eleven Justice calls out.

"Thanks, bro!" Jonas shoots back in what he probably thinks is a really smooth way.

We come to a table set up next to the doors leading to the gymnasium and sign in. I scan the guest book quickly, trying to spot Liam's name. I see Peishan's name near the top of the page but no Liam. My stomach sinks ever so slightly. Even though Liam isn't my date, I was looking forward to seeing him in a tux. And, okay, I was looking forward to having him see me all dressed up and wearing makeup instead of the usual bare faces we have to go to school in. Interesting that he and Peishan didn't come here together.

"Don't forget to vote for the Spring King and Queen," the boy manning the table says, pointing at a large box.

Jonas and I shuffle toward the box, pick up a card each, and write down our votes. Next to the word "King" I write down Liam's name. No hesitation there, he's the perfect Spring King. Then there's the queen. Hmm. I should write down Peishan's name, but gah. I squeeze the marker and then force my hand to write her name. I don't want to be the kind of jerk who doesn't vote for a perfectly nice person just because I'm jealous. Peishan's name comes out as a jerky scrawl, but it's written. I fold up the paper and drop it into the box.

"Ready?" Jonas says, smiling down at me. The kind of smile that would send most hearts racing.

I force a smile back at him. "Sure."

And with that, we go through the double doors.

I have to pause to take in the amazingness of the place. Mingyang's dances have always been pretty humble affairs, the decorations done by the student council and usually involving a lot of balloons. But Xingfa's Spring Dance is in a league by itself. There is no way that students could've done these decorations. The walls have all been covered by soft silver-and-white curtains. The ceiling is draped with the same cloth swooping here and there, dotted with a thousand twinkling lights so it resembles a magical night sky. There are a dozen towers of beautiful flower arrangements. Lilies and roses and orchids drip from massive vases, their scent filling the room. A live band is in full swing, the music loud enough to fill any uncomfortable silences but not so loud that one would have to shout to be heard over it. A stage has been set up at one end of the gym, the sides wreathed with flowers. There's a large buffet on another side and sofas on the other. Clumps of students occupy most of the sofas, and still more are milling around the buffet. Nobody is on the dance floor yet.

"There they are," Jonas says, nodding at one of the sofas.

I glance over to see Jonas's meathead buddies. Great. I don't even bother with a pretend smile as Jonas leads me to his group of friends. The guys are all manspreading, of course, and the girls are perched demurely on the very edge of the sofa. They all look amazing. I notice fancy, blinged-out watches that probably cost more than one year's tuition, blinged-out handbags, and jewelry with stones so big I hope they're fake but, knowing this crowd, I'm willing to bet money that these are all real diamonds and sapphires and pearls.

"Hey, bro!"

"Brooo!"

"Braaaah!"

Is there anything more obnoxious than guys calling each other "bro"? Or maybe I'm just annoyed because it's Jonas and his jerk friends, the very same people who have called me Crazy Kiki for the past two and a half months. They glance at me and smirk at each other.

One of them elbows Jonas, still grinning, and says, "So you really brought Crazy Kiki, huh?"

The back of my neck boils.

"Hey, c'mon, man," Jonas says. "I told you guys, she's not crazy, she's pretty cool."

Elon jerks his chin at me as a greeting. "Yo, Kiki. Can't resist Jonas after all, huh?"

Jonas smiles at me like this is somehow a huge compliment to me. He wiggles his eyebrows. "Yep, told you guys, it was bound to happen sooner or later."

Jesus, this is why he wanted me to go out with him. To prove to his cronies that, like everyone else, I'm no match for his charms. I want to lunge at all of them and punch the smug smiles off their smarmy faces, but I'm so close to the finish line now. I force myself to take a deep breath and ignore the guys.

I scan the sofa for an empty space, but though there should be plenty of space for everyone, the guys on it are manspreading so hard they're practically doing the splits. I guess I'll just stand, then. I try to make eye contact with the girls, hoping to at least make polite conversation with them, but they're all too busy chatting with one another to spare me a single glance. Even though Jonas thinks that by dating him I'm elevating my reputation, the truth is, it hasn't done shit for me when it comes to these people. I will always be the "crazy" outsider who doesn't know her place.

As Jonas is enveloped into his group of friends, I'm left to one side, forgotten for the moment. On one hand, yay for not having to endure small talk with Jonas! On the other hand, ack, this is so awkward. I grip my purse in one fist and rub my elbow with the other and try to look super casual as I scan the room.

"Kiki! Over here!"

I glance around to see Trissilla waving at me from the buffet table. Next to her is Zoey. I look over at Jonas to see what he's up to. His head is dipped low as he talks to his friends. It's as though he's completely forgotten my existence. Just the way I like it. "I'm just going to be a minute," I mumble. Nobody even looks at me, so I lift the hem of my mermaid dress and hurry over to the buffet table in little steps.

"Glad you made it!" Trissilla gives me a one-armed hug when I get there. Her other hand is balancing a teetering tower of mini burger sliders and cocktail shrimp. "Grab a plate before the horde gets to all the good stuff."

"The sliders have wagyu patties and foie gras," Zoey says through a mouthful of food.

"Wow." I am genuinely impressed, and so, so relieved to be with Triss and Zoey instead of Jonas and his friends right now. I pray that Jonas won't notice that I'm not with him for at least another fifteen minutes.

Triss hands me a plate and I survey the decadent spread before me. Damn this stupid mermaid dress, it's not going to allow me to eat more than a few bites of food, so I'll have to be strategic with what I choose.

"Hey, ladies, what's good here?"

I look up to see Peishan standing on the other side of the buffet table. She looks amazing in the emerald dress that we found a couple days ago, her hair swept into an intricate side braid and her lips painted immaculately in a dark red shade. My throat seems to close up on its own. Liam isn't going to be able to take his eyes off her.

"Sliders," Triss and Zoey say in unison.

Peishan nods and takes a plate, then turns and passes the plate to someone behind her. It's a guy who I think plays the trombone in the school band. Or maybe he plays the flute? I don't remember. "Here," she says to him.

"Thanks." He grins bashfully, and I stand there confused, because there are some serious vibes going on between these two right now, and I do not understand it.

"Hey, Tommy, how's it going?" Zoey says.

Tommy nods at her. "Great. Who did you come here with?"

"Klodiya." Zoey cranes her neck to scan the gym. "She went to the bathroom—oh, there she is." She waves into the growing crowd, and we turn to see Klodiya, wearing a silver jumpsuit, walking in next to . . .

Oh god. It's him. Liam. And he looks—there are no other words for it—devastatingly handsome. I mean it; my soul disintegrates at the sight of him, because he looks so freaking amazing and it is just too cruel. I don't want to be standing here watching him greet Peishan, so I edge away from the buffet, though I do pause long enough to grab a foie gras slider. I slink behind a decorative tree with silver and white leaves and crystals and chomp into my slider mournfully. My first-ever fancy dance at a fancy school and I'm miserable—wow, this slider is really good—but I'm still really sad. Though I'm not above taking comfort in wagyu sliders.

"Hey."

I'm so surprised that I nearly choke on the chunk of slider in my mouth and am reduced to a coughing mess for the next five seconds.

"I'm so sorry," Liam says. "Are you okay?" He pats my back as I cough, and when the coughs recede, his hand remains there on my bare skin, its warmth spreading throughout my entire back. Then he seems to notice it and yanks it away with an embarrassed clearing of his throat, as though he burned his hand.

"Um, so." Liam shoves his hands into his pockets and bares his teeth at me.

"Is that supposed to be a smile?"

"Is it not coming out as a smile?" he says, his mouth frozen in a half grimace.

I bite my lip. "It looks like you're about to have a stroke?"

That breaks the awkwardness, and we both start laughing. Then the laughter ebbs away, and we're left with a heavier, more expectant silence. There's so much unsaid between us, and I don't quite understand it, because I'm the only one with something to hide here.

"So, uh," we say at the same time.

"Sorry," I say quickly. "You go first."

"No, you go."

"Okay, um . . ." Of course, by then, I've forgotten what I was about to say. No doubt it was something stupid anyway.

"You look really nice," he blurts out. Then he clamps his mouth shut like he hadn't meant to say that.

My entire face bursts into flames, and I'm glad that Mami insisted on having me slather on a thick layer of foundation at home. "Thanks. You look nice too." Then guilt overwhelms me. I don't want to be the kind of person who hits on someone else's date. "Um, so does Peishan. That color looks amazing on her, right?" I say desperately.

Liam's eyes soften. "I didn't come here with Peishan."

My breath lodges in my throat, a pocket of air that I have to cough out. "You didn't?"

He shakes his head.

"Who did you come with?" My mind is flailing, throwing random thought after random thought at me. *No wonder she was with that band guy! What's his name again? How could you have forgotten it? You only heard it, like, two minutes ago! It doesn't matter what his name is. Randy. It was Randy. It was not Randy. Oh my god, stop freaking out internally!*

"Nobody, actually." Liam clears his throat and takes a single step toward me, and I'm suddenly struck by just how close we are standing to each other. The air between us turns electric. "Um, can I ask you something?"

I can only nod, not trusting myself to speak.

"Are things between you and Jonas serious?"

Somehow, I manage to shake my head. "In fact, I'm pretty sure tonight is our last night as a couple." The words feel slimy coming out of my mouth, even though they're true, but it feels wrong being, like, *Hey, I'm about to break up with my boyfriend (even though said boyfriend is basically a fake boyfriend), so please be ready.* "I mean, I didn't mean that to be, like, 'So let's get together.' Not that I don't want to—uh, not that I necessarily want to either—but—" Oh my god, somebody stop me, please!

"I'm really glad to hear that."

His words stop me dead. Our eyes lock, and for the first time, I sense nothing in our way. Just us, and the naked truth between us: that I like Liam, and he likes me back.

"I don't want to be the sort of asshole who comes in between a couple," Liam continues, "but since you said you're breaking up with Jonas, I, uh, I just wanted to say, I'll wait." He smiles and looks down at his feet for a second before looking back at me. "I'm good at waiting."

I swear I'm about to float away. Everything feels so light, my limbs weightless, my hair flying up. I'm like Peter Pan, soaring through the clouds and playing among the stars. Dimly, I sense myself nodding. I don't know the words to convey to him how brilliantly happy I'm feeling, and I don't think there's a need to say anything, because we understand each other, we get it. We smile so hard at each other that my cheeks start to ache, and I don't care, because I've never felt this joyous, as though my insides have been replaced with bubbly, sparkling glitter.

Just then, the music stops abruptly. The spell breaks, and Liam and I blink and look around, as confused as everybody else seems. Someone taps on the mic. *Thud, thud.* As one, our heads turn to face the stage, where Jonas, of all people, stands.

"Hellooo, Xingfa!" he calls out, completely comfortable with all the attention.

My mouth drops open. Honestly, just when you think Jonas couldn't possibly be more obnoxious, he proves you wrong. I bet he's going to start singing or, worse, rapping.

Jonas swings one hand dramatically and a screen descends from the ceiling. Or maybe he's about to do a presentation on all of his fancy cars. He puts the mic back up to his mouth—probably touching his lips, ew—and says in a husky voice, "This is a tribute to my girlfriend, Kiki Siregar."

Goose bumps erupt all over my skin. Dread uncoils deep in my guts. Oh no.

"Hit it, guys!" At that, a video starts playing, cast onto the giant screen. And it's so much worse than I expected. Because it's a recording of our *Warfront Heroes* gameplay. Jonas starts narrating in this stupid, deep narrator voice. "Some of you may know what this is. But for those who don't, it's *Warfront Heroes*, an online shooting game. That's my character you're following. And here it comes—" On the screen, a rogue suddenly appears out of thin air and stabs Jonas's character in the back. There is a collective gasp from everyone. The rogue stabs Jonas's character until Jonas's HP bar is empty, and as soon as he collapses in a lifeless heap to the ground, the rogue begins to dance over his dead body. Jonas rolls his eyes at us. "That rogue is Dudebro10, my archnemesis. As you can see, Dudebro10 started to follow me around in-game, killing me whenever he found me."

"I can't believe this," Liam mutters.

I should ask him why, but I've lost the ability to speak. My mouth is a desert, my throat feels like someone has put their hands around it and started squeezing, and I swear my heart has clawed its way into my stomach and is continuing to dig for the floor. This is bad. This is so bad. I should go up there and—I don't know—tackle Jonas off the stage or something. But my feet refuse to move.

"I know that guy," Liam continues, more to himself than to me. "Dudebro10, that's my friend. This is so weird."

"At first," Jonas continues, "I was so mad. Every night, I would log on to *Warfront Heroes* and hope that I wouldn't run into this assho—uh, this guy. Heh, sorry, teachers."

Gentle laughter ripples across the crowd. They're all completely enamored by Jonas, listening to his every word, their eyes wide and full of interest. And I still don't know what I'm going to do.

"But night after night, Dudebro10 found me and killed me over and over again. I couldn't play the game. I reported him to the mods, but they did nothing. So I did the only sensible thing: I took it into my own hands to find out who Dudebro10 is in real life. I thought he was going to be a twelve-year-old boy in Thailand or something." He gives this self-deprecating laugh, and the crowd laughs appreciatively. A couple people even clap. "But what I found shook me. I mean, literally. I was *shook!*" Jonas does one of his dramatic pauses, turning his head slowly from left to right, his gaze sweeping across the crowd. "Because Dudebro10 isn't some random kid. Dudebro10 isn't even a dude."

"What?" Liam mumbles.

All the blood drains from my head. I feel dizzy. "Liam—" I choke out. "I need to tell you something."

But my voice comes out so tiny that Liam doesn't hear me. He's staring openmouthed at the stage, and god knows what's running through his head. He takes out his phone and unlocks it, muttering to himself. He begins typing rapidly.

A second later, my phone vibrates in my purse with a text. I ignore it, gripping my purse handle tight with sweaty palms.

"Dudebro10," Jonas says in a low, let-me-tell-you-a-secret voice, "is a girl. And she goes to this school."

A murmur rises like a growing tide across the crowd. Liam types furiously into his phone. My phone vibrates again and again, message after message coming from him, and still I remain frozen, still I do nothing, say nothing, my voice gone.

"And when I found out exactly who Dudebro10 was, I"—Jonas takes a deep breath—"fell for her."

"Ooohh!" the crowd gasps.

Jonas smiles, scratching the back of his head. "That's right, I fell for her, because wow! What a girl. Any feminist would immediately fall for her, right? And so of course, I went to her house, and I said, 'Kiki Siregar, will you be my girlfriend?'"

He might as well have set off fireworks in the gym. Everyone starts talking at once, the noise level in the gym rising like a tide, but none of it matters to me, because when I look over at Liam, I find him staring at me with an expression of utter shock and betrayal. My insides twist painfully.

"Liam—"

But Jonas isn't done yet, oh no. "It was basically a real-life enemies-to-lovers story. You guys all know how much Kiki hated my guts." He laughs. "First day in school and she was already on my ass in class, weren't you, babe?" He winks in my direction. "But love wins. Every. Single. Time. She can't resist this, what can I say? And I had to do this. I had to tell you all the truth, because I feel really bad for starting that whole

'Crazy Kiki' thing. I'm here to tell you guys that she isn't crazy. I mean, she's sassy, amirite?" Jonas laughs. "But not crazy. And she definitely shouldn't hide in the dark. Someone like her has to enjoy the limelight. Come on up here, babe. To my beautiful, feisty girlfriend, Kiki!"

Every pair of eyes in the vast room is suddenly on me, the weight of all their gazes pinning me down. I can practically taste their expectation, hear the thoughts running through their heads. They're all waiting for me to rush onstage and hug or kiss Jonas and thank him for the romantic reveal. They don't know that he's just destroyed everything I've been so careful to protect.

I keep my eyes on the only person who matters to me right now. "Liam, I wanted to tell you—"

"You—you're Dudebro10?" His voice cracks, nearly breaking, and it nearly undoes me.

Somehow, I manage to nod. "But I can explain—"

Liam's mouth twists, and without another word, he turns on his heel and strides away. Everything inside me screams at me to go after him, but I'm rooted—truly, it feels as though roots have sprouted from the soles of my feet and dug deep into the ground—and I can do nothing as Liam walks away from me.

"Baaabe," Jonas calls from the stage, his arm still outstretched.

Everyone watches me, starry-eyed from what they think is the most romantic thing they've ever witnessed, and this is what makes me snap: the fact that they think what Jonas just did is amazing and not ridiculous. Shame bubbles up from deep inside me, hot and red and thick. I've told myself to be patient, to be quiet and benign so I wouldn't call any attention to myself again, wouldn't get on the wrong side of my new schoolmates, but all that has gotten me is this freaking mess. I can't bear to be here, to hear the judgey murmurs that are already rippling through the crowd. *Why isn't she going up to him? Why isn't she more grateful? Why doesn't she know how lucky she is to be dating Jonas Arifin?*

It's too much, all of it. A sob chokes out of me, and I clap a hand over my mouth. My muscles unfreeze, and I sprint away from the crowd, running for the exit, my vision blurred by hot tears. It's over, everything is shit, and I fully deserved this.

CHAPTER 19

I can't possibly remain on school grounds. It won't be long before everyone rushes after me to continue enjoying my humiliation, and I sure as hell am not about to hop into Jonas's car. So after I burst out of Xingfa's main gates, I keep running, which is quite the feat, considering that form-fitting mermaid dresses aren't built with mobility in mind. Still, I manage to do a thigh-squishy waddle all the way to the main road, where I finally stop long enough to order a GoCar.

"Your GoCar will be here in four minutes," the app announces, and I groan out loud.

Might as well be a whole eternity. I don't have a choice, though, so I stand there, my chest heaving, my gaze skittering back to the dark silhouette of Xingfa now and again. Nobody comes after me. But just as I'm about to breathe a sigh of relief, my phone judders in my hand. It's a notification from TikTok. Someone's tagged me in a video. Dread unfurls in my gut. My phone vibrates again. And again. More TikTok notifications. An Instagram notification. Another Instagram notification.

I don't want to look at any of this stuff. But my thumb moves on its own accord and taps on the top notification. It directs me to a TikTok of Jonas on the stage, talking about Dudebro10. Then the camera swivels off the stage and locks onto my stunned face in the sea of students, gaping at Jonas. The caption reads: "Org yg paling tdk tau diri didunia #CrazyKiki #BestBoyfriend."

It translates roughly to: "The most oblivious person in the world." But *oblivious* here isn't being used as "ignorant," it's being used to describe someone who doesn't know her place, who thinks she's better than she really is. That's how my schoolmates see me. Someone who doesn't know how good she has it.

The next TikTok has similar content—Jonas onstage making his speech. The caption reads: "Pls how can anyone not love himmm?! 😭 #CrazyKiki."

I should stop, I know I should, but I tap on the next notification, and the next.

"Omg wtf just happened #CrazyKiki."

"What does he see in her??? #CrazyKiki."

"LMAO look at her stupid bitch face!! #CrazyKiki."

The phone screen suddenly turns dark and the name "Eleanor Roosevelt Tanuwijaya" appears along with the phone icon. It takes a moment for me to realize that Eleanor is calling me. I don't have it in me to have any sort of phone conversation right now, so I hit the red phone icon, but my hands are shaking so hard that I accidently tap the green one instead. "No!" I cry.

Too late.

"Ci Kiki?" Eleanor's voice comes out of the speaker. "What's going on? Are you okay? You're kinda blowing up all over my feed. . . ."

In the background, Sarah Jessica calls out, "Some people are tagging Lil' Aunties on these posts."

The mention of Lil' Aunties Know Best is what does it for me. I break, letting out all of my shame in a torrent. "I don't care about Lil' Aunties!" I yell.

Eleanor and Sarah Jessica abruptly stop whatever they were saying, and their shocked silence spurs me on. "I wish you'd never asked me to join, and I wish you didn't rope Liam into joining—" I hate myself so much right now, it's overwhelming, a rushing river of rage and humiliation and grief drowning me. If only I was never enrolled at Xingfa, if only I'd stayed at Mingyang. None of this would even have happened if Sharlot hadn't met George Clooney. And the thought of this, the realization, is the last hit of the hammer. I drive the nail right into Eleanor Roosevelt's heart. "I wish I'd never met you or your brother!" With that, I hit the End Call button. When I look up, I see that my GoCar has arrived. I have no idea how long it's been there, the driver gaping at me through the open window. I ignore his shocked expression and throw the back door open.

"Uh, you're not drunk, are you?" he says as I slide in. "Because if you are, I'm not driving you anywhere. I don't want to have some drunk teen vomiting in my car."

"I'm not drunk," I manage to mumble, right before I dissolve into wrenching sobs.

"Um . . . ," the driver says. He gulps audibly, but when I

continue weeping, he sighs and puts the car into drive. Thankfully, he drives the whole way in silence, the only sounds in the small car my uncontrollable sobs as my heart cracks all the way open.

"Kiki! You're home so early," Mami calls out as I step inside the front door. She hurries over from the living room, her face aglow with excitement. I take some pleasure at the way her eyebrows shoot up before knitting together. I'm glad she's not getting the arrival she expected: me with Jonas, arm in arm, her dreams of her daughter dating some billionaire hotshot smashed into jagged pieces. "What happened? Are you—have you been crying?"

I take in a shuddery breath, and the fact that I can't even inhale without my breath flapping and fraying, threatening yet more tears, makes me even angrier. "This is all *your* fault. You enrolled me at that stupid school to fulfill your own ambitions, and I will never forgive you for it," I hiss. Hot tears spring into my eyes, and I hurry past Mami, ignoring Papi as he gets up from the sofa. I rush up the staircase and make sure to slam my door shut, just to drive in how angry I am, before locking it.

The knocks come a few seconds later, because of course, my parents don't understand—or won't understand—the universal cues for "Leave me the hell alone." So I do the only thing I can. I shout it at them. When they continue knocking, I grab a cushion off my sofa and fling it at the door for added effect.

Thankfully, after that, the knocking stops. I huff a relieved/ disappointed sigh (I'd been prepared to turn full banshee on them) and flop very dramatically down on the sofa. I thought I'd cry some more, but my eyes have run out of tears, which is somewhat inconvenient, because I still have all these squishy emotions inside me.

With a frustrated cry, I push myself up, trudge to my desk, and fire up my computer. Time slows, my heart thumping at least three times a second, as I wait for my computer to start. I click on the *Warfront Heroes* icon, and I swear it takes literally forever to load. While waiting, I tap out a message to Liam on my phone.

Kiki: Hey, please let me explain

Kiki: It's not what you think

Kiki: Liam, please

No reply. The app says that Liam hasn't been online since 8:42 p.m., which is over an hour ago now. *Warfront Heroes* finally loads, and I quickly open up my Friends list and locate his name. I double-click it and type out a message.

Dudebro10: Hey, it's me. Kiki. I just want to explain everything to you. Please give me a chance to do that

I hit Send, and an unfamiliar tone beeps at me. A notice pops up in the middle of my screen: *You are not on Sourdawg's Friends list. Message not delivered.*

My breath catches in my throat. I'm not on Sourdawg's

Friends list? That's not possible, that—realization *thunks* with the weight of an anvil. He unfriended me on *Warfront Heroes*. I release a choked sob. Maybe I could—I could do what I did with Jonas and try to locate Liam on a battleground, but what good would that do? He *unfriended* me. Somehow, this is the thought that hurts most of all, the one that carves up my insides and leaves me completely empty.

I'm barely aware of shutting down my computer and turning off the lights. All I recall is slouching, zombie-like, from my desk and crumpling into my bed without bothering to take off my dress or my makeup. I have just enough energy to wrap my duvet around myself and turn into a cocoon before I slip into a deep, exhausted sleep. Maybe when I wake up, all of this will turn out to be nothing more than a nightmare.

CHAPTER 20

I wake up to the sound of my phone ringing. Groggily, I grope around in my bed, but it's nowhere near me. With a groan, I push myself up, wiping off the trail of drool from my cheek and blinking in the dark. My god, what time is it? There is no daylight streaming through the gaps in my curtains, so it must be the middle of the night. For a beat, I sit there, confused. Then it all comes back to me in a painful, overwhelming rush. The Spring Dance. Jonas's speech, outing me as Dudebro10. The look of absolute betrayal and hurt on Liam's face. I gasp and hurry out of bed before belatedly recalling that I'm still in Mami's mermaid dress, which catches around my thighs and makes me tumble in a distinctly ungraceful pile on the floor.

"Ow!" I scramble up and waddle to the sofa, where I locate my phone stuffed between the seat cushions. I mash the green phone icon. "Liam? Liam, I'm so glad—"

"Uh, not quite."

"Huh?" I put the phone away from my ear and wince at the bright light scything into my eyes. Turns out the phone call is a video call. How did I not notice that before? It takes a moment for my mind to catch up with what I'm seeing. "Sharlot?"

"Hey, cuz!" She waves at me. "How's it going?"

Even though we've spent the last few months chatting on the WhatsApp group, Sharlot and I haven't video-called each other in . . . well, ever.

"Uh . . ." I blink again, trying to shake off the last dregs of drowsiness from my head. "What time is it?" I tap on my phone and find the clock. "Dude, why are you calling me at three in the morning?"

Sharlot gives a sheepish grin. "If it makes you feel better, it's noon here." She gestures to the blindingly blue sky behind her.

"It doesn't make me feel better, no." I pinch the bridge of my nose and shut my eyes.

"Well, and George pointed out that if you were asleep, then your phone would be on Silent mode and it wouldn't wake you." Sharlot moves her phone to show George waving at me and giving an equally sorry grin.

"George was wrong," I say flatly.

"Yeah, we figured that out. Although you should always remember to turn your phone to Silent mode before going to bed," Sharlot nags.

I sigh. "Why are you calling? Not that I don't love hearing from you, but why are you calling at three in the morning?"

Sharlot's expression turns serious. "Eleanor might have

called me. Well, actually, she called George, and when George refused to meddle, she called me. She's threatening to call my mom next if we don't get things sorted out with you."

At the mention of Eleanor, guilt stabs me in the gut, hard and deep. "Oh god," I murmur, covering my face as I recall all those horrible things I said to her last night. "Is Eleanor okay?" I manage to choke out.

"Why wouldn't she be?"

I search for any traces of sarcasm on Sharlot's face but find none. I'm so ashamed of myself I can barely get the words out. "I sort of said some really mean stuff to Eleanor last night. A lot of crap happened and I lashed out at her."

"Yeah, she told us you weren't your best self."

That is so Eleanor Roosevelt that I can't help snorting, and the small laugh somehow triggers the tears, and to my horror, I find myself sobbing once more.

"Oh, Kiki!" Sharlot cries. "I'm so sorry, cuz. Are you—oh, what am I saying, you're obviously not okay. But it will be okay, I promise you it will be."

This only makes me feel even guiltier. I've been keeping the whole bullying thing from Sharlot for no good reason, and now here she is, calling me and being so sweet and supportive. Through my sobs, I manage to choke out, "No, it won't! How can it be okay? You don't know what I've done. And what everyone is saying online—"

Sharlot's gaze flattens. "Uh, really? You're telling me, of all people, that I don't know how things can possibly be okay? Have you forgotten what happened to me last year?"

"Oh yeah." That brings out a shuddery laugh from me. I

have to admit, Sharlot had it pretty bad last summer, when the entire nation branded her a scheming, gold-digging slut.

"Yeah, I see the memories coming back to you. Please, you're basically talking to Monica Lewinsky. Nothing can touch me now." Sharlot smirks, flipping her hair over her shoulder. "And I'm here to tell you that it will get better. You will get through this, because you are one bad bitch. You helped me get through my mess, I'm going to help you get through yours."

"But you're not even here!" I wail. When Sharlot's life crashed around her, she'd been staying at my house and I was able to literally pick her up off the floor and shove junk food in her face until she felt more human. But I'm all alone. Waaah, poor me.

Sharlot gives me a sad smile. "True, but hey, you can call me anytime, and I'll call you all the time and I'll hold your hand virtually, okay? We can do a Netflix party and binge on junk food if that's what you need. Kiki, I know it feels like the entire world hates you right now, but trust me when I tell you that none of it will last. Whatever they say about you, you know deep down inside that it's not true. Only you know what the core of you is made of. So don't let them take you down, cuz. Not like this."

This only makes more tears flood my eyes, because god, for the past few months, I've been fighting so hard not to let all the #CrazyKiki stuff erode me. But between people constantly calling me crazy and me lying continuously to Liam, it's taken a toll on my self-confidence. "I don't like who I am now." The words come out in a shocked whisper, and I realize with a start that it's true. I don't even recognize who I am anymore. Who is this girl who's trying so hard to be liked? Who lies to her best friend? Who lashes out at her friends and her parents instead of talking things through with them?

"Oh, Kiki. I know. I hated myself too when it was happening. But please remember that before all the shit that everyone threw your way, you liked yourself, right? Because I know you, and I know you're amazing."

I think back to who I was before I moved to Xingfa. Back when I was at Mingyang, with Cassie. I wasn't anywhere near perfect, but yeah, I liked that girl much better. It never occurred to her to not speak her mind. She never had to make herself feel small to make boys comfortable. I nod at Sharlot, and she smiles.

"You are not who they think you are," she says gently.

My mouth parts, because wow, that's so true. I'm not #CrazyKiki. Neither am I Jonas's meek girlfriend. None of my schoolmates knows me, except maybe Liam, and even then, I've been hiding under layers and layers of lies.

"I think I have a lot of explaining and apologizing to do," I finally say.

Sharlot's forehead scrunches up with concern. "Okay, but not to the wrong people, right?"

I smile. "No. After I'm done apologizing, I will be ready for a battle with everyone else."

"That's the Kiki I know."

♡

Papi jerks awake into a kneeling position, arms out defensively, when one of the floorboards in his bedroom creaks under my foot. "Stop, thief!" he shouts. Next to him, Mami grunts, then resumes snoring.

"Papi, it's just me!"

"Kiki? Wha-what time is it? Are you okay?"

It hits me then that maybe I should've waited until at least after daylight before barging into my parents' bedroom. But I'd been so overcome by the need to talk to them.

"Um, I think it's almost five in the morning?" I say with a grimace.

Papi reaches out to the side table and flicks a lamp on. Mami grunts and shields her eyes.

"What is it?" she groans. "Did you have a nightmare?"

"Seeing that I'm no longer three years old, no, I do not need comforting from my parents from a nightmare." The words come out so caustic that even I wince at my tone of voice. "Sorry. I didn't mean to be so . . . mean. I just—" I take a deep breath. "I've been struggling for a while, and honestly, I'm kind of really mad at you guys."

That gets their attention. Both Mami and Papi sit up and stare at me. "You're mad at us?" Papi says. "Why?"

"Because!" I flap my arms before reminding myself to remain calm. "Because you transferred me to Xingfa."

Mami sighs. "Sayang, I already explained to you why—"

"Yes, I get it. You wanted me to be in a school of rich kids, you wanted me to learn discipline, etc. But you never asked me how I'm doing there."

They both look confused. "Of course you'd do well," Papi says. "You're wonderful, your friends love you, your teachers love you—"

"Actually, my teachers hate me and I don't have any friends. Well, I did make friends with a few girls, but that didn't happen until very recently, and probably only happened because they felt bad for me."

For a few moments, Mami and Papi simply sit there gaping at me like goldfish. If I hadn't been so sad and the subject matter weren't so close to my heart, I would've laughed at their blank expressions.

"But—" Mami splutters. "You—you're popular!"

"I *was* popular. Back at my old school. The school you didn't think was good enough for me."

Mami shakes her head. "Kiki, I know you think I transferred you to Xingfa because I want you to climb the social ladder and get a rich boyfriend, but that truly wasn't why we did it."

I narrow my eyes at her. "Reeeally."

"Well, okay, I did hope that you'd find someone as nice and eligible as George Clooney. But the real reason is because Papi and I—we thought you needed to learn what our society is like. Mingyang is great, but it's just so . . . liberal."

"Which is good," Papi adds hurriedly. "But we also wanted you to learn how to survive in a more conservative setting, because like it or not, the rest of the country—heck, most of Asia—is quite conservative. And we thought it would be good for you to learn how to fit in while you're still at school."

I get what they're saying, but frustration gnaws at me at

the unfairness of it all. I'm having to learn to "fit in" the way that only girls are expected to. "I get it," I say finally, "but I think I've learned that I don't actually want to fit in."

"Kiki—" Mami sighs.

"No, I don't, not in an environment as toxic as Xingfa. Do you know what the other kids there call me?" My voice cracks, my face burning with both anger and shame at having to reveal this to my parents. "Crazy Kiki."

Papi's jaw hits his lap, while Mami's hand flies to her mouth. "What?" Mami gasps.

"There's a hashtag and everything. Look." I take out my phone, open up ShareIt, and do a search for #CrazyKiki. There are over a hundred posts with that hashtag. I pass the phone to Mami and look down at my feet, unable to meet her eyes. I know that this is for the best, that I should be truthful with my parents to make them understand what's been going on with me, but it doesn't make the revelation sting less for me. It hurts, ripping apart their perception of me. I know that they've both always been proud of me; they love telling people how loved I am by both my classmates and my teachers. When Sharlot visited last summer, I saw the way Mami's eyes lit up whenever I gave Sharlot advice on what to wear and how to behave. They saw me as a natural leader, and to expose my weakness to them is painful.

"This—" Mami is scrolling down with lightning speed. Then she glances up at me, and I freeze because she's wearing an expression I've never seen before. I've often seen Mami irritated, or put-upon, or even snappish. But I've never seen her this incandescent with rage. Her face glows with the heat of her anger. She's gripping my phone so tightly that I wonder if she's going to crush it. "This . . . ," she hisses again. "These are posts from your schoolmates? Xingfa kids?"

I nod and hold out my hand for the phone. "There's more."

"More?" Papi says, aghast.

I open up TikTok and search for the hashtag again. "There's more that I haven't told you." And here comes the hardest part. Telling them about my deception, the way I've been playing games for over a year as a boy, and how Jonas found out about it and effectively blackmailed me into dating him.

Mami looks like she's going to be sick. "You mean Jonas Arifin—*that* Jonas—forced you to—"

"Kiki," Papi interrupts, his face a mask of pain and rage, "did that boy do—? Did he make you—"

"No!" I shout quickly. "No, no. He was decent enough—ha, it's weird calling Jonas decent—but he never made me do anything I wasn't comfortable with physically. We never even kissed or anything. Well, he did request that we hold hands, which was not great, but . . . you know, on the whole, I could live with it."

Papi squeezes his eyes shut for a moment, pain crossing his features, then he opens them and gazes at me with so much tenderness that I find myself getting all teary again. "I hope that you never again have to say 'I can live with it' when it comes to dating a guy."

I manage to croak, "Thanks, Papi." Then I clear my throat. "Anyway . . ." I fill them in on everything that happened last night, Jonas exposing me and Liam storming out and me running away, and I show them the videos on TikTok. Mami watches with a hand over her mouth the whole time, and Papi's hands are clenched into white-knuckled fists.

"Good grief," Mami says. "Kids are monsters." Then she hurriedly adds, "Not you, of course."

That gets a small smile out of me. "Of course not me. I'm a delight."

At that, Mami utters a half sob, half laugh. "You are. You are a delight. And I can't believe what these monstrous kids have done to you."

"A little bit over the top, but I'll accept it. To be fair, though, I think they're just following Jonas's cue."

"God, I could kill that boy," Mami growls. "But, sayang, why didn't you report him and his cronies to the teachers? Or—I don't know, the guidance counselor? Don't they have one of those?"

"I tried, but the principal only blamed it on me and basically told me I should change myself to better fit in with the rest of the school."

Papi nods solemnly. "The rice stalk that stands out gets the scythe. That's a well-known Chinese proverb. Traditional Chinese culture values the cohesion of the group as a whole; individualism is not as encouraged as it is in modern times."

I narrow my eyes at him. "Pretty sure it's a Japanese proverb."

Papi shrugs, looking rather sheepish. "Well, I'm sure the Chinese have something similar."

I can't help smiling at him. "I'm sure our ancestors have something similar, yes."

"Well," Mami huffs, "I think we are all in agreement that there is no point in discussing rice stalks right now. I am ready to rain down hell on this awful school." And sure enough, she really does look like she's ready to march with all the bluster and indignation that only a Chinese mother can summon and tell Principal Lin exactly what she thinks of him and Xingfa.

For a moment, I'm tempted to let Mami do just that. "No, Mami."

They both frown at me. "Why not? They think they can just bully our daughter because they—" Mami rants, while at the same time, Papi says, "I'm calling Seventh Aunt right now. She'll know what to do; she's a lawyer."

I raise both hands and gesture at them to stop. "Okay, okay! And Papi, you don't have to always say Seventh Aunt is a lawyer every time you mention her. She's my auntie; I know she's a lawyer." I take a deep breath. "Anyway, I think I have a better idea of how to handle this. Because I'm very sure that Xingfa is used to parents complaining about this and that. They're going to know exactly what to say to beat you down. But with my way, they're not going to know how to react."

Mami narrows her eyes at me. "It's not illegal, is it?"

"No!" I gaze at them pleadingly. "Please trust me on this? Once I'm done, you can complain all you want to the school."

Mami and Papi look at each other, and in that moment, I know that this is exactly the kind of relationship I want to have one day. One where we can convey an entire conversation with just one look. They nod at me at the same time, then Mami yawns and tells me to get out of their room so she can catch a few hours more of beauty sleep.

By the time I go back to my bedroom, the sun has fully risen, fresh morning sunlight streaming through my windows, bathing my room in sweet golden light. It feels hopeful some-how, a new start. I smile and utter a tired but happy sigh. After talking to Mami and Papi, the giant boulder of resent-ment that has been crushing our relationship for the past few months has lifted. I didn't expect them—especially Mami—to be so horrified on my behalf. I was afraid that they would tell me it's all my fault, and I'm so unbelievably grateful to find out that I've been wrong about my parents. But I'm not done talking and apologizing to people. I take out my phone once more and open up a video call on WhatsApp.

The call goes through, and the first words I hear are: "Ex-cuse you, a lady simply does not answer calls before nine!"

I grin. "Eleanor Roosevelt, since when are you a lady?"

The video on the screen shifts to show Eleanor blinking blearily at me. Despite her sleepy state, her smile is as imp-ish as ever. "Ci Kiki! I knew you'd call. That's why I kept my phone on, you know."

"You knew I'd call?"

Eleanor rolls her eyes so aggressively I wonder if it makes her dizzy doing that. "Please, of course I knew. I knew you'd feel bad about all the nasty things you said to me and Sarah Jessica last night and you'd be so overcome by guilt and you wouldn't be able to live with yourself if you didn't apologize, and I was right! Hey, Sarah Jessica, I was right." The video swings around crazily, then it shows a mess of hair next to Eleanor. "I convinced Sarah Jessica to stay over last night so we could both witness you groveling for forgiveness."

I don't know whether to laugh or feel mortified by this. But when I pause to think about it, I realize that I shouldn't have expected anything less from Eleanor. The only way out is through the tunnel. Gotta swallow whatever pride I have left and own up to my assholery. "I'm glad that you and Sarah Jessica are both willing to hear me out. I'm so, so sorry about all the things I said last night."

Eleanor smiles smugly while, next to her, Sarah Jessica yawns.

"I haven't been honest with you," I say with a sigh. "I only really joined Lil' Aunties Know Best because I wanted to find out who my online bestie was. And he turned out to be Liam, by the way. Once I found out, I wanted to quit, but then Jonas found out I was his online troll and decided to date me, so . . . yeah, it's all a mess, and none of it was your fault. I'm so sorry that I took out my anger on you."

The smugness melts away from Eleanor's face, and the smile she gives me now is a real one, shining with warmth. "Thanks, Ci Kiki. See?" she says to Sarah Jessica. "Told you she's not a raging asshole."

Sarah Jessica appraises me coolly before shrugging. "Okay."

"Thank you for accepting my apology. Can I just say, you two are terrifying."

Eleanor nods with a smirk, as though what I've just said was the biggest compliment she could ever receive.

"Just so you know, we were both bullied when we first started at Xingfa," Sarah Jessica says flatly. "Well, I was bullied a lot longer before Eleanor found me and rescued me. We know the signs. We were aware that you were being bullied and we thought Lil' Aunties might be able to help."

My heart swells and clenches painfully at the thought of

plucky Eleanor and quietly brilliant Sarah Jessica at the hands of bullies. But of course, it makes sense, because neither of them fits the mold. Both of them are rice stalks that stand too tall. Gah, damn it, Papi. Now I'm going to have that stupid proverb in my head forever.

I hesitate for a second before going for it. "I have an idea on how to address the bullying at Xingfa, but I'm going to need your help. I know I've been horrible to you both, but can you help me?"

They both smile at me like hungry sharks. When I tell them my plan, Eleanor Roosevelt rubs her palms together and goes, "Mwahahaha."

Oh god, what have I gotten myself into?

CHAPTER 21

The last thing I thought I would want to do on Monday is step foot in Xingfa, but I'm actually looking forward to it. Okay, well, I'm mostly dreading it, but potayto potahto. I'm dreading seeing Jonas and his cronies, but at the same time, I remind myself that I'm not going in alone. I have Eleanor Roosevelt and Sarah Jessica, who are formidable forces. I filled Peishan, Triss, and Zoelle in on everything, and they are totally on board. We're going to be okay. Maybe.

Outside my classroom, I deposit my phone as usual in the phone basket and keep my eyes on the floor as I step inside, ignoring the loud whispers and glances and stares thrown my way. Elon says in a stage whisper, "Heeere comes Crazy Kiki!"

With superhuman effort, I ignore him, resolutely keeping my eyes on my feet until I get to my desk. A couple of minutes later, the seat next to me scrapes back on the floor and I look up to see Liam. For a split second, our eyes meet, then he looks away, busying himself by taking his books and pencil case out of his bag and arranging them on his table. My heart twists painfully. I want more than anything to grab him and make him listen to me as I explain everything, but I know now's not the time for that. Later, I tell myself.

"Hey, Kiki!" Jonas calls out as he strides in with all the confidence in the world. "Can we talk?"

My mouth turns dry. I prepared for this moment all yesterday, but reality hits a lot differently, especially with everyone in the classroom watching us. Liam glances over, his jaw tightening, but then he looks back down at his desk. I ignore the sharp pain jabbing at my stomach and look Jonas dead in the eye. When I speak, my voice comes out loud and as clear as water. "I have nothing to say to you, Jonas."

There are a few gasps, and Jonas's chest swells. He's probably about to tell me I'm crazy, but just then, our Form teacher, Mr. Tan, walks into the classroom. Everyone rushes back to their seats, and Jonas calls out for the class to stand and greet Mr. Tan.

"All right, kids," Mr. Tan says when we're all settled. "Is everyone ready to present their game to the rest of the class?"

Most of us nod and murmur, "Yes." Heat rushes from my stomach down my arms. I can practically feel every pore on my skin opening up. This is it. I raise my hand. Mr. Tan's eyebrows knit together.

"Yes, Kiki?"

"My group would like to go first, Teacher." Already, I'm standing up and walking to the front of the classroom, not giving Mr. Tan a chance to say no. Behind me, I hear Jonas go, "Wait, what?" but Peishan says, "Don't make a scene, Jonas." I can almost feel Liam's eyes boring into my back like laser beams. He must be wondering what the hell I'm up to, but thankfully, he doesn't protest.

"Ah—" Mr. Tan sputters, clearly flustered.

I raise my iPad and start my presentation. The large screen behind me blinks to life and shows the first slide of my slideshow. Mr. Tan is obviously astonished. "How did you—"

"I didn't want to waste any of your time, Teacher, so I took the liberty of hooking up my iPad to the projector before class started." Actually, Sarah Jessica was the one who connected my iPad to the system, but he doesn't need to know that. "Thank you for assigning us this project, by the way. You're a great teacher." I say all this firmly, with confidence I do not have. I read somewhere that if you say things in a polite but firm manner, people are more likely to let you have your way. And I don't know how true that piece of advice is, but it's working on Mr. Tan. He straightens his tie and, after a second, nods at me to go ahead.

I turn to the class and my smile wobbles, because holy shit, standing at the front of the classroom with everyone's eyes riveted on me is terrifying. *Deep breaths,* I remind myself. *I can do this.*

"Um, hey, everyone. A few of my friends and I prepared something that I'm going to share with you. Ah, to start with, a few of you may know that I play an online first-person shooting game. What does this have to do with anything? Well." I take a deep breath and go to the next slide, which shows almost a dozen screenshots of private messages.

"These are screenshots of messages I received while playing as a girl online." I go through each photo. "Rape threat. Death threat. Rape threat, rape threat, this one's more of a vaguely weird sex joke, more death threats . . ." I force myself to look at my classmates, taking in their shocked expressions. When I spot Liam's face, it makes me falter, my words catching in my throat. He looks—I don't even have the words to describe his expression. He looks like he could tear apart an entire world with just his hands. Is he mad at me? Well, that's pretty obvious. The real question is, what is he specifically mad about? Me lying to him about being Dudebro, or me hijacking our group presentation?

It doesn't matter, I tell myself. I need to do this. I owe it not just to myself but to all the girls who have helped me get here. I force my attention back to the presentation. "This isn't unique. Female gamers are harassed on a daily basis, and reporting it doesn't do any good. I was punished for reporting my online harassment. In the end, the only way I could think of to avoid being harassed online was to pretend to be a guy. So I created a fake profile with the most male-sounding name I could think of, and surprise, surprise, suddenly, no one had a problem with my gameplay. People treated me with respect, just because they thought I was a guy." My eyes meet Liam's as I say this, and I pour all my emotions into my next words. "I didn't mean to deceive anyone. I just wanted to play without getting rape threats."

Liam swallows, his jaw moving as he clenches and unclenches his teeth. What's going through his mind? His eyes close for a moment. My guts sour. I want to throw up. I want to run out of here.

But then Liam opens his eyes, and what's inside them isn't

anger, it's pain. He gazes at me with an expression of such acute sorrow that tears rush into my eyes. Then he nods at me and mouths, "I'm sorry."

It's as though a balloon has just been inflated inside me. I could float away right now, I really could. I nod back at him and bite back the huge grin that's threatening to take over my face. I'm not done with the presentation yet. I clear my throat and keep going.

"If you think this only happens in-game, think again." The screen changes, going to the next slide. "These are screenshots of messages I have gotten from people I know in real life. My fellow classmates." I nod at them, noting with some pleasure that many are squirming, their faces red with shame. "Notice a pattern? They're all tagged with #CrazyKiki." I turn to look at Mr. Tan. "That's my nickname here. I got it because I dared to challenge Jonas's vision for our group project."

Mr. Tan looks aghast. Or maybe he looks angry? I can't tell. I quickly launch back into my presentation before he regains enough brain space to interrupt me.

"This, by the way, was what Jonas wanted our group to go for." The slide shows Jonas's mock-up of his proposed game with the ridiculously curvy woman carrying huge guns. "I was tired of having the only female characters in games be overly sexualized. But voicing a different opinion led to me being called crazy."

Jonas is sitting so low in his chair that he looks like he's in danger of sliding off at any moment.

"You might think that calling a girl crazy is no big deal, but what you might not know is that it quickly became part of my identity here. It created an unsafe environment for me, because when I had a very legitimate problem, I was dismissed because, hey, she's crazy! I'm crazy for not wanting to be Jonas's girlfriend. I'm crazy for speaking my mind in class." My voice rises with passion, with anger. "I'm crazy simply because I exist as my own person." My words ring with power, vibrating in the shocked silence of my classmates.

"Now let's talk about Jonas." I turn my gaze to Jonas, and he actually flinches. "The perfect boyfriend. So romantic how he called us a real-life enemies-to-lovers story. Well, you know what? Sometimes, people are enemies because one of them is tormenting the other, which was exactly what Jonas had been doing to me before he found out I was Dudebro and decided it would be cool to date me. I made it clear to Jonas that I wasn't interested in him, but because I'm Crazy Kiki, nothing I say is to be taken seriously, right? My nos are only there as obstacles for Jonas to overcome. Well, you know what? Fuck you, Jonas."

There is a collective gasp, and Mr. Tan starts forward, saying, "Okay, that's enough, young lady—" but Zoelle, Triss, Peishan, and Klodiya all jump out of their seats and form a protective line between me and him.

Jonas jumps out of his seat, saying, "This is bullshit!" and in a split second, Liam's right in front of him. Jonas snorts. "Move out of the way."

Liam shakes his head. "Nope." My head almost explodes into a million happy pieces, because, oh my god. Liam is standing up for me! Literally, might I add.

"You can't stop me." Jonas tries to shove him away, but Liam stands there unmoving, blocking Jonas's way.

By now, I have to raise my voice to be heard over the commotion. "I reported the bullying and harassment to Principal Lin but was told it was harmless good fun and to be flattered because it means that Jonas was interested in me. So there you have it, this is the truth about Xingfa and the people in charge of it. Why are we letting this happen? I guess it's much easier for the school if a harassed girl keeps her head down and learns to accept abuse, but I am done keeping my head down. I'm done swallowing my anger and pretending that everything's okay. I'm not crazy just because I speak my mind. I'm a person with rights equal to those of everybody else here, and I am done staying silent to make boys feel comfortable."

Silence. A bead of sweat trickles like an ant down my back. I swallow. Well, I did my best. And now to make my exit and—

Someone starts clapping. It's Liam. Peishan, Zoey, Triss, and Klodiya all follow suit. Before I realize what's happening, it spreads to the rest of the classroom. Not everyone joins in, but enough people do to make my eyes sting with tears.

"This is outrageous!" Mr. Tan screams.

Making my presentation and sharing my truth has unlocked something in me. I've empowered myself. It feels like I've finally found my old, confident self, the one who doesn't fear speaking out for herself. So I can't resist saying, "Did the presentation go over your head, Teacher?" Mr. Tan literally turns red. I've never seen a human in real life do that before. Time to make my exit.

But before I can leave, I see Liam walk toward me, his grin so wide that it basically eats up his entire face. My mind explodes into a thousand chirruping thoughts. He holds out his hand. Without really realizing what I'm doing, I put my hand in his. Holding hands with him feels so right, like coming home after a long journey. Peishan, Zoelle, Triss, and Klodiya walk out of the classroom behind us, followed by a handful of others.

Outside, I see that students have crowded around their classroom windows and are staring at our tiny procession. There's a moment of panic before I recall that Sarah Jessica, in all her terrifying brilliance, hadn't just hacked into our classroom computer; she hacked into the entire school system so my presentation was shown in every classroom at Xingfa. She also managed to hack into the sound system to broadcast my narration in real time. In my wildest dreams, the entire school comes undone, everybody rushing out of their classrooms to congratulate me. But of course, nothing like that would ever happen at Xingfa. Instead, they stare silently as we walk by, but here and there, I catch girls giving me a thumbs-up, or nodding or winking or mouthing "good job," and my spirits flit up to the sky. I can only hope that sharing my truth has lit a fire under them. A tiny flame, for now, but I hope that it will grow with time, that more and more girls will speak up, and that others will support them.

"What the hell is going on?" Principal Lin thunders, striding through the hallway. He's heading straight for me, and everything inside me squeaks, but somehow, I stay rooted to my spot, my feet planted firmly. He stops two paces away from me, breathing hard. "In all my years as principal," he sputters, "I have never—never!—met such a disrespectful, disobedient student. You're expelled!"

Part of me wants to quail, to drop my gaze and apologize. I guess the traditional Asian teachings of respecting my elders no matter what they do still lives on inside me. But I've grown past that now. I can unlearn the harmful things I've been taught. I am my own person. I lift my chin and meet Principal Lin's eye, unflinching. "You can't expel me."

"What?" he snorts. "Oh yes, I—"

"Because I quit the school. My parents sent in the withdrawal form this morning, along with a formal complaint."

Surprise flickers in his eyes before he manages to recover. "Well, good. Good riddance."

"I quit too," Liam says.

We all gape at him. Including me. "Liam—" I say, at the same time as Principal Lin says, "What?"

"I quit as well," someone else in the crowd pipes up. The sea of students parts to reveal the slight frame of Eleanor Roosevelt.

This time, the blood drains from Principal Lin's face. "Eleanor," he whispers. "Hang on—"

"I already told my parents, and they agreed," she says cheerfully. "They were honestly shocked at how unsafe the environment here is, all thanks to you."

I gesture at the dozens of cell phones aimed at us. "There are going to be a whole lot of videos on social media about this mess. I uploaded my presentation online, so everyone knows exactly what happened here. I'm guessing that you'll lose more students in the coming days."

"That's—that's perfectly fine, our waiting list is notoriously long. . . ."

I don't bother waiting around to hear more of his bluster. With one last smirk at him, I turn on my heel and march out of the school with my friends beside me.

We stop outside the school gates, pause, and give one another the biggest WTF look ever. There's a pregnant moment of shocked silence, then one of us giggles, and that does it. We all start laughing, and even as I laugh, tears flood my eyes and my entire body feels like it's caught fire.

"Did we really just do that?" Eleanor Roosevelt shouts.

"You guys—" I have to pause because I'm so choked up. "I can't believe you guys did all that for me."

"That's a bit much," Peishan mutters. "It wasn't just for you. I was also standing up to the many years of sexism I've had to suffer through in this hellhole."

"Right." I laugh, wiping my eyes.

"What now?" Sarah Jessica says.

"Well, we did just quit school," Zoelle says. "So I guess we go home?"

"No way! I'm on an adrenaline high," Eleanor Roosevelt says. "If I go home right now, I'm only going to be a menace. We need to go to a cake shop to celebrate!"

I grin. "I know just the place." What better way to give

Xingfa the middle finger than to go to Cake Ho in our uniforms?

Phones are whipped out and drivers are called. Liam clears his throat and says, "Hey, can we talk for a sec?"

My entire body turns into one giant heartbeat. Somehow, I manage to say, "Um, yeah, of course."

As we walk away from the group, Eleanor Roosevelt stage-whispers, "Get it, Ci Kiki!"

I'm going to need to have a word with this kid later.

We go under the shade of a large beringin tree. There's an awkward pause, then everything comes out of me in a torrent. "Liam, I am so, so sorry. When I created the Dudebro profile, I didn't foresee making an actual friend in the game. I mean, all I had known until I switched to playing as a guy was abuse, so I really wasn't in there to make friends. Until you. I didn't mean to deceive you like that, Liam. I wanted to tell you the truth so many times. I was dying to tell you the truth about me, but as time went by and we revealed more about ourselves to each other, it just got harder and harder. And I told myself that maybe it was better this way, because we weren't ever going to meet in real life anyway."

Liam snorts. "True . . ."

"But then I moved to Xingfa and I found out that Sourdawg was a student there too, because the universe is a giant asshole."

That gets a laugh out of him, and I laugh too, through the tears in my eyes, because really, how out of this world can our situation be? "I tried using the Lil' Aunties service to find out who Sourdawg was. And meanwhile, you and I were becoming friends in real life. Liam, I liked the version of you online. You were one of my closest friends. But I didn't expect to fall for the version of you in person."

The laughter dries up. Liam stares at me, his mouth parted slightly. I'm burning with embarrassment and my mind is screaming, *WTF why did you say that whyyy,* but I keep going. "You're even better in person. You stood up for me in class, you make me laugh, you make me . . . you make me feel like myself." I have to pause, because saying the words out loud is a revelation to me as well. And at the end of the day, aside from his hotness and his charm, the thing that made me fall for Liam was how, when I was buried in a sea of mockery and contempt, he was the one who reminded me of who I was. The one who reached into the darkness and pulled me out.

When I speak again, my voice is heavy and thick with tears. All my life, I've embraced a sassy attitude, especially toward guys, never letting anyone see the cracks in my defenses. But I don't want that chasm between me and Liam. I want to be completely honest with him. "I—what I didn't expect was to fall in love with you." There. The full, naked truth. My heart before him, completely exposed, offered up to him. He could break it if he wanted to, and I would let him.

Something warm and firm envelops my right hand. I look down to see Liam's hand around mine. He gives it a small squeeze, and when I look up, he's smiling at me with such tenderness that a lump forms in my throat.

"You don't owe me anything," he murmurs. "I'm the one who should be apologizing to you. I had no idea what you had to go through as a girl on *Warfront Heroes.* I—I don't know, when I found out you were Dudebro, I didn't even pause to consider why you'd done it. I just assumed you did it as a joke. I should've known better. And you know what? There was a part of me that thought: *She's Dudebro? That's . . . kind of the best damn thing. It makes so much sense.* When I was seated next to you, I don't know how to describe it, but . . ." He takes a deep breath and brings my hand up to his chest. "That first day I saw you in class, the moment I saw your face . . . I felt like I'd come home."

I can't believe what I'm hearing. Against my palm, I feel the steady beat of Liam's heart. I know that he is saying the complete and honest truth too. No more walls between us. Every card on the table.

"I fell in love with you at first sight, Kiki," Liam says. "I only agreed to participate in that ridiculous matchmaking scheme because I wanted to spend more time with you."

"What? No, but—" My head spins, everything swirling inside it—hope and disbelief and the everythingness of it all.

"And the whole time, I thought: *There's no way she's into me.*"

A shocked laugh burbles out of me. "But!" I don't even know what to say next.

"I love you too, Kiki Siregar."

It's as though my veins are rushing with some magical, sparkling cider. I feel a sense of weightlessness. I swear my feet leave the ground and hover above it. I look into Liam's eyes, and there's no guile in them, no laughter, just the core of him, exposed and vulnerable. I meet his honesty with my own, letting him in, letting all my carefully constructed walls crumble. Nothing left standing between us but the truth, our truth. I take a step forward, pressing the length of my body up against his, and we're so close to each other that the rest of the world falls away. Our lips meet in a soft, sweet crush, his hands warm on my back, and I wrap my arms around his neck and let myself fall, fall, fall into him.

EPILOGUE

Dudebro10: Wow

Sourdawg: Yeah . . .

Dudebro10: That's a lot of blood

Sourdawg: Wow, you can actually see brain matter on the ground. Nice headshot

Dudebro10: Mwahaha!

Sourdawg: Ugh, honestly tho, IDK about this game. The gore's making me queasy

Dudebro10: Yeah, I'm not a fan. On to the next one?

Sourdawg: Yep. Hey

Dudebro10: ?

Sourdawg: You look rly cute in that top

My cheeks wrestle with my mouth to keep the smile from taking over my face. I can feel the heat rising up the back of my neck, all the way to my ears, and it's next to impossible to keep my eyes locked on my computer screen. *Don't look up, don't—*

Our eyes meet over the tops of our screens. Liam waggles his eyebrows, and I can't help bursting into delightfully embarrassed laughter. Oh my god, this boy. He reaches around the side of his laptop and puts his hand over mine, its warmth enveloping me, trailing up my arm and making my heart thump in a sweetly painful way. Together, we get up and walk around the desk, and he puts his arms around my waist, pressing me up against him.

"Do you think it's weird that we still chat online even though we're, like, right in front of each other?" Liam murmurs.

It takes a moment for the words to sink in, because I'm so distracted by the movement of his lips. They're so close to mine, I can practically feel the magnetic pull of them.

"Are you objectifying me again?" he says.

"Huh? Sorry, what? I wasn't listening, I was—"

"Busy admiring my face? Can't say I blame you." He laughs, then grimaces when I punch him in the arm.

"Anyway, yeah, maybe it's weird to chat online when we're in the same room, but I dunno . . ." I shrug. "I kind of like it."

"Same here."

"So are you nervous about starting at my old school tomorrow?"

An eyebrow shoots up. "Me? Nervous? Have you seen how cool I am?" But then he gives me this sort of nervous grin and says, "Sort of, yeah. But everything you've told me about it sounds amazing, so I'm not too nervous."

"Well, don't worry, I'll be right beside you."

A slow smile plays on his irresistible lips as he gazes at me.

He pushes a lock of hair gently off my face. "You do realize you're the one who makes me really, really nervous?"

I quirk my eyebrows up. "I do, huh?"

In answer, Liam takes my hand and puts it against his chest so I can feel exactly how fast his heart is going. To be fair, mine's not exactly doing a slow crawl either, but I'm not about to tell him that. Instead, I raise myself onto tiptoes, inhaling the scent of him, marveling at the everythingness, all the pieces that moved just so in order to lead us both here, in each other's arms, and I close my eyes and kiss the boy I've been in love with for a really, really long time.

ACKNOWLEDGMENTS

Is it clichéd to say I did not see this book coming? Ha! I thought I would write a fun, fluffy book filled with laughs, but when I sat down to write the outline of Kiki's story, it ended up being much more serious than I expected, and I actually became teary eyed at the end. Poor Kiki has had to go through so much to find her happiness, and I just wanted to give her all the hugs! I wanted to address the sexism that is still rife in the places I grew up in, and I hope that I've done this topic justice.

My sweet, wonderful goddess of an agent, Katelyn Detweiler, was one of the first people to read Kiki's story, and I can't describe how encouraging and supportive she was. Thank you, Katelyn, for reading the many iterations of the outlines and brainstorming with me. Your comments of "Omg poor Kiki!!" were such a delight to read. And yes, poor Kiki!

I can't thank my editor, Wendy Loggia, enough for her brilliant notes. The draft I handed in to Wendy was an erratically paced mess, and Wendy very gently and patiently nudged it into a much more coherent story. I had the good luck of meeting Wendy and her beautiful family in person, and it was one of the highlights of my publishing career, something I will remember fondly for many years to come. Thank you too to Alison Romig for holding my hand throughout the editing process and helping to get this book into shape.

The whole team at Delacorte Press made this book possible. I never thought I'd be able to publish a story set in Indonesia, especially one at a school in Indonesia, but this amazing, magical team made it possible.

And to you, my wonderful readers. Thank you so much for coming on this journey with me. So many of you have written to me about how much reading about Sharlot and George Clooney meant to you, and I hope Kiki's story will touch you in the same way.

ABOUT THE AUTHOR

Jesse Q. Sutanto grew up shuttling back and forth between Indonesia, Singapore, and England and considers all three places her home. She has a master's from Oxford University, but she has yet to figure out how to say that without sounding obnoxious. Jesse has forty-two first cousins and thirty aunties and uncles, many of whom live just down the road. She used to game, but with two little ones and a husband, she no longer has time for hobbies. She aspires to one day find one (1) hobby.

jesseqsutanto.com

On sale now
from bestselling author

JESSE Q. SUTANTO

jesseqsutanto.com

JESSE Q. SUTANTO

"There's a kind of magic to Sutanto's writing. . .
She tackles complicated issues of culture
and family ties while also creating convoluted
plotlines that'll make you squeal with laughter."

–The Wellesley News

For a complete list of titles,
please visit prh.com/sutanto